First published 2017 by Solaris
an imprint of Rebellion Publishing Ltd,
Riverside House, Osney Mead,
Oxford, OX2 0ES, UK

www.solarisbooks.com

UK ISBN: 978 1 78108 510 3
US ISBN: 978 1 78108 511 0

10 9 8 7 6 5 4 3 2 1

A CIP catalogue record for this book is available from the
British Library.

Designed & typeset by Rebellion Publishing

Printed in Denmark

UBO

STEVE RASNIC TEM

SOLARIS

For Melanie,
Always

Man seeks for drama and excitement; when he cannot get satisfaction on a higher level, he creates for himself the drama of destruction.
— Erich Fromm, *The Anatomy of Human Destructiveness*

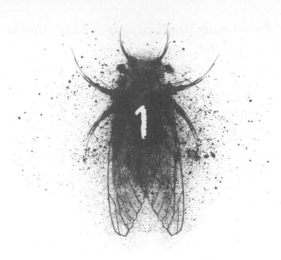

Now in Ubo, he felt as if he'd not just fallen into but passed through the rabbit hole.

Every resident had a similar memory of the journey here: a dream of dry, chitinous wings crossing the moon, the gigantic insects so like roaches or cicadas dropping swiftly over the houses of the neighborhood, and then hooking him with a spur through the base of the thumb, yanking him out of his life for a trip into the distant stars. They all had that same impossible recollection, some sort of shared nightmare or mass hallucination. Each had passed out or had suffered some gap in memory, although many were lucky enough to have gone to bed or nodded off reading or watching television. For some there was a vague recollection that a window had been left open or forced open from the outside, or in a few cases the walls of the house or apartment had actually dissolved, providing easy access for their kidnapping.

Specifics varied. For some it was all the eyes looking at them. For who could trust eyes like that, staring at you out of the dark on the other side of the bed? You could never know what really occurred in the stream of thoughts passing uninterrupted, even in sleep, behind such eyes.

For others it was an obsession with fingernails, how at any moment those nails might turn into claws and dig into flesh. Some claimed they'd seen nails lengthen and expand, turning into a hard sheathing covering hands, arms, torsos.

Most recalled despair that they might never find their way home again.

In a few instances they had had a notion that they'd done something terrible that day, or had wanted to, or had first realized that they were capable of performing some dreadful act.

Dark membranes and scabrous exoskeleton passed through walls and windows in some manner magical or scientific like a deck of dusky and baroquely-ornamented cards fanning themselves from one hidden world into the next. Then, spreading their wings over the bed where he curled against the love of his life, they'd separated him from his wife of ten years and yanked him out of the world.

In almost all these memories long horned lobes ascended into the broad ebony heads framed by multi-faceted eye globes. From each side of the head protruded vicious-looking mandibles. Their forelegs and back legs were armed with jagged protrusions, and their thick black and dull-gray hides were spotted with barbs.

There was also the smell which wasn't quite a smell, and the sense of a scummy dark effusion that made you want to avoid contact at all cost.

Some of the residents claimed to have been awake during the final stage of the journey. They said the name Ubo came from an aerial view of the ruined complex that made up this experimental hell which shaped the letters U, B, and O. Daniel had no memory of this, no memory of waking up at all during the long journey, and yet he too had known the name immediately upon awakening. Strange as the story seemed, it had always rung true.

They all wore skin-tight uniforms the color of snail skin, with a dark mottled pattern over the shoulders and back. Daniel thought they looked like animals preparing to shed their hides. They gathered in small groups to wait and pass the time. These groups tended to go everywhere together, eating together, sleeping in close proximity like tribes. And each tribe seemed to have its own particular conversational obsessions.

It was the stench of the place that originally convinced Daniel that Ubo was no dream, even though "dreamlike" was an impression he was never quite able to shed. But no dream could have been that extended or detailed, that vivid. And in the early months of shock and confusion after his arrival, those inescapable smells upon awakening reminded him where he was.

He'd been there long enough that familiarity had lessened the effect of those terrible smells, but they could not be ignored. Picking out individual olfactory sources was a futile game, but one his tribe played from time to time.

"A slaughterhouse, I think," was John's assessment. John was huge and bearded, an unusually dramatic presence in their relatively small community. "I visited one in Berlin in my youth. You never forget the lingering smell of blood as it turns, and this underlying rot because the facility could never be completely cleaned. The animals, too, when they became frightened, gave off this peculiar smell. Ammonia, I believe. People do as well, of course, when they know they're about to die. They piss themselves." He laughed loudly. Daniel always thought of him as their Falstaff: larger than life, a drunken and deranged Santa Claus type, as played by Orson Welles. But with something worn and tired deep behind the twinkle in the eye. What was the line? *"We have heard the chimes at Midnight."* Henry the Fourth Part Two. Whatever Shakespeare had meant by that, Daniel was sure it had happened to all of them.

"P—please, we just a—ate," Bogart said muddily. His real name was Alan, but assigning alternate names to each member of his small group had become a habit of Daniel's. But it was also self-protection; it took the sting out when they disappeared, which they all did eventually—either they wouldn't come back from a scenario or they wouldn't be there when he woke up in the morning. There was no particular logic behind the name assignments—a vague resemblance, perhaps, or the result of some anecdote. Daniel didn't know these men well enough to suggest they were anything like their namesakes. But there was a power in naming, even if you didn't know your secret name. Somehow over time the names began to fit in odd ways, as if he had sensed something about them he couldn't have put into words. Bogart had turned out to be as secretive as a gangster, and wouldn't tell Daniel his real name when they'd first met. "I'd r—rather not say. The guards…" He shifted his dark eyes. "They m—might hear."

Charles, their red-headed comrade with the little beard, became Lenin in Daniel's mind. Lenin thought Bogart might be an infamous criminal, perhaps even famous enough they'd be asked to *play* him at some point. Daniel just figured that Bogart was afraid if the roaches knew his name they'd have more power over him. Daniel was pretty sure the roaches already knew everybody's name. They knew everything else.

"You should know where your food comes from, my friend. It shows respect for the animal," Falstaff said.

Lenin made a disgusted noise. "Do you really think that pink protein paste they feed us came from any living thing? From some chemist's vat, most likely."

"Sewer smells, what else could it be?" Walter said. Daniel had assigned Gandhi as Walter's new name. The resemblance was approximate—Daniel doubted that Gandhi had ever been this thin. "Piss and shit, obviously. Don't tell me that after all we've been through you're too shy to say the words!" Gandhi stretched out his neck and gestured broadly with his arms in emphasis. Daniel noticed the scars running lengthwise on his wrists, spreading up his neck from his chest like flesh-colored vines.

Falstaff laughed. "You'd think with all these scientists in charge, the roaches could build a better sewer." That the roaches were scientists, that they were studying the residents for violent tendencies and dynamics, was their agreed-upon theory. It made perfect sense, given the scenarios they were each forced to act in.

Most importantly, it provided a semblance of an answer to the question of why they had all been brought here.

The other men did look uncomfortable, with Lenin glancing at the brown smears on the walls. "That's just paint, I think," Daniel said. "These random, foul-looking streaks about, the spots on the floor, I think it's deliberate. They want us to feel like we're in a degrading environment. It might even be a separate study all its own.

"Come to think of it, the roaches probably pump in an artificial stink. They want to make things seem as awful as possible—it heightens the scenarios. And maybe they think it'll bring out our own violent tendencies. A few weeks back I played a guard in the Khmer Rouge. We forced the prisoners to eat our feces, but then we had to smell it on their breath when we tortured them. When they brought me back here I could still smell it, taste it in the back of my throat. So bad."

It bothered Daniel that he knew trivia like this, that Stalin had hated kitchen smells, which is why he always kept his living and working quarters far removed from the sources of his meals. Playing the parts of murderers could be quite educational.

"I remember that scenario," Gandhi interrupted. "I smelled it. I smelled it, too."

"Exactly," Daniel said. "The roaches are manufacturing the smell and pumping it in." It sounded ridiculous even as he said the words, but it was a modestly entertaining theory. Which he didn't believe. Whatever the source, he was sure this was what Hell smelled like.

"They're n-not roaches," Bogart mumbled. "Well, of c—course they're n—not, but I mean they don't a—actually resemble roaches, that's j—just what we all c—call them. They resemble c—cicadas, gigantic cicadas."

"Ki...ki..what?" Falstaff said.

"C—cicada," Bogart said. "They make that loud s—song on hot s—summer nights, especially in the South. S—sometimes the locals c—call them locusts, but they're not t—true locusts.

"Who cares?" Falstaff said.

"Everything m—matters here," Bogart sounded less and less like Humphrey Bogart the more passionate he became. "Every d—detail has some m—meaning, if we can just f—figure it out. These are relatively b—broad creatures with their w—wide and triangular oversized h—heads. A roach's h—head would be m—much smaller. And the b—bodies? No c—comparison, the cicada's being relatively b-bulbous like these, and see the w-way they come to a k—kind of point at the end?"

"Like the ass on a large bee," Lenin said. Falstaff snorted.

"Yes, b—but again, they're not really c—cicadas either. The o—ones observing us, the scientists..."

"They look ridiculous in their lab coats." Gandhi spat. "They don't even fit."

"No, they d—don't. I s—suspect the c—coats are for our benefit, or rather, r—reference. The scientists have those h—huge multifaceted eyes..."

"You can see your face in each one. I hate that! The guards' eyes are smaller," Falstaff said, "but they've got those huge mouth parts, and swollen forelegs with the serrated edges. I've heard they've taken off a man's head with those, two or three, although I've never seen it personally. You don't dare tangle with one of those—you won't survive it."

Bogart wrinkled his mouth. "I've also h—heard that for p—punishment they can wrap one of those f—forelimb c—claws around your thumb and r—rip it right out of your h—hand, that several c—captives were punished that w—way on their initial t—trip to Ubo. Supposedly there are a n—number of m—men here missing t—thumbs, but I've never s—seen one."

Gandhi waved a thin, fragile-looking hand. "It's just another story they tell you when you first get here. An old man told me the thumb would grow back eventually so the roaches could torture you all over again. They're just stories they tell to scare the new arrivals, that's all."

Lenin interrupted. "But can we agree to continue to call them roaches? Because that's the word in our heads, and the other's too, well, odd."

The others readily agreed, then fell into silence, waiting. For this was the waiting room. Although the men sometimes referred to it as the commons area, it was really just this big room in the middle of everything where they waited for their next dramatic assignment.

Daniel stood up and walked around. There were few opportunities for exercise here. Although in his next scenario he might be running around creating mayhem, he'd actually be lying on a platform back in the labs, the roaches swarming all over him as if he were an accidentally-dropped morsel of food, taking readings and—he didn't actually know what all they did, simply that it felt unpleasant afterwards.

The five of them always sat in a circle facing each other in the waiting room. It narrowed their focus, and the grouping provided them with a sense of security. And after six months or more of virtual catatonia following his initial arrival, Daniel had them to thank for leading him out of it.

The room itself was enormous-more than a hundred feet in length, half as wide—and a ruin. It looked to have been a factory originally. Much of the floor space was open, but the concrete and tile floor was pitted every few feet with small impact craters. Daniel remembered photographs of Sarajevo after the siege. The ceiling was missing large sections, with bare wiring and insulation hanging down, some of it melted into ghostly screens of translucent plastic stalactite. Although a great deal of the debris had been swept up, there were still large regions chained off, gaping holes in the floor surrounded by layers of plaster, rotted trim, blast fragments, burnt mechanical parts, and melted masses of the unidentifiable. Whenever residents felt inspired to clean up those areas they were warned away by a rapid deployment of the giant roaches brandishing their serrated and swollen appendages.

Even the so-called clean areas were marred with scorch and rust, dark friction trails, crash scars, and black fields of mold. He'd seen similar footage of abandoned industrial structures in Detroit.

Other groups of residents were scattered around the room, huddled together, backs turned like Daniel's own group, or occasionally barricaded behind crumbling concrete and steel pillars and overturned furniture. They glanced warily at him and the other groups. Territorial squabbles and accusatory outbursts were common, although during his time here Daniel had never seen any actual combat. The roaches would have quickly intervened, and no one wanted that. Even though he'd been here for a relatively long time (although apparently nothing matching Falstaff's stint), the visceral reaction he experienced in their presence was debilitating. It made you want to peel off your skin.

The wide archway at one end of the room led to the bunkrooms and cafeteria, and presumably other barracks and other populations of residents beyond. It was rumored there was a small section for women only, but Daniel had his doubts. He certainly hadn't seen any women since he'd been here. Falstaff's explanation had been simple, "Women don't kill nearly as many people, so the roaches aren't as interested." The vast majority of the residents were men in their late twenties, with a few middle-aged, and a select few much older. Two or three appeared to be in their late teens, with no one under eighteen as far as he could tell.

Wherever anger and irrationality were factors, he imagined males any younger would skew the results. Bad enough they had so many in their twenties—those he tended to avoid. Perhaps it wasn't fair, but he'd always assumed the residents had been chosen for a reason. As to why they'd chosen him personally he had no idea.

Several roaches—the mammoth, guard variety—milled about in the area beyond the arch, dragging their oversized appendages on the floor, spinning around now and then like dogs chasing their tails. Their mere presence kept the residents from wandering too far.

At the opposite end of the room was a long wide slot of a

window at about chest height. Numerous roach heads were visible peering in from the other side. These creatures were of the smaller variety, who walked around upright and wore the lab coats—no more than tattered capes really, of some thin shimmering material. Because these were the ones seen just before each scenario began, they'd been labeled "scientists" or "doctors" by the residents.

Of course there was no way of knowing whether any of these suppositions were true. Falstaff, however, was definite. "Trust me. I've been here a long time. The way they stare at us, I think they've probably got us all pretty well figured out by now. They're the ones in charge."

Daniel had noticed that at certain angles the heads of the roaches shimmered with a flickering striation effect. It occurred to him that they might be wearing some sort of protective suit, without which they would be unable to breathe. It was a constant tug on his attention. It suggested an alien environment. Where exactly *was* Ubo?

Daniel wandered over to the bank of windows which provided the sole view from the waiting room of "outside." He did it for the direct sunlight, not because he particularly enjoyed the view. Many of the residents appeared to avoid it after the first few visits.

One of the surprises he'd gotten the first time he'd gazed out these windows was the understanding that they were more than twenty stories up in the air. Each reminder of this fact disoriented him. The facility had always felt like a dim, buried, underground sort of place. To look out a window and see a vista felt somehow contradictory here.

Even if that vista had largely been destroyed. It was obvious that a significant portion of the sprawling structure they were in had collapsed. The ground below them contained shattered walls and support beams several levels deep. An avalanche of dozens of floors of staircase sections had made a convoluted mass of steps that led nowhere. The building that remained looked as if a gigantic bite had been taken out of it and the mouth's contents spat out below.

The area around the building appeared to have been scraped down to bare earth and gravel. Hundreds of yards beyond were the ruins of more buildings, mostly destroyed, not enough left to speculate as to their original appearance. Beyond that a drift of haze, smoke, and flickering talons of flame. Daniel craned his neck to look up at the sky: more, darker smoke, but sometimes there were reddish clouds near molten in appearance. Many days a misty rain came down, and often a steady fall of fine light gray ash.

There was a commotion behind him. He turned, already accustomed to the sound. Several of the enormous roaches had entered the room, their claws clattering across the floor. With impressive efficiency they separated certain men and herded them back toward the arched entrance, the residents hurrying themselves to avoid any contact with the guards.

The morning round of scenarios had begun. They didn't take you daily, but it was more frequently than every other day. Still, it seemed random, as the roaches never announced their schedule, or anything else. The roaches didn't speak.

Daniel saw the huge bug headed his way, and ran to stay ahead of it. He did not exactly dread playing his part in these experiments, even though they were often unpleasant. Invariably they were stimulating, and they allowed him to go beyond himself at least for a time, to escape what his life had become.

High drama, excitement, was everything to the human organism.

If not love, then cruelty. If not goodness, then evil.

2

SOMETIMES IT HAPPENED this way. Daniel—non corporeal, a mind in a bubble—hung over the figure below. It was as if he had died, and having left his mortal flesh, paused for a final goodbye.

But he had no idea if he believed that was the way it happened. Probably he didn't—if the mind of man imagined it, at best it could only be a vague grasping after the truth.

And that figure below was *not* him, and he was not leaving, but arriving. He was simply reluctant to take the final leap into a stranger's mind which could only mean more anguish and hellish confusion, and yet another delay before he might get back to leading his own life again.

Not that Daniel had any choice. Behind him was the weight of a thousand mad insects, pushing him to complete his mission, to slip into the stranger's mind and experience the dynamics behind his violence, however poorly Daniel understood it. The assignment was never that clearly articulated but it was apparent that was what was expected. He made no report—there was no need. The roaches watched everything that happened to him.

He could feel insect parts invading his brain, working their way into his motor centers, into the prefrontal cortex and basal ganglia. The insects, the roaches, had a *need* to know.

Still, he resisted. He'd gone through dozens of these, maybe hundreds—he really had no idea. Hundreds of personal Hells. He floated, and the longer he floated the more he knew, the more he absorbed from the character he was to play. Mid-Sixties, Austin, the University of Texas. Climbing the tower.Daniel watched as the young man climbed the steps steadily, without rest, arms and legs captured by the precise, military rhythm. This young man was in good shape, and admired precision, and loathed the very imprecise thing that was happening inside his head.

Unable to resist any longer, Daniel was sucked inside.

Going into a personality was much like diving into a pool. You immediately sank to the deepest, coldest, scariest part—the part you didn't like to think about—before returning to the relative safety of the more manageable surface layers. In this case the deepest, scariest part was the almost robotic, emotionless determination.

Daniel began to sweat more profusely, his heart racing, his legs and lower back straining as he pulled the dolly with the heavy footlocker up the stairs. He saw that he was wearing khaki overalls. He had a vague notion to stop, to get out of this body, this life, to go lie down somewhere. It was *hot*. But everything had already been decided. Two floors so far, he thought. One more to go. He'd supplied himself well. He was satisfied that he'd done everything he needed to do to prepare for a long siege.

He kept staring at the words printed on the footlocker:

L/CPL. CHARLES J. WHITMAN
USMC - 1871634
Marine Bks.
Navy 115, Box 32-A
FPO, NY, N.Y.

Beneath him, at the bottom of the footlocker, two small, thin arms were straining, wobbling, trying to help him by pushing the footlocker up the stairs. A pale face appeared alongside the footlocker as the little boy put his shoulder into the job. Blond hair so light it was almost white, glowing as if electrified. Daniel had a vague vision of a photograph drifting up out of the inky darkness, eventually floating on the surface: the little boy at two or three, playing on the beach, holding on to two rifles taller than he. They were his father's guns, C. A. Whitman's. Guns had always been the old man's thing—he'd taught the boys how to shoot at a young age, but of course Chuck and his brothers had never been good enough. Well, now guns were Chuck's thing, and he was far better with them than his father ever had been. Later, after it was all over and the bodies had been carried away, his father would say, "Those guns aren't to blame for anything."

As Daniel perspired he felt Whitman's growing presence in his skin, the sweat spreading from one part of his body to another as Chuck Whitman travelled with it, cooling suddenly, chilling him, and leaving Daniel's flesh dusty-feeling, soiled. A strange sensation. Then he felt the thoughts, the desires, the long-dead rages taking over.

Chuck remembered reading comic books as a kid and thinking how great it would be to have super powers. Maybe you could just point your finger and a building would blow up ten miles away. Or you could look up at a plane flying high overhead and reach out with your mind and bring it down.

But you didn't need any super powers if you had the right firearm and the necessary skills. You could remove a pigeon's eye at a hundred yards, stop a heart at five hundred. Add to that the proper stronghold, a fort or a tower, and you could accomplish practically anything. Just two weeks ago he and Kathy had visited the Alamo in San Antonio. What those brave men did from that half-assed fort he could do far better from the top of the UT tower. One skilled man could hold off an army from up there, for an indefinite length of time.

He would never say that he loved his guns. His dad probably did—in fact Chuck was sure he did. But Chuck appreciated what a gun could do for you. A gun was the great equalizer. It made you as good as any other man. He felt pretty fabulous about that. What was his was there waiting for him to make the right move. Let somebody dare think he didn't deserve it.

People weren't going to understand why he killed his mother. They were going to think that he resented her, that some of his dad had rubbed off on her in some way in his mind, but nothing could be further from the truth. That woman was a saint, and deserved being turned back into energy. Matter could neither be created nor destroyed. It could only be transformed. Looked at in that way, even destruction seemed comforting, simply the means to a greater end. Mayhem had a holy purpose—it could turn you into a superhero, maybe even a god. A God of Mayhem, now that was a thing to be.

His mom was in heaven now, part of the vast source of energy that fueled every human being. Wasn't that a better place to be than this Hell on Earth?

And he loved his wife, he really did. She was a good person, and he was sorry that she had to work so hard to make enough money to support them both. Over and over he had recommitted himself to treating her better and controlling his temper and not hitting her. He only stabbed her as many times as he did to make sure he got the job done. Better that both his mother and his wife be in a better place of pure energy than to be ashamed of him and what he was going to do that day.

"Can we *rest*?" the little boy pushing the footlocker whined. Chuck hated whining and he hated the scrunched up face the boy made when he whined.

"No. We've got one more floor. Then we're going to do what we planned to do. Don't be a quitter, boy. I'll throw you down those damn steps if you quit on me." The boy didn't say anything but he went back to pushing the footlocker up the stairs. Chuck rubbed the back of his neck. The crisscross of insect scratches like stitches in his skin ran straight up his neck and across the back of his scalp. The sweat oozed into the scratches and made them burn like his head was on fire. He pulled out the white bandana and tied it around his forehead. It would keep the sweat out of his eyes so he could shoot better. He tossed a second bandana to the boy so they would match. He was feeling impatient now but he waited while the boy fumbled with it and put it on. He had it on crooked but there was no time to fix that now.

Chuck's shirt was soaking wet. He probably stank by now. He'd put some spray deodorant into the footlocker but he couldn't take the time just then, so he reminded himself to use it later. He also couldn't take the time to make an actual physical note about it so he hoped he would remember. He'd been very distracted lately.

He hoped that later, when they wrote about it, they'd put down that he'd been an altar boy. Also that at 12 he was the youngest boy in the country to make Eagle Scout. That was important. Maybe he'd have time later to write that down in a note. And maybe he should mention his piano playing.

Of course he'd wanted to be more. He'd wanted to be *lots* more, but sometimes you have to work with what you're given. Thank God he was a great shot.

He didn't have to worry about a job anymore, or good grades, or what his mother wanted today, or what his father would say, or if he could be a good enough husband to Kathy or not.

And Kathy, she'd been Queen of the Fair in Needville, Texas. Maybe he'd write that down, too. Probably the prettiest girl around.

Hated his father, of course. Old C.A. Maybe he'd put that down, just to make sure they knew why he was probably doing this, even though he wasn't completely sure himself.

"Hurry up, boy!" he shouted down to the kid. "We've got a schedule to keep! Don't you *dare* make me late!"

Daniel came out of it for a second. Had Chuck almost passed out? The stairwell was empty, cold. But there was still a kind of ghost here, a memory that was more than a memory. Chuck Whitman was a ghost of a memory that still haunted this place. He'd left his stain behind in the air.

Daniel felt insect legs scrabbling, an oily smell as they tried to regain control. Mandibles clicked against his flesh damp with a cold sweat. The ghost drifted in and out of his skin as his breathing grew ragged. Daniel became more excited as Chuck—large and again in charge—re-exerted himself and marched up the steps of the tower.

Daddy had been a self-made man. Chuck had wanted to be, had started out to be, but Daddy just couldn't leave it alone, couldn't stop picking at him. Not that Chuck didn't want to be perfect—he just had to get there his own way.

"Pick it up! Pick it up!" he shouted at himself and the boy struggling to lift the end of the footlocker. They had a schedule to make. "Don't make me throw you in the pool!" Chuck had just turned eighteen when Daddy did it to him, for celebrating drunk. Chuck'd almost drowned. Sometimes he thought that would have been a better way. But you go with what you've got. Chuck knew he was going to be famous for doing a terrible thing. Imagining the press grilling old C.A. about what his son had done made Chuck smile.

He had to get that receptionist out of the way before he did anything else. A rifle butt to the back of her head and a crack across the eye put her down so he could drag her behind the couch. That couple came down from the observation deck while he was standing by the couch. The surprise of it shook him a little, but then they left—they hadn't seen anything. He barricaded the stairway. The boy kept jabbering at him about more people coming up.

Chuck took the sawed-off 12 gauge and shot the two boys trying to open the door. Then he fired a few more times through the grates at the other people. He was annoyed—none of this was planned. He barricaded the door to the reception area. He started out onto the observation deck, stopped, walked over to the receptionist lying behind the couch, took aim and shot her in the left side of the head.

He was proud of how well he'd outfitted his footlocker. He could hold out for two days easy with all those supplies. As he went through the items and laid some of them out the boy got more and more excited, clambering around like a monkey until Chuck had to give him the back of his hand. That shut the boy up some, made him move a little more cautiously, but clearly he was no less enthusiastic than before.

Chuck'd packed that Randall knife with his name on it, a Camillus hunting knife and the Nesco machete in its scabbard, and even a hatchet, if it came down to it. It would take him at least a couple of days to go through the 700 rounds of ammunition he'd brought, but then they'd send somebody to pull him off the tower unless they decided to blow up the tower with him in it, which would be spectacular, but foolish and unlikely. Maybe they'd even send some fellow Marines in to do the job. Then he'd have to go at it hand-to-hand. He wasn't as good with a blade, but a knife fight made a cool picture in his head.

He pulled out the Channel Master 14 transistor radio, which would be handy for monitoring the response by the local authorities. Notebook and pen, in case he needed to leave any more notes. Light green towel, white jug of water, red jug of gasoline, rope and clothesline, and that terrific Nabisco toy compass he'd sent away for when he was thirteen. Of course the boy snatched that up right away and Chuck had to snatch it back with a scolding.

Canteen, binoculars, matches and a lighter with extra fluid. He had a vague idea he might have to turn the gas jug into a bomb but wasn't sure if he could do it right. Anyways now would be a good opportunity to try that out.

Alarm clock to wake him up when he needed to rest, pipe wrench and flashlight and two rolls of tape, gloves and earplugs. Also that Mennen spray deodorant—he didn't know whether he should use it now or not. He just didn't want people saying he'd smelled bad. The boy picked up the toilet paper and started running around the deck with it. Chuck wondered if he might have to throw the boy off the tower at some point.

He wasn't sure if he had enough food. He'd brought twelve cans of it, plus a couple cans of Sego condensed milk, bread, honey and Spam, some sandwiches he'd already made, Planters Peanuts and raisins. Sweet rolls. But maybe he'd be way too busy to eat.

And of course he had a goodly selection of firearms. His favorite was the scoped 6 mm Remington—that's what he was best with. He'd also packed a 700, an M1 carbine, .357 Magnum, Luger, and a Galesi-Brescia. He hoped to use them all, but you never could tell. You had to stay flexible.

He was feeling more mellow now that it was almost time. He placed his hand gently on the boy's shoulder and guided him around the deck, explaining to him how they were going to go from shooting station to station, firing a few times from each so that the people below would think there were more snipers up on the deck than just the two of them.

Back at the starting point Chuck looked at the boy and nodded. Then he raised the Remington, gazed down the scope at the figure crossing the South Mall of the campus, let go of his breath and pushed back the trigger. He expected to feel something—excitement, elation, completion—but he felt nothing when the girl fell. Then he shot the fellow leaning over her.

He aimed for the center of the chest with each one. He didn't want to risk missing with a head shot. He moved his targets east, to the Computation Center. He glanced at the boy, dressed identically to him with his white bandana and brown khakis, also shooting from the rainspouts around the deck. Chuck went westward and sighted along Guadalupe Street. He shot a fellow off a bicycle and started checking out the store windows. He shot somebody coming out of a newsstand, someone else hiding behind a construction barricade. He was perfection at last.

Suddenly people were shooting back at him. He peered through one of the rainspouts—he saw Texans hiding behind trucks and cars, rifles raised, firing his way, chipping the concrete all around him. It was just like the Alamo. He almost laughed. All them good ole Texas boys, taught by their fathers from an early age how to use them guns. He switched to the carbine and returned fire. Killing America, one bullet at a time.

He heard the drone of the small engine, looked up in amazement as the small plane approached and a man leaned out and opened fire. King Kong all over again. Chuck shot back as if he was waving off a mosquito and the plane retreated.

He shot a few more figures, maybe—now he wasn't so sure. Before he was like God raining down bullets. Now he was just struggling to take back control. It was proving harder to get off an accurate shot. But on the south side he picked off someone who had stood up behind a car.

Maybe if Daddy had just spanked him more. Some of them would say he got off easy. He'd kept telling himself to *be gentle* with Kathy. He'd written it right down in his notebook: BE GENTLE.

He tried to let everything leave his head. He had nobody left to worry over him, nobody left he owed a thing to. There was nothing he need worry about anymore. Finally, he could escape himself. Erase himself.

The people down there, they had no idea. They had no idea as to whether they were safe or in danger. They had no idea of his range.

Someday people would just walk down the street, and they'd have a hundred different rifles pointed at them. Someday that's the way it was going to be everywhere.

Two men ran into range, Chuck tracking them. He missed the first, and the second jumped out of range before he could pull the trigger again.

An old man bobbed into view. Chuck squeezed the trigger with a groan. But the old man had changed his mind, fell back just in time. Chuck began to weep. He squeezed the trigger again and again and each bullet erased a portion of his name.

Four roaches rode past on a four-seated bicycle. Chuck blasted the back wheel apart and the roaches tumbled haphazardly. He took more shots but the bullets bounced harmlessly off their armored hides.

There were neighbors and relatives, and people he was only barely acquainted with, and those were blasted too, taken apart shot by shot, squeeze by squeeze, spirited away.

Chuck looked up into the clear blue sky. He thought he'd heard another plane. He heard the sound, the drone starting somewhere deep inside his belly, but he didn't see the plane. Still he tracked the sound moving overhead with his eyes, smiling.He just couldn't smile enough today. Then the black plumes of smoke came drifting overhead. He noticed the blue highlights, smelled the faint trace of phosphorous in the air. And as the ghost of himself pulled away from his skin, leaving it sore to the touch, he remembered that his name was Daniel, and that he was in Ubo.

The policemen came around the corner, guns blazing. There was a misfire, and Daniel changed position. He looked around for the boy but he couldn't find him. Good.

Something slapped him in the head. He looked up, trying to figure out which of the men had shot him. Then the next one took him out.

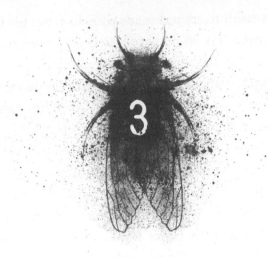

3

DANIEL WOKE UP staring at the ceiling. Oddly hung over, he was convinced he'd done something terrible, but not sure of the details. His head was full of images of people falling. He had an urge to wake Elena up and tell her about his complex dream. Then he started crying, because he'd begun to remember the scenario, and all the people he'd killed.

The paint on the ceiling blistered and stains spread, mold-colored and rust-colored like some exotic soup. He heard a rapid panting, and he thought to ask her to get the dog out of the bedroom. But they'd had to give away the dog, because Gordon was allergic to dog fur and the smallest thing might set off a respiratory attack. He reached out to touch her, as he always did when awakened in the middle of the night, in the darkness needing confirmation that she was real and that she was alive. But this time he could not find her.

He sat up. The motion sickened him, constricted his breathing. There was a skim of filth on his skin he couldn't wash off. Sourness slathered his tongue. He began to choke, turned to throw up into the plastic basin attached to the side of every bed. He splashed the running water onto his face and rubbed it into his eyes.

But he could still hear the panting. Several bunks away a man sat hunched over the side of his bed, chewing at his wrist and then using his teeth to strip threads of skin from his blood-slicked forearm. The man was insanely focused, pushing his teeth forward and attacking the flesh aggressively. The pattern didn't look random—a stark, tribal design was emerging—an expressionistic face—it certainly *could* be accidental, and he could be seeing patterns where they didn't exist. That's what human beings *do*, he thought. He looked around for the roaches, saw several dark heads in the observation window, their antennae waving.

"They'll step in if they think he's going to bleed to death," Falstaff said behind him. Daniel turned around and blinked at the enormous man filling the next bunk. "That's Barker. He's done this kind of thing before. He reacts badly to his roles."

Daniel looked at Barker again. A low, terrier-like growl came from under the panting. "I don't think I've seen him before."

"Really? How long do you think you've been here?"

It surprised Daniel that he was so unsure of the answer. "A few months."

"No." Falstaff flushed. "Sorry, but it's been much longer. Over a year, year and a half at least. I was here when you came in. At least that much."

Impossible. If he'd actually been gone that long, his family would think he was dead. They'd be trying to move on with their lives. But it couldn't be. Admittedly he was a little fuzzy about the beginning, but that seemed only weeks ago.

"You were out of it at first. They usually are. There's the shock of the transition, and the pull of the family left behind. You feel acutely responsible. Some never recover—they're damaged permanently from the time they arrive. For that reason I don't think the roaches use everyone they retrieve. Well, I know, they don't." He nodded at Barker. "He was probably in the infirmary when you first got here. The roaches shouldn't even bother with anyone less than stable—they make unreliable subjects. Not that the roaches would ever listen to what I have to say."

"What are they testing? How long it takes us to break?"

"We've played the most dangerous human beings who've ever lived. Why did those people do what they did? The roaches must think we're a terribly troubled people. We live in Hell but we aspire to Heaven—that's the drama of being human. The disparity makes us troubled, even insane at times, but we pretend not to be just to get through the day, work our jobs, care for our families."

Daniel glanced at the observation windows. The roach heads were gone. He wondered if he and Falstaff were being recorded. "If this were a science fiction movie, I'd think they were testing us to see if the human race was worth saving."

Falstaff laughed. "Let's hope it doesn't come to that."

A groan came from somewhere deep in the building, rising into a howl that must have been open-mouthed and wrenching. "What *is* that?" Daniel hoped he wouldn't have to hear it ever again.

"Our werewolf," Falstaff replied. "He does that from time to time. Our Gilles de Rais. A fifteenth-century Breton knight. A serial killer of children, I'm sorry to say, hundreds of them. The poor fellow's name is Henry—I never caught the last name. He was a nervous, agitated type, but fairly harmless, I think. Gilles de Rais was the first role he was given after he arrived. He never completely came out of it."

The howl came again, louder than before, ending with a cracking, tearing sound, as if the vocal cords had shredded. "Can't they stop him?" Daniel covered his head with the blanket.

"Not without killing him, and I suspect they'd prefer to continue studying him. Eventually his voice gives out."

Even as the last word left Falstaff's mouth another howl began, this one so fractured, so human, that Daniel could only grit his teeth and fill his head with some random interference until the weakened voice died.

"They've l—lied to us! They've lied to us a—all our l—lives!"

The blanket-covered lump in a bunk several yards away had hatched, and there was Alan, his Bogart, eyes glassy as he shouted at an invisible audience.

31

"Alan! You're back in the barracks now!" Falstaff shouted at Bogart.

"B—but they've b—been lying to us!" Bogart's volume was only slightly reduced as he stared at Falstaff.

Falstaff looked somewhat shaken. He said nothing for a moment, then asked, "Who, Alan? Who has been lying to us?"

"Everyone! Everyone t—telling us how to be a m—man, what we're s—supposed to do, how we're s—supposed to feel, what w—women are supposed to mean. I have two d—daughters—!" He pinched his face, snagging bits of skin in his fingertips and pulling, as if trying to rearrange or remove his features. Daniel could feel the anxiety like a blast rippling across the room.

"Alan!" Falstaff yelled over him. "Who were you last night? Who were you playing?"

Bogart/Alan stopped babbling and looked fixedly at Falstaff. "S—Speck. Richard Speck. B—born To Raise Hell. I had n—n—no feeling, like always. Just nothing while I d—did, well, whatever I thought I o—oughta be doing. I s—should have, I shoulda been one of them. I w—wanted everything they had." He spoke in a heavy Southern accent, with a thickness in his throat. His eyes appeared to be in some other place. "I w—wanted them, but they r—reckoned I was a p—pig. I d—disgusted them, and you know what? D-damned if it didn't just m—make me more d—disgusting."

He did something with his hand, brought it to his mouth, the fingers curled and open, took it away. A pantomime of drinking. "I b—broke in, whenever I c—could, took what I could. Course they was always c—catching me, putting me back in a c—cell. I'd been d—drinking heavy that n—night, so heavy I was just s—syrup. I could h—hardly get my h—head off the floor. When I left the bar I just w—wanted a woman to clear my head.

"It was the lights, y—you know? I just f—followed the lights up to that house. I had my g—gun out, and I asked her where her c—companions were, and I forced my way in.

"I told them I wasn't going to h—hurt them, that all I w—wanted was their m—money. That's what my m—mouth said. But I was feeling pretty s—sick, and the sick was thinking s—something else, I r—reckon.

"I made them s—sit on the l—linoleum floor f—facing me. I looked at each one of them. They give me their m—money, then S—Shirley, my ex-wife, she c—come in. She c—couldn't a been there, but she was. I put the g—gun to her cheek. Course later I f—figured out she weren't S—Shirley, b—but by then it was too l—late. I cut a sheet into strips and t—tied them all up.

"Then t—two more of them n—nurses come in. They was all n—nurses. These two screamed and r—run into a bedroom. I pulled my knife and ch—chased them through them b—bedrooms, stabbing and having sex, it all kinda r—run together, that's the way it w—went, until it were all d—done." Bogart fell silent then, sounding sleepy, exhausted, his head down.

"Alan, it was just another part. That wasn't you. You were just along for the ride." Daniel was surprised by the gentleness.

Bogart raised his head. "R—really? Is that t—true?" There was an eagerness in Bogart's voice that embarrassed Daniel. "None of it was m—me?"

"Absolutely… none of it." Daniel could detect a note of hesitance. The big man stood and grabbed Daniel by the shoulder. "Let's get some air." He couldn't mean outside, and the windows were all secured, but Daniel stood up anyway.

The walls of the barracks were off-white with random, rose-colored blotches and some darker more unpleasant blotches. Some sections were missing surface layers, fading to a patchwork of stone and faded brick with the odd bit of antique wood and iron filigree attached—but nothing complete, nothing to indicate what the original piece or function had been. The ceiling was the most damaged—thoroughly water-stained and unstable.

Unlike the floor of the waiting room, the surfaces of the barracks were well-swept. But the deteriorating ceiling left a light fall of pale dust every morning on bed blankets and exposed heads.

Besides the bunks and basins a rusted-looking, metallic cube construction stood in the middle of the room where sustenance could be obtained in paste shaped to suggest various categories of food, but more suggestive of lubrication than nourishment. The roaches' observation windows were similar to the ones in the waiting room, but there were a few more of them, and they were well-staffed by the dark insectoid heads. There were no windows to the outside.

A baroquely-ornamented door, like something from a church, was embedded in the wall near one corner—a dark toilet sat tucked behind. He rarely had the urge to go—he assumed it was the malnourishment. A larger door at one end was left open so they could go out at any time, the top hinge cracked so that the door tilted from the vertical.

But there was nowhere to go, as far as he knew, other than to more devastated areas of the old factory. The other areas he'd seen were empty of everything but debris and the occasional heavily-mandibled guard, and the floors were partially collapsed, so to wander there seemed pointless. The door to the waiting room remained closed and locked until the roaches decided to open it.

There were more empty bunks in the room than there had been earlier in the week. But some of the residents might be in the scenario rooms, or in the waiting room, transferred, or in the infirmary, or being punished. Daniel tried not to write anyone off too quickly. Sometimes residents died, he believed, as they all talked about. Occasionally there would be evidence of a particularly black smoke coming from one of the factory chimneys.

Falstaff led the way across the barracks. Residents were rousing themselves, sitting up—some from ordinary slumber, some having recently come back from a scenario. Daniel could tell these by the faraway look in their eyes, the pale patches around the forehead and mouth, and the tendency to move lips silently.

One was staring at him coldly. A man in his late twenties, black hair and pasty complexion. A bright red rash covered most of his face. His eyes were scarlet pinpricks in dark hollows, embers that darted constantly about as if seeking something combustible. He'd seen the fellow before—he looked worse every time. His name was Carter, or Clark... no, Collier. Collier had been here a long time.

On the next bed a younger man avoided looking at him. He'd been placed here just before Daniel went on his last scenario. Short dark hair with red highlights, combed straight out from the scalp. Eyes diamond-shaped. Dark lips. Not red, but he wasn't sure what the color was. Thin, wiry body that contorted itself in sudden fits. Max—that was the name.

"Dan'l?"

He spun around. The chubby figure squatted Buddha-like on his bunk. Raymond P. Smythe, age fifty-two, late of Louisville, Kentucky, as the man had told him several times.

"I used to have that problem, myself, with them after-images, comin out o' one of them devil's lives. It's like a little fire and brimstone hangs on to your coat tails on the way back from Hell." He shifted his hips and grinned at Daniel impishly. "By the way, you rememberin me now?"

"Vaguely... yes, yes I do."

"Now that's mighty fine, Dan'l. Used to, it'd take you days, or whatever passes for days here, just to get the vaguest notion about where you were. But I don't suppose you member that?"

"No... not at all."

"Well, as God's my witness, that's the truth, if you can count on anything in this upside-down promised land." Raymond grinned, and it was as if the sweating red beach ball of a head had split open, a corn cob of gleaming white teeth instantly filling the wound. The beach ball bounced a few times up and down on the neckless trunk, then the corncob appeared to turn sideways a bit. "Hey now, what's the matter, Dan'l? You look a little peak-ed. Dan'l?"

He'd collapsed to the floor when it hit him. "He knew! The first one he shot—she was at least eight months pregnant, and *he knew*."

"Aimed directly at her belly, didn't he? Shot right through her unborn baby and murdered it. With his skills, no way was it an accident!"

Daniel was vaguely aware of Falstaff's arm around his shoulder moving him along. He was vaguely aware of how good it felt, vaguely aware of sobbing uncontrollably. It felt so good to lose control. "Did the woman die?"

"She survived," Falstaff said. "She was eighteen, young and healthy. But she couldn't bear any more children after all the damage. And that was her fiancé leaning over her who was killed."

"Oh Jesus Jesus Jesus..."

"Daniel, let's get to some fresh air."

"Have you played Whitman, too? Have we all done *that*?"

"We've all done things, we've all been in those roles. We're all in this same boat together. It's the roaches."

"No! It's us! We couldn't do those things if we didn't have that already inside us. Nobody could make you do such things if it weren't already there!"

Raymond was suddenly standing in front of Daniel and Falstaff blocking their way. "But the point is none of us ever did things like that before. I don't think any of us *could* have done those things if them damned roaches hadn't taken us. That's what matters, Dan'l. It's not us. It's them *roaches*."

Daniel wanted to believe this, but how did Raymond know? He didn't know Daniel. He didn't know what Daniel was capable of in his heart.

"He doesn't seem that devastated by it. Not to me." This from a sleepy-looking bald headed fellow a few bunks away.

"Keep it to yourself, Scott." Raymond walked back to his cot. "I'm getting tired of listening to that kind of trash from the likes of you."

Scott looked offended. "I just know how bad I feel after one of these things. And he doesn't look like he feels that bad."

"That's enough, Scott," Falstaff warned. "No more."

Scott grimaced, or smiled. Daniel remembered him now. Scott's eyes suddenly widened. "What was that?" he shouted, then burst into laughter. "Stay away from me, bitch!" he screamed.

"Let's keep walking," Falstaff moved him toward another door in the wall by the observation windows. Because of its proximity to the roaches, Daniel had always stayed away from it.

The door opened into a hallway nearly clear of debris. At the end another door and a stair led upwards. "Are you strong enough to climb these steps now?"

"I'm okay," although he wasn't actually sure. "What's up here?"

"You'll see."

After a flight Daniel asked, "Did you mean what you said? That we're not personally responsible?"

"That's not exactly what I said. But I do believe that just because you do something terrible playing one of these roles doesn't mean you'd normally do it, under any other circumstances. We're just inserted into these evil creations to bring our human understanding to the narrative."

"To figure out why they did what they did?"

"It's hard to say what the roaches hope to get out of this process. Unless they're actually the sadistic gods we sometimes think them to be." Falstaff turned around and sat down. "Let's take a break. I don't get the exercise I used to." He sighed, but Daniel didn't think he actually looked that tired. He stared at Daniel. "There once was a famous comedian, Louis C.K.? He used to do a routine about how the biggest danger on the planet to women was men, how he couldn't believe they actually consented to date us, to continue the race because men were, well, so dangerous, I believe that was the gist. Hilarious, hilarious stuff."

"Sure, I've heard the routine, fairly recently, I think. I never thought of him as that famous. What do you mean 'once'? Did he die recently? How long have I really been away?"

Falstaff blinked, grimacing. "No, no—I didn't mean that. I think I'd imagined he'd said it a long time ago. Maybe because it's so, wise, I think. It's very perceptive, what he said, what it says about the dynamics between men and women."

"Oh, I suppose. It seemed a little exaggerated to me. Funny but, it overstates, don't you think? Like most humor? I know I'm not dangerous like that, certainly not to a woman."

Falstaff was silent for a few moments. "It's not an accusation leveled at any *specific* male. It's about what challenges us, what we have to overcome, the things we've always been forced to live by. It's-it's what Alan said, something about how men have always been fed this poor approximation of the truth. About how we've *all* been immersed in a lifelong distortion. And what that's done to men, and to most human beings. It's made us more... dangerous. Do you have a daughter?"

"No."

"Neither do I. But if I did, I'd be afraid about what she might encounter. It embarrasses me."

They started to get up, then Daniel said, "There was a young boy with me, with Whitman. He participated in the shootings."

"A doppelganger."

"Doppelganger?"

"It happens sometimes. There's someone else in your scenario, some persona who commits some of the crimes. It takes some of the pressure off you."

"It didn't make me feel any better."

Falstaff shrugged. "It works differently for different people. Did he look like anyone you know?"

Daniel couldn't think about it for very long without a thrill of anxiety riding across his skin. "No," he said firmly. "But it reminded me of myself. I was never as angry as I was when I was young. My dad would have to calm me down. 'There's nothing more dangerous on the planet,' he told me, 'than an angry young man.'"

They took another flight of stairs. The deterioration was more pronounced. Paint peeled from the walls like leaves and fronds wilted and the color drained out. Stair steps were cracked, the treads missing large chunks. Rusted brick-a-brac clogged the darkened corners of the landings.

They reached the final landing, a final door. "Wear these." Daniel slipped the sunglasses on as Falstaff pushed open the door.

The roof of the building was much larger than Daniel had expected—going on for hundreds of yards, it was vast, a rambling stretch of stone and tar and metal and some fibrous material he did not recognize with a rotten, blasted surface. Loose debris lay scattered over everything. It was like some abandoned, ruined beach.

Besides numerous pipes sprouting from hidden sources deep inside the building, and duct ends of old rusted ventilation shafts, he could detect the remnants of foundations across broad stretches, and here and there an actual piece of a wall, indications that at one point there had been additional rooms up here, maybe even a partial level.

There were also crude lean-tos and makeshift loungers, a number of crudely assembled shelters, an array of furniture dragged up from the levels below, and gray-uniformed residents lying around in the sun, and only a short distance away the roaches doing their own lounging, their gleaming carapaces reflecting brilliant green and blue fractal patterns that hurt the eyes.

Most appeared relaxed, apparently glad that sunshine and moving air were possible in this strange prison. But consternation and irritation were evident in some of the isolated small groups. An older man and a woman—the first female he had seen since coming here—were screaming at each other so furiously he couldn't understand what they were saying.

A man in his seventies, wasting away in a voluminous robe, and a younger fat man were seated together. The fat man was stroking the old man's emaciated face and hands, speaking in soft murmurs, then reaching out with clawed fingers and digging into the old man's chest, the fingers coming away slightly bloodied.

"Father and son, I believe," Falstaff said.

Here and there were some solo performances in the crowd: a man sitting on a broken piece of stone sculpture, quietly nibbling at his left hand. A young woman walking repeatedly to a shiny piece of metal, staring at her reflection and bursting into tears.

As they got closer to one edge of the building the roaches far outnumbered the residents. They watched silently and, like the soulless soldiers Daniel suspected they were, slowly turned their heads with those enormous multi-faceted eyes. A few were half-hidden in the debris, betrayed only by a barbed black leg straying around a corner, or a section of dark carapace showing behind gaps in a wall or through metal mesh. Several lounged ridiculously on steps or benches, their stiff legs erect and suspended in mid-air. Daniel almost laughed.

"Daniel!"

He ran into something hard and immediately felt the salt taste. He looked up past hard black branches with daggers attached, to his face mirrored hundreds of times in the black facets of the globes. A smell like rancid motor oil and urine. He was rigid, and thought he might scream.

But only the antennae moved, drifting fractionally in the still air. Daniel turned and walked away from the enormous roach.

"Notice how they've gathered around the edges, as if shielding the air space," Falstaff pointed out.

It was true. The roaches appeared to have strategically placed themselves along the perimeter of the roof, blocking the residents from accessing the building's edge. On one side he saw the gleam of water and a boundless emptiness of ocean, and on the other a wide stretch of dirt and then a distant, ragged jumble of concrete and brick ruins. He was startled. He'd had no idea they were near an ocean.

"What are they doing? Are they afraid the residents might try to escape?"

"I think it's more along the lines of suicide prevention. Although what's to prevent a roach from taking the leap I don't know."

Daniel determinedly looked away from the roaches and the residents, lifting his eyes toward the sky. It was mottled with dark clouds, smoke or pollution, and slight traces of a shimmer, as if it were all cooking. Then further away, hovering above a more distant rubble, gray and red, with sudden plumes of black.

"Feeling as if you're in the crosshairs?" Daniel nodded nervously. "It's a common notion people have up here on the roof. Remind you of the Charles Whitman scenario?"

"Yes, yes it does. But from the victim's point of view."

"He was the first, or the first we remember, to shoot strangers randomly that way. Death from the skies. It's because of him that American police departments established SWAT teams."

"But an aberration," Daniel insisted. "Not everyone does things like that."

"I suppose not. But one of our more famous American writers—I'm sure you studied him in school—he's part of the literary canon as they call it—Harry Crews, he once wrote after visiting that Texas Tower that he knew that all over the earth people were resisting climbing the tower. That all of us have a Tower to climb. And to deny that you have your personal Tower is to risk the possibility that you might someday climb it."

"Harry Crews? He wrote *Car*, right? About a fellow who eats a car? And *Feast of Snakes*? Great stuff, but you don't study a writer like that in school, at least not where I come from. You discover him at a sleazy newsstand, or in a box of used paperbacks at a garage sale."

A darkness came into Falstaff's face. And something odd was happening with his mouth. "I suppose. He's just a writer... I admire very much. I misspoke." In the bright afternoon air his face shimmered with vague shadows and Daniel had to look away.

4

THE INSECT VOICES at the back of his brain might have taken him anywhere. Often there was a time just before the dream was over and a new scenario began that he thought they may have taken him to some prehistoric place and left him there, some lost landscape of hard shell and claw and bodies torn and leaking. They'd sent him to where they wanted him, to where he needed to be. They'd left him with barbed, narrow legs in his thoughts, hard exoskeletons at the periphery of his vision.

Daniel came to again while staring up at the sky. The smell here was worse than Ubo, worse than anywhere he'd ever been. He could see blackened, crumbling brick buildings in his peripheral vision, moist and dripping, a thick red sky. And all he could smell was that stench of raw sewage. He wanted to look down and make sure he wasn't standing in it, but the character he had entered was singularly focused on that sky and wouldn't allow it.

Daniel was surrounded by a wall of noise, beating against him from all sides, and yet his character had somehow turned it off, refusing to hear it. It was as if his new persona had eaten him.

A black plume of smoke thrust itself across the red sky, stalled, then began to dissipate into air already heavy with particles. This left some patches of sky looking oilier than others; he could see the small green and purple and blue rainbows that oil makes in a puddle.

Then the head snapped down and around and the sound came rushing back in: an incredible clatter, layer upon layer of thousands of rattling carts and buggies pouring down the kennetseeno streets, metal shod wheels on cobblestone, and their vibrating shells all sounding as if they were shaking themselves to pieces, punctuated by the more pleasing rhythm of the horses' iron-clad hooves. Then there were the sellers, the street criers, their shouted words overlapping until he had no idea what they were saying, except the periodic exclamation of "Buy! Buy! Buy!" And then lording over them all the melodic notes of the bell tower at Christ Church, pealing out the hour.

Christ Church? And all this smoke and sewage, buggy rattling. London in the Victorian era, certainly. Early industrial London, incredibly filthy city. He never would have believed the amount of pollution that could be generated by coal, tons and tons of it burning all the time, if he hadn't been seeing it himself.

Spitalfields, his character thought, as if in answer. And the chapel. *Whitechapel*. And Daniel felt his own thoughts falling away into tatters as an old rage tore up out of the deep shadows and consumed him.

A ballad monger stood on the corner, his broad sheets tied around his hat, his head dropping back (*slice, slice!*) as he began to bellow,

"*Now Mrs. Potts says she, I'd let the villain see,*
If I had him here I'd sure to make him cough,
I'd chop off all his toes, then his ears and then his nose, And I'd
make him such a proper drop of broth,
His hat and coat I'd stew and flavor it with glue, Blackbeetles,
mottled soap, and boil the lot,
I've got a good sized funnel I'd stick it in his guzzle,
And make humbug eat it boiling hot..."

And all around him the folks was laughing and jostling, speaking of Jack the Ripper. Well, that weren't his name, now was it? But he didn't like the name his bastard of a pa give him, so Jack would do, all jolly the way they said it now, or all full of fear the way they said it at night. Happy Jack—though he'd never been happy as far as he membered—or Sad Jack or Rippin Jack it was all him. Never mind wot they said in the papers. He didn't read them, just heard about them, and their lies, because he'd never writ any of them letters, or called hisself Jack. But Jack, Happy Jack would do.

Oh, he knew how to read and write well enough—one of his pa's old customers was a proper gent, some kind of professor fell into drink and become a lushington. He stank of hair oil, his bloody whiskers all curled up in bacca-pipes. Before he died—a do down one night with a holywater sprinkler bashing his noggin—he taught Jack plenty, including things Happy Jack wouldn't think about. But Jack never liked the way the read and the writ words felt in his head, all bumping around and hurtful like a tin cup full of stones. Each word like a new voice in his head, and him with too many in there already. The "mad multitudes," to quote Milton, the way the professor always done.

But the words kept coming none the less, with all their temptations and colorful suggestions. There was that other bloke the professor was always quoting, now wasn't there? Something Blake? "Sooner murder an infant in the cradle (a terrible thing!) than nurse unacted desire."

Jack never set out to be no trassewno. He never wanted to hold a candle to the devil. He weren't born evil, no matter wot the papers or the ballad criers said. Oh, he knew life. He'd done his share o' area diving round the Chapel, some beak hunting (he dearly loved them chickens!), bug hunting, a bit of blag. But he weren't a bludger at first. All that bloody business come after living too many years in Hell, hearing the church bells every day and thinking about wot they promised, and then getting none of it. The Chapel were a long ways from Heaven.

Then a film come over Jack's lamps, like it done most days ahead of sunset, betwixt three and four. Soon enough you'd hardly see your hand in front of your face, even with the gas lamps on, with all the black bits in the air. But Jack got dark afore the rest. Jack got dark with the sun still blazin high. He could see all them other blokes walking about in the afternoon of their day when for him it was nigh midnight. Not like he favored the dark, or being alone and such. The dark left him with a sick feeling in his belly and salt on his tongue, with all the times he membered living there, no matter the time of day.

So he started moving, running in his big gallies into folk, knocking em down, not cause he was of a mind to hurt nobody but cause he wanted to run out of there, run out of London if he could. Folks shouted at him, cause they knew him, though they didn't know him as Jack.

The ripper distracted, Daniel floated up through the swirl of madness, past the thoughts of *bloody hole, filth and scum and a rotting taste going down as deep as the lungs*, as if seeking a gulp of clean air. He'd never experienced such chaos in a character before, not even in a murdering thug like Jesse James or a monster like Caligula, both clearly reasoning people compared to this one.

He was playing a character and the character was part him and part what the roaches had been able to find out or recreate. But the experience of being inside a character was always different, and sometimes even varied widely over the span of a single visitation.

Sometimes, like this time with Jack the Ripper, you were swallowed completely, so there seemed no difference between Jack's thoughts and your thoughts, and looking out Jack's eyes was the same as looking out of your own, and you smelled the stench with Jack's nose, and when Jack raged that was you raging as well.

These were the hardest characters to shake later, when you woke up back in the barracks. You'd feel the most guilt over what Jack had done, and you'd have flashbacks into the character at the most inopportune times, like when you were eating dinner, or thinking of the family you'd left behind, and you'd curl up into a ball on the floor, knowing that a hundred showers wouldn't wash all that filth away.

Other times it felt as if you were riding within a bubble inside your character's brain. You could hear everything, and feel everything, but that was still you inside the bubble, horrified by everything your character was doing, and yet you were forced to watch. Their rage was not your rage—in fact when they raged against their victims, it also felt as if they were raging against you.

But if you were lucky, the walls of that bubble might be thick enough that you didn't hear everything your character said, or see everything your character did, and sometimes you could even close your eyes and pretend you were back home with your family, no matter how hard the roaches tried to yank you out of there.

An invasion of nausea rose out of the ripper then, draining any thought of an earlier- or later-day London, or of a Daniel or Jesse James or Caligula or of any other lifetime. There was only this…

He was here and now, trapped here in Jack, Happy Jack. Once again a tide of salt water lapped at his throat as he emptied himself of Daniel, was drained of any memories of a time or a place other than this. Inside the dark part of his eyeballs he could see a roach-head, black eye-globes glistening, barbed legs sawing against his tender brain tissue. A skittering through his head as the roach-thoughts clawed, digging for some kind of understanding of why Jack done what he done. Like Jack had any idea at all.

Whitechapel High Street. A man with a rough old face, his patchy white beard like some kind of infection, goaded a small drove of cattle down the street toward the slaughterhouses at Aldgate. Deerstalker cap, brown kecks and a cutaway coat--even all that dunnage couldn't hide the filthy white hair on the man's face. Jack imagined that if he stripped off the coat he'd find more hair running the fullness of the man's body, matted with cow shite and other filth.

47

Jack stared at the cuffs of the man's trousers. They was so badly frayed he wondered if a dog had chewed them, or the man's own cows when he slept with them. Mud speckled him from his cracked leather crabshells to his beard-eaten face. Jack could see the tiny balls of mud--or maybe they was shite--clinging to the ends of the man's whiskers, as the horns of the lead animal snagged Jack's coat. An explosion went off in Jack's head, as much terror as anger. And suddenly he was God bringing the mayhem down on this transgressor.

Jack punched the man on the shoulder. "On yer way! Outta the street!" The old man raised his cane, looking startled, unable to speak. Jack punched him in the face. He felt the nose give way like it was made of eggshell. Blood spurted from one nostril, thickly painting the beard. Jack rocked back and forth on his feet, acting the bruiser, hitting at the old man, who was now trying to maneuver himself behind his cattle. Jack slapped out at his face, but a shoulder got in the way. The old man stumbled back against a cow, and Jack tried to pursue him around the lead animal, careful to avoid the horns. The cattle stirred restlessly, moaning deep in their throats.

"You!" Jack turned to see the copper splashing toward him through the stream of sewage in the lane. "Stop!"

Jack turned to the old man with a grin, nodded once at the blood spotting his coat and waist-length beard, then hit him again, this time tagging a cheek. He could feel the crisp crack of bone beneath the mushy face afore the man went down, nobbled. The cattle bolted ahead of him as Jack ran, laughing. The brief beating had gotten his blood up, made his palms sweat, his lungs flutter. He'd have to get the tension out now; there was just no helping it. A fist fight or some quick work with a shiv, anything to raise his head a bit, keep the blood up. He laughed out loud. He howled, then bayed at a startled old lady in a black hood. His palms itched. His throat was so dry he knew he could down a full flagon on the run. He could smash gents' heads and tear into ladies' faces with his teeth. Spit em out and dance on the soft parts. Bloody, bloody kids and dollymops with their soft bits turned out. All their hanging down parts spotted with black soot and the sewage from the streets. Can't be leaving your soft parts hanging. He'd found that out a long time ago. Asking for it if you did. The only way to have anything would be to raise the blood and spit and beat on it, break off the filth. Scratch it out. Then you'd be a giddy one, living higher than the steeple. You'd be a giddy bloody king, you'd be. Nobody gives it to you. You expect that and you're lying in the street, letting the blood flow till it's cold. The rich and the lovers and the famous gents all got their blood running hot. Jack'd found a way to get his blood hot, too. They had no idea. Helpless as cattle in the street.

Armored wings fluttering, barbed legs dancing in the shadows, antennae kiss to his lips...

Jack slowed to a stop after a couple of blocks. He picked up an old felt hat some swell had lost and ripped it with both hands, gnawing at the damp material. Felt like badger meat, or squirrel maybe, after it's been left to soak. Tough but chewy. He bit his lip hard and sucked out a little bloody salt. No copper'd catch him, not that way, and not here. Who'd care anyway, in this sty?

It was a spiderweb of alleys and courts here. A shroud of dark shadow lay over everything, a blackish scum. Looked like shite, and Happy Jack liked to think it was shite. He imagined he smelled it all the time, even in his sleep. And throughout most of the area there was also a heavier layer--greasy rags and trash ancient when Jack's judy of a mother was born, all glued together with liquid sewage into a kind of caul that slipped into all the cellars and slopped up into the house if you wasn't careful. A separate country it was, a different world, even with the East End but a short distance from Bishopgate and the Leather Market and the Bank of England.

Jack knew the secret, though. They wasn't human beings. How could human beings live six or seven or even twenty to a room? Rooms and rooms full of them lost souls, all the rooms of Hell.

He stopped, bewildered, then began to cry to himself. He let the tears wash out the gray city, and for a moment even the stench was missing from his enormous head, his skull full of the mad multitudes. He'd kill them all, he would. He'd kill them all. They was children dying… they was dying everywhere.

"Yer borned dead…" his flummut daddy once told him. "They bring your bloody carcass into this wurld and they slap ye good 'n silly so's you'll live and they do pretend pretty yer alive but you was borned dead…"

A scratching at his brain… their damned hard barbed legs. Wings across his eyes. Their enormous eyes always watching.

He membered that time he'd followed one of the ladybirds plying her trade on his street—she'd flashed her Miss Laycock at him and musta figured he'd pay her for the privilege—down down through a basement kitchen stinking of sin and the corruptions of the flesh, through a narrie hall moist and red, when she pulled him into her kes and turned her back, lifting her dress to show off her Nancy, pushing its plumpness against his Nebuchadneezar, and him about to do her in, he stepped off and messed around in his trousers looking for his shiv, when he seed that wee foot tucked under the edge of the bed, pulled on it and the dead tot slid out, its eyes closed and mouth open--that wee angel singing his way into death, a brown-stained bundle too small even to raise a stench. Jack looking down at it like it was a wee puppy drowned, and her turning round saying she had no knowledge of the thing. Leaving it to Happy Jack to dispose of.

Jack got out quick, forgetting her well-deserved murder.

They was mothers here in the chapel, death-mothers all, who'd turn their children into the streets at night because they let their rooms for whoring. Leave their own baby children out till past midnight, out there with the loafers and criminals to sleep with em in whatever staircase, doorway, dustbin, or loo they could find. But at least that was more money for the children than being a sackmaker for a farthing each or tuppence farthing a gross matchbox making.

Jack swung his foot at two shy-of-ten year coupling in the pathway. Connected right solid, but he felt no pleasure in it. He started thinking of the Eddowes woman, and what everybody had said. Ripped her up like a "pig in the market," they'd all said. "Her entrails flung in a heap about her neck," they'd said, their eyes gleaming.

Maybe he done it that way. He couldn't member it rightly. But if they got them particulars from the papers they got em wrong.

Jack made his way toward his doss on Flower and Dean Street. His pa run that one, and even though he was the very devil Jack knew he was lucky to have the free deb and not have to pay the four pence, which was more than he had most days. All he had to do was not speak to the man or let on that the warden was his pa. But everybody knew anyway, seeing as how he didn't have to show no tin ticket to get his bed.

They was some Irishmen round the front door smoking their short pipes, a couple old women with walnuts in their hands, a fellow in tar-smeared trousers tearing up a piece of gray chicken with his dirty fingers, stuffing it in his mouth, watching against them what would steal it. Two children dressed in a mismatch of rags huddled against the wall close by. They'd been there the day before—Jack figured they was dead or sleeping but he didn't want to be the one to check. He went down the steps into the area. His pa was there in his little booth. They locked eyes but neither said nothing. Jack walked into the kitchen and the big fellow with the burnt face and no name tossed him a bit of the herring he'd been toasting. The stench of it filled the downstairs. That was the way his pa sometimes give him some food—always from somebody else's hand. A fellow might think the old man was bang up to the elephant, except that very same day he might betray Jack, fill his bed with some stranger so that Jack had to go somewheres else or fight for his bed.

Two old fellows was sitting at the table spreading the broads. Jack didn't know the stakes, but there was a couple of gen on the table. When they seed Jack one of them covered the shillings with a rough hand that looked mashed and crooked. Jack didn't care—he never stole in the doss house.

There was a bunch of others lying around on the benches, coopered. One skinny bloke he'd seen afore, and he couldn't figure how the fellow was still breathing air. He had a head like a lamb been sheared, starved, his wrinkles crisp as folded paper. He breathed like he been punched with every gulp.

Jack climbed the stairs to the beds—another way he was treated special. Every other soul had to wait. The broken windows patched with rags and paper. Hardly no air, even through the ones they could open, and everything stinking from no proper washing. He found the old bed where they said his ma used to sleep, and his, the one he still had. Seven foot long but not even two across, a four foot tall wood partition on both sides. Like a coffin, though he never understood why a body needed such a thing. When you ain't gonna wake up who cares where?

He was beginning to feel a might glocky and went back downstairs. He got that way sometimes, not wanting to sleep in the room with all them other people. He waited until nobody was in the downstairs hall, crouched down, and pulled aside a couple of boards under the stairs, crawled in like a snakeman on a burglary. The vein he was in was dark and smelled like the world was dying, same as it always had.

In the first stretch he didn't have a lamp, but he didn't need one. He'd known the way almost since he was born, after his pa stuck his ma in this hole, her being pregnant and him not wanting nobody to know.

So she'd laid in here until she died, him inside her. Pa said he found Jack like he'd just crawled out of her filth hole, like the rutting and the birthing and the dying was all the same to her, and here Jack was still hanging by the cord. And it might ha' been that way, but there was no way for him to know now for positive.

Over the years Jack had dug it out further. It went down in under the foundations between the buildings, widening out as it went until you couldn't stand but you could almost. Finally he got there where he kept a lamp and some food, a bed of straw and rags, a few secret treasures, all to hisself. Most would think it a terrible place to be, some kind of way station along the road to Hell, but he still felt safer than upstairs with all them others watching him dream. It was a quiet place where he could bury hisself in sleep.

Did she scream in pain when she brought him out of one dark and into another? Or was she screaming in pleasure, or maybe there weren't no difference no more? Did she know she'd even had him? Sometimes Jack could conjure up her voice and he'd lie there for hours listening to her speak. Born from a dead mother, that was Jack's story. It was a short one, but it said all that was needed. And it always made him grin.

Oh, Jack had always been a grinner. His pa reckoned it were a tic because of the way Jack was born. Growing up he tried to control the grin, but the flesh above his upper lip bunched and fought him all the way. It pinched his nostrils, making him look like he was always smelling a bad smell. And the more he got excited, the more he felt about anything, the more he grinned. Happy Jack was a grinning fool.

That's why he grew that dark moustache. The grin was always under there, but now nobody else could see it.

He felt the roaches' legs at his lips, stiff wings brushing his thighs. He began to cry as the roach mounted him, carrying him deeper into the darkness, but at least he could sleep, come at the cost of one of them awful dreams.

"Jack? You asleep, Jack?"

He opened his eyes. "Ain't my name. Least not one anybody else can use."

The other eyes stared back. "Sorry. Penny for a suck?"

Jack struck out but there was nothing there. Then he saw the lad, half there and half not. But the boy was just a child, doing what others taught him. He needed to be patient with the lad.

Jack had no idea what time it was outside. Down in here it was always night time, dirt time, dead time. But he was too awake to stay dead, so he climbed out of his hole and went back out into the chapel.

This was when they come out. The haybags with that particular look about them, the dollymops and the judys and the night flowers and the three-penny-uprights what had no money for a doss, or the ones what had given up, now waiting for Fate to come and decide. The ones so plain about it--the death waiting in their soft parts. The death mothers. The teeth mothers. Dry wings raking, scraping the back of his brain. *Oh mother of God forgive me as I...* he whispered softly, as to a dream.

"Come on, Jack. Time to do your business." The lad walked ahead of him, leading him down the path. They'd done it all his life, leading him down one path or the other. But Jack followed, the London Particular so thick he couldn't find his hand afore his face. "Come on, Jack," the boy kept repeating. Jack followed the voice.

Hands kept coming at him out of the soup, like the walls and the dark itself had growed em. It was all he could do to keep hisself from slicing them hands off, but he wouldn't be distracted—he had to follow the lad. The lanes was full of lurkers, mumpers, and gegors with them hands out, griddling him for some coin or some food.

He'd battered a few at first... no knives then; he hadn't yet seen his calling. They'd bend over and spread their dresses for him in the alleys, and then he'd push their faces into the wall and beat em there. He took no pleasure in it. That was the point. Not a thing he done was about pleasures.

He'd started a long time ago, just a lad hisself, tearing up whatever he could get his hands on, acting the master of mayhem. His pa kept him locked up most days, said he couldn't trust him round the belongings. Then there was Jack's little parties in private, down in his secret place or in some quiet lane with the mice and the birds, all done serious-like, like he was a surgeon, or a priest in a church. Taking things apart weren't much different from putting them together in the first place, now was it? And God done both, two sides of the same hand. God the Father and God the Mayhem. But them little parties just didn't raise the blood no more.

Happy Jack thought he could see blazing white pantalettes and bloomers hanging in the dark, with just ever-so-much soiling. He thought of dead bodies casting off their clothes underground, like snakes shedding skin, all them unmentionables leeching to the top… barbed black legs and antennae raking at him passionately… Happy Jack could not escape from Hell. He could not love enough. *Where was the lad now*? He stumbled into one hidden court after another looking for him. No kingdom of peace for Happy Jack. No smiling family. No loving wife. No child to carry on his face. Just the dead mothers, always in his way, stopping him. So he'd turned around and gone a different way.

"Don't be a mewler, Jack," the lad said out of the soup just ahead. "You'll need some dash-fire in your belly if you're to survive the chapel."

Jack went off his onion then, couldn't believe the boy's bloody cheek to speak that way. To Jack of all people, who'd had to endure the fires of Hell afore he got to that babe's age. He commenced a run into the fog, bellowing like a bull and mad as hops. Course he couldn't find him, the boy having enough brains to run off by then.

He run into the usual collection of beggars and whores instead, his boots mashing the softer bits of them unfortunates, and the times being what they was he heard more than the usual portion of screaming, what with the whole populace down with the vapors over this Jack the Ripper affair, and just for a spell he forgot it was him they was referring to. He weren't no big toad—he was just doing what he had to do. They all had their own stories about what he done.

Had he really eaten the kidney of that Eddowes woman? He didn't think so. He was disgusted by the very notion. They was saying he cut open the bodies and made off with his little souvenirs, and maybe sometimes he did. Sometimes he'd find things he didn't understand when he'd opened them up, things what made him curious. So maybe he'd put em in a pouch and take em home with him. He'd usually forget about em afterwards, or lose em. He thought probably the rats what was always visiting him made off with them souvenirs.

Sometimes he'd smell the bits, putting em against his face to see how soft they was. They smelled the way he spected women to smell. Sometimes he'd look for any dead babies they might be hiding. Something about sorting through all the pieces made him feel like he wasn't all by hisself. He'd loved nary a woman alive.

He might ha' eaten that kidney. Sometimes he liked the taste of piss. But probably not.

Daniel swam up, gagging. Jack stumbled on his way through Hell. Mandibles tore open the back of his head. Mandibles and antennae and sharp sharp barbed legs dry hardened wings sharp as a razor for slicing off sections of the brain. In a frenzy they bore him down into the filthy street, their quick jabs growing fainter as they injected him, the memories and the stories and the speculations feeding back into his head, the sap rising up his spinal column easing him, erasing him, until Daniel was swallowed up in his own bile and he was Happy Jack once again.

Happy Jack. From Hell.

So excited he was that he quite bit through his bottom lip on the right side, and spent several minutes sucking the blood, almost desperate to keep the salt and iron taste flowing, priming his taste buds. He had never known a woman completely. They couldn't all be nasty whores. He had never known pleasure. He had never known a life outside his own skin.

The women in the street taunted him, dared him, their invitations framed in lace and painted lips. It was the paint that infuriated him most, making it obvious they knew all too well what they was doing, what they set out to do. Their special crime was that they made it all too obvious what it was all about, all that tedious waiting for your final hour and the death neverending. They drifted in and out of the dark alleys, the shadow holes, as in a fever dream. Sluts and pus-wells all.

Confronting the harlots had become gradually more difficult. Their dirtiness fascinated and repelled him--how unbelievably, beautifully dirty they was. The ground made into flesh. Like they had to dig themselves up every night for their lust time. Each time it was more of a chore to get the same ecstatic effect. They seemed far more in control of the event than he, drawing him further and further into their enticements. The death-mothers weren't likely to release him anytime soon.

He'd been watching Mary Kelly for months. Something special about this one, his feelings for her. Most of the judys was plain, washed-out things. Not her—she still had a freshness and good looks on her. He'd spent many a night sitting across from her lodgings at Number 26 Dorset Street. Or following her in the shadows as she left The Queen's Head pub. The lodging-house keeper, John M'Carthy, knew his pa, and had told Jack quite a bit about the woman, thinking Jack was less than he was, and the man liked to hear hisself talk. Her room was number 13 and had its own entrance onto the narrow street.

It was the fact that he found her so attractive that threw Jack off; he couldn't make himself go in and just dispatch her. Not like that. And that drove him mad. For in all other ways she was like every other whore what brought a poor whelp into this world, and everything what was wrong about the chapel. She was dead, she was walking around meat; she just didn't know it.

Most of the houses around her was full of whores, most of the windows boarded, and opposite Miller's Court was that doss with three hundred beds, filled every night. Her pretty face kept her busy—Jack counted several customers a night. She was always working Aldgate and Leman Street. She had a broken window, stuffed with a rag, and Jack had seen her reach through, push back the ragged muslin, and unlatch the door several times the past few days. Looked like she'd lost the key.

Maybe he best be careful; never afore had he hung around so long. But no one knew what he looked like. He'd heard he was pale, then he was swarthy, slight moustache, heavy or none, long dark coat, red coat, hunter's coat, light waistcoat with a thick gold chain, trousers and garters, red handkerchief, a foreign look, a twinkle in the eye—every man Jack of em seed something different, suspected a different neighbor or renter, father or doctor or reverend or husband-to-be. Anyone could ha' done them crimes— that's what drove em all crazy.

Jack had visited Mary Kelly's window the past few nights for a peek, when he knew she was gone. A bed, a chair, two tables. That was all. Some lace hung up by the window, a touch of the girl still in her. He caught himself wondering what it might be like to be living there with her. It made him angry with hisself; he might as well hope to be an angel up in Heaven.

He thought she might be pregnant. He had a special sense about such things. He could smell it on her.

Here the babies was all dying and the slut was bringing another dead child into the world. Jack could see it dangling blue-faced from its cord, wrapped around her waist like some prized belt. He reminded himself—this harlot was like all the rest.

In the darkness of the filthy street a child was softly crying. Jack looked around but could not see the babe. He wondered if it was drowning, half-dead under a pile of filthy rags, left abandoned in some darkened doorway, or what. The young ones had no chance. Their dead mothers was raising a nation of children with no one, a nation of staggerers wandering them alleys alone. They had to be stopped.

Teeth grinning a blade, scummy eyes shining under the gaslight. The lad had returned, standing in the darkness behind him. Happy

Jack whirled about and reached for him. The boy was starved, and the largeness of his hunger stopped Jack. The boy's eyes burned, pushing him.

"Do it," the boy said.

"No, not tonight."

"Don't be a mewler, Jack. You're going to feel good with this one. You're going to feel quite a bit more than yourself."

Mary Kelly wandered back from the public houses on Commercial Street about quarter to midnight. She couldn't manage more than a drunken wobble. She had with her a short, fatty pig of a man, ragged sleeves and a billycock hat, thick moustache, still carrying his beer from the inn.

"Goodnight, Mary," someone said out of the darkness. A woman's voice, but it could ha' come from anywhere. Jack's own head maybe? But he couldn't be bothered thinking on it, so busy he was watching his love and his hate dancing around with the filthy bulldog of a man.

"Goodnight," Mary called out. "I'm going to have a song." She then began to sing "Only a violet I plucked from my Mother's Grave when a Boy." It was ugly and off-tune but it was still like a needle going into Jack's heart.

Happy Jack watched her reach through the broken window and unlatch the door, then drag the fat sack of meat in with her. A short time later the pig stumbled out and went his way.

Jack turned toward the shadows. Tiny teeth gleamed. And somewhere a child was crying. At that moment he doubted Mary Kelly would resist; she wouldn't have it in her. For she was already dead, now wasn't she? And Happy Jack had come. Death would be too beautiful for her to refuse.

The paving stones beneath his feet was slick with human filth. He felt hisself stumble, and a pale arm come out of the filth and righted him. As far as he could see: dead bodies lolling in the alleys and doorways, their pale flesh beautiful in the moonlight. He and the lad stepped over them easily, the soft body parts rubbing against their progress. He and the lad. Happy Jack and the babe. Duly ordained and intent on their mission.

Happy Jack. Happy Jack. He walked to the broken window and reached through the space into the darkness of Mary Kelly's room. He unlatched the door, stepped there, and was through.

She wore a thin chemise to bed. He couldn't see her face in the darkness. He suddenly thought he might swoon with the power he had over her--he didn't know how he could bear it. Once again the world was his and everyone had to know this. She didn't know she was already dead. Happy Jack had a duty to tell her. He had a way to excite her.

With each stroke he felt he was erecting something higher, building a monument in his heart with each thrust and twist as the blood thickened and raced, ran up his veins and exploded out to mend the world.

Once, maybe twice, maybe even a third time she said it. "Oh! Murder!" But very softly, as if she really didn't care. Jack doubted anyone else could hear her.

The first thing he knew of it there was two chunks of flesh lying on the table in front of the bed. How had it happened? Where had they come from? Then he looked back at his love in her white jawbone, white cheekbone, white-tooth grin. Smiling at his love for her. Wanting to reach down inside her and seize that love, bring it out for all to see, embrace her in a way she had never been embraced before, as he had never, ever been embraced. The throat had been cut clear across with a knife, nearly severing the head... but letting loose her grin. Both meaty breasts sliced off the trunk, and he started to go into the belly.

And the boy was asking him for the knife.

Jack stared at the boy with his grin, puzzled, thinking how wrong it'd be. Then handed him the knife.

The boy was all grin, thrilled with participation, as he began the work: hacking and slashing until the nose was all gone, and Happy Jack thinking Mary was lucky she didn't have to smell the chapel no more, didn't have to smell her own dying. The left arm hung, like the head, by a flap of skin only.

Mary Kelly's leg was suddenly grinning at him, speaking with harsh white and red sounds, and Jack seed the knife digging a trench to her bone. Happy Jack moved closer as the belly was slashed across and down, reaching in desperately to find the babe drowning in his mother's filth, digging frantically, sure the lad would kill the new baby as well.

He had to pause once he was inside her, feeling the soft, warm wetness of her. Soothing as a baby's touch, as old silk underwear falling apart in a trunk, as an old felt hat caught between the fingers. Again he bit into his lip and brought up some salt taste for comfort. He reached for the baby, for Mary Kelly's love, determined to hold it, keep it, take it back with him to keep in his secret place under the ground.

He could not find the child alive in all that bloody flesh, even though he heard again and again its soft cries for help. He pulled away from the corpse-mother, suddenly afraid of the boy with his knife. Jack looked down at the flesh in his hands, Mary Kelly's liver, and placed it ever-so-gently on the bed between her feet, as if it was the babe. The boy looked back over his shoulder at Jack, grinning foolishly. And for some reason Jack found himself thinking of Christmas, and how a boy belonged with his toys and not in a Hell like this, and Jack giggled crazily, and reached in, and deep inside him Daniel managed to close his eyes, refusing to look.

When Daniel opened them again Happy Jack was staring into Mary Kelly's face. Only the eyes were human. He'd ha' blotted out the eyes too, their stubborn insistence on life turning his insides into a tortured twist, but he didn't dare step past the grinning boy. He stepped back as the boy held the bloody knife out to him.

And then he had the knife in his hands, Mary Kelly's eyes was on him, and the boy had again disappeared. Happy Jack sobbed as the barbed legs and mandibles raked away at the back of his skull in almost frantic rhythm. Something was breaking away here.

"My name..." he cried and fell to his knees, sobbing, unable to complete the sentence or look at the bed.

Instead he gazed at the window. At dark mandibles and barbed lobes rising into two shadow faces framed by large, multi-faceted eyes.

5

Daniel woke up on the floor by his bunk. He had his hands up and in front of his face. He stared at the red line as it moved down his right forefinger and began to spread across his knuckles, widening gradually until it was a thick swatch of blood. He turned. Mary Kelly's entrails steamed on the floor beside his head. He could feel the heat coming off them. What he did... He bit his lip and tasted salt. "*My God!*"

"Daniel!"

What he'd done, he'd ripped her, he'd felt inside her, touched inside her, touched... "*My god!*" The things he'd touched... "*My god my god!*"

"Daniel, you're back in the barracks. It's over." Daniel moved his eyes, saw Falstaff hovering over him. "Who were you last night?"

"The Ripper. Jack the Ripper. Or whatever his real name was."

"Oh. Upsetting stuff. He was like a shark, wasn't he? A human, butchering shark."

"How he saw women... I couldn't bear to think I had even a shred of those feelings inside me. I adore my wife. I loved my mother. I..."

He saw women's torn and bloodied lingerie hanging from the ruined ceiling, jeweled with cobwebs and spider eggs. Discolored and fake-looking manikin parts. A baby hung from the webs.

"You were playing a part. Now you have to shake it off. Many of us have ghosts of those feelings, stray notions and longings, but it doesn't mean we would do those things. We're not the people whose parts we're forced to play. You and I, we have food prep duty this morning. That'll help take your mind off it."

It seemed ridiculous that the roaches with their advanced technology should still require hands-on food preparation. Until Falstaff explained it to him.

"You've noticed they have humans handling the food? They never let roaches handle the food?"

"How do we know that roaches didn't handle the food before it got to us? It's just some kind of paste-more like mechanic's lubricant than any kind of proper food. It certainly looks like the kind of thing that a roach would have handled, or made, or thrown up, actually."

Falstaff made a face. "Don't be grotesque. Humans need to eat, they expect to eat—things go wrong if they don't eat—but they don't like thinking about where their food came from. But if they were to see the roaches handling the food, they would probably turn it down. They might even starve themselves."

"How do you know this?"

"It's the only thing that makes sense. The roaches don't even train us to do the job—it's passed down human to human."

The paste came out of three different dispensers: one with the symbol of a cow, one with the symbol of a fish, one with a leaf symbol. All the paste was of an identical, slightly grayish color, but the textures and flavoring varied. The vegetable paste tasted of greens. The fish paste tasted fishy. And the meat paste could have been chicken, beef, or pork—depending on your mood. To further individuate the offerings, the "cooks" cut the paste into a variety of shapes as it solidified, then ran it through a dye-and-flavor apparatus one batch at a time.

"Wait," Falstaff said. "That was vegetable paste."

"Yes."

"You applied the meat dyes to it."

"I doubt it makes much difference. It all tastes oily and greasy anyway."

"We'll see. I'm not greatly enamored of roach cuisine, either," Falstaff said. "But at least they've solved the food problem for themselves."

"I'd still like a good steak from time to time."

"Have you ever heard the expression, 'Meat is murder'?"

Daniel stared at the entries assembling into individual packages. "I won't argue with the ethics, but people have to eat. You were right. People don't like to think about where their food came from."

HE'D BEEN A summer child, Daniel's son. Oh, he was born in winter and might one day die in winter for all Daniel knew, and the last few years before Daniel had been yanked off to Ubo, Gordon had had the look of winter hanging about him. His hair was dark and fuzzy in a way that reminded you of coal, skin pale and translucent as plants grown with too little sun. And frozen eyes, shiny with their hard layer of ice, unmoving eyes that could accuse you like no other.

But he really should have been a summer child. He would have been had Elena and Daniel been able to make love that cold October when Daniel lost his job and Elena had first understood that the life she was going to have wasn't the one she'd signed up for. It was the first time they had gotten into trouble with their marriage, the first time they had been unable to talk each other out of worry, make each other feel safe again. From that moment on their pain had taken them down separate paths.

Although Daniel had been sure the marriage would be good again—it *had* to be, as he could not imagine a life without her—the estrangement shook him. He went back over the things he had said, the things he had done, determined to fix anything he had cracked or broken.

And so Gordon was conceived the first week in June during a hot spell in Miami. They'd gone there so that Daniel could look for work. The air conditioning in their cheap motel had broken down. They'd stripped but still couldn't get to sleep. And although things between them would get much better over the next few years, Daniel would never forget that they'd had Gordon simply out of frustration and a desperate need for comfort.

Gordon was born in Denver in March, during the worst snow storm in ten years. People talked about how global warming was obviously a fraud when they still could have such temperatures. The car lodged in a snow bank on the way to the hospital and Daniel was sure the baby would be born right there in the freezing automobile. But Gordon waited for the hospital to make his entrance, and from then on avoided the cold. Daniel could tell even in that initial cry—sluggish and forced out, as if he were afraid the winter would force its way into his body through his open mouth— that this child would hate the winter.

Gordon wanted to be a summer child: it was there in the set of his shoulders as he concentrated on a new project full of artificial color and light, in the tentative corners of his smile on the first really sunny day of spring, in his eyes the first time they saw a drive-in movie together, just the two of them, Daniel and his boy Gordon.

But all these gestures of promise and light were finally absorbed in the paleness of skin, a certain flaccidity of tissue that erased the boy's smiles. As Gordon grew older he settled into being a quiet and somber child. The cold organism that had wrapped itself around Gordon's heart had decided to smother anything else, and no wishes, lies, or dreams were able to stop that.

This boy here, the youngest resident Daniel had seen in Ubo— where there were no fathers or sons—had the same dark hair, the same paleness of skin, but the ambient light gave the skin a reddish, healthier tint. The black hair shone as if sprinkled with tiny jewels, from silica trapped in the strands, he guessed, and infrequent washing. The boy pretended to be at the beach with the bright blue sand bucket he carried and the short-handled shovel. Daniel went up to the roof of Ubo every day he could, which was where he first met him.

The boy glanced up at Daniel and the resemblance to his son snatched his breath. Then he pointed at the object between his feet, half-covered with filthy debris. It was the corpse of a small aquatic bird, its beak open, eyes closed, left wing bent awkwardly underneath. Birds sometimes crashed onto the roof. Few flew or walked away. The boy poked the bird's body with the shovel.

"Bird's dead," the boy said.

Daniel nodded, not sure how to handle this. But he thought he should say something. "Too bad. How did it happen?"

"I didn't do it!" The boy looked up at him defiantly, his lower lip puckered out.

"I didn't say you did... son. I just thought you may have seen it happen."

"No... I was just here, then there it was by those old cans. Dead. It won't ever move again, be alive again."

"That's right."

"Why can that happen?"

"It just happens, I'm afraid. It just happens that way."

The boy nodded. Then with an irritated little grimace he began digging up the debris around the bird as if trying to bury it in the roof. There was a great deal of dirt and debris here, but Daniel didn't think he could get deep enough to bury even a small bird. Finding damp, darker dirt underneath, the boy began to dig more violently. It seemed to Daniel a primitive reaction.

Daniel nodded again, feeling incredibly stupid. "That's too bad. Are you going to bury it?"

The boy bent over the bird with knitted brow, as if this were an extremely difficult question. "Maybe. I guess so. But maybe I oughta 'xamine it first, though."

Daniel crouched beside the boy, looking at the dead bird intently, as if he were just as interested as the child. And maybe he was. He reached and, absentmindedly, began to pick sand grains out of the boy's thick black hair. The boy looked up briefly, then turned back to the bird, apparently not minding.

"Why did it die?"

Daniel shifted uncomfortably, then sank his knees onto the roof and leaned closer. "I don't know... disease most likely. Maybe a heart attack. I've heard that birds have a lot of heart attacks..."

"Where's the blood? Didn't it have any blood in it?"

Daniel touched the bird gently with the boy's shovel. The blood appeared to be gone, and he'd seen animals in this state before, usually off the side of the road. But he couldn't really explain it—the question, a very good question, had caught him off guard. "I'm... not sure. I think maybe they get dehydrated. That means the sun dries them out once the heart isn't pumping anymore, or the lungs breathing. They turn... sour, I guess is the word. Like if you take a tomato out of the refrigerator and forget and leave it on the windowsill."

The boy nodded, then suddenly, vigorously poked the body with the shovel. The breast feathers depressed with a rubbery, sickening movement. "Will I die like that?" he asked in a near-whisper. "I mean, somebody'll find me on a beach or a sidewalk somewhere, and think I was just sleeping, 'till they poke me and I don't wake up? I mean, just like that, like something broke?"

Something caught in Daniel's breath then. Like a failing bird's wing desperate for some small wind. "Well, we don't know if that's what happened to this bird. Maybe he was having a good time, doing tricks in the air, racing another bird. Birds don't last long, you know—they die pretty quickly."

"Yeah." It sounded like relief. It made Daniel slightly nervous. "Maybe he won't be so lonely now."

"Why do you think he was lonely?"

The boy shrugged. "I don't know. All birds are, I guess."

He was smiling now. "Least maybe he was being excited when he died. He was... mad or something."

"I think you may be right."

Again, he looked so primitive, with his ragged shorts and face set over a problem he couldn't begin to understand. Maybe the boy *would* have known if the bird had been lonely. And maybe children did share a certain kind of loneliness with the first humans—it wasn't all that long ago that they had been a part of a wholeness that included everything in their universe. But then you're born, and your eyes open onto yourself for the first time and see that you are separate and alone. But you want to go back to that all-encompassing love, and gather up the parts of you for a return trip to paradise.

But there was no turning back the clock. And that made you angry, made you want to tear the whole world—your house, your crib— apart. The child would always be that naive, painful part of you still aware of your first separation, when the shadow of violence slipped out. And that would make anybody furious.

It made you mad that the child was so naive, that he could not see the danger, and could not see the danger from you, your hands, your fists. Sometimes you wanted to kill that part that refused to grow up.

"Maybe I wouldn't *mind* dying so much, you know, mister? How would you know?"

Daniel grabbed his shoulder. "Don't say that-you have no idea what you're talking about." The boy looked disdainfully at the hand on his shoulder. Daniel pulled away and sat down on the roof facing the boy. "Where are your parents?"

"Dead, maybe. I don't know. Maybe I'm the one—I fell asleep one night and then I was here. And now I have to pretend to be other kids I'm not."

"Anybody to take care of you?"

"They've all gone away. What's it like, mister, being dead? Are we in Heaven, or are we in Hell? Are we like gods, or are we like monsters?"

Daniel bit his lip. "I don't know. What do you think it would be like to be dead? Do you think it would be like this? Because I'm afraid you'd be wrong. You just wouldn't be—at least that's what I believe."

"I don't know for sure, but maybe it might be kinda exciting. It ain't that easy to die, is it?"

"Usually not."

"Then you gotta be doing things that are risky, things you shouldn't do."

"Well, not always."

"And so maybe you're doing exciting things when you die, maybe the most exciting stuff you ever done, mister."

Daniel stared at the boy in exasperation. "What's your name?"

The boy grinned. "I don't know. I guess I lost it coming here. You can call me anything you like."

From Gordon's first days Daniel and Elena had had definite ideas about their son's education and their obligation to instill certain values in him. To that end there were no toy guns in their house, no tanks or other combat equipment, no toy weapons of any kind. Gordon's television viewing was carefully supervised, and programs with heavily violent content weren't permitted him, including most Saturday-morning cartoons. Comic books and magazines were similarly scrutinized before Gordon was allowed to have them. This program started when Gordon was two years old. Daniel and Elena were determined that he have a repertoire of better solutions to his everyday problems than the aggressive ones his parents had grown up with. He'd be a better kind of person.

It wasn't long before it appeared that Gordon had an even greater fascination with weaponry than the average kid. His playtime fantasies were dark and violent, full of monsters and colorful deaths. Children, Daniel concluded, were a mystery.

Children were human beings, but they weren't "like us"—they weren't adults. And few adults treated kids as if they were fully human. They treated them like animated dolls, robots, pets. The adults used unnatural tones and vocabulary. They referred to them as "cute," or "noisy." Parents were amused by the walks and dances that mimicked the human, but certainly didn't duplicate it with much accuracy.

Children lulled you, made you think of them as small cuddly humanoids, but something would change, and the child would suddenly speak to you in an anguished, strangely human voice, and you felt ashamed.

Daniel vividly remembered one night becoming aware of soft moans from Gordon's bedroom, interrupted by wet coughs and hiccups. He went into the bedroom and a wail from under the comforter made him turn on the light.

"Gordie ..." He pulled the wet and trembling child from the tangled mass of bedclothes and embraced him fiercely, wiping awkwardly at the damp face with a corner of the sheet. "It's okay, love. Daddy's here... nothing to be afraid of. Nothing wrong here."

"... bad dream..." Gordon gasped out between sobs.

"Oh, but it's gone now. The dream can't get you now, sweetie. Daddy won't let that happen."

Gordon gazed at him sleepily. "They were trying to get me."

"Who?"

"The man and the woman. We were in the bathroom and they held knives to my belly and all the skin started coming off me and... they didn't have no faces, and I was bleeding too much. I started yelling but that came out blood, too, all big and bubbly."

Daniel held onto his son. After a while Gordon fell asleep. Daniel gently slipped him under the covers and kissed him, and as an afterthought tucked Flat Duck under his arm. Then he returned to his chair in the living room, where he brooded for hours.

He'd never thought of children having nightmares that bad, and over the next few months discovered that Gordon had a variety of them. Suddenly his son seemed a tiny container of horrors. Small cuddly humanoids should never have such dreams, nor should robots, nor dolls. Was it his fault, Gordon picking up Daniel's own anxieties? But the source of Gordon's fears remained a mystery.

After they had been told of Gordon's heart condition Daniel thought he had at least a reason for the mysterious dreams and fears. This small thinking machine had created a compelling image or two to explain its hidden defect to its human masters.

Each night Daniel went into his son's room, allowing the light from the living room to illuminate the bed in the corner. Each night he would walk over to the bed and stand a moment, watching carefully to make sure that the small chest was rising and falling as it should. Then he'd lean over and hold his son awkwardly through the covers, repressing the urge to climb up onto the bed and sleep with him.

"There's still much we can do," he whispered to end the ritual, and damned himself for a liar each time. It seemed the best he could do was imagine the worst.

6

DANIEL HAD BEEN forced to endure many trips into the minds of soldiers during combat. It had become a constant theme in his compulsory role-playing, so apparently it was a primary area of interest in the roaches' studies, but at least in Daniel's case the results were mixed. It was almost always a frenetic and fragmented experience, frequently brief, as he was jerked out of these scenarios for a variety of reasons including bodily trauma and death. He wondered if the roaches had been unable to get a stable read of these personalities because of the volatile nature of most combat experiences. The stray thoughts he caught were like unstable bombs threatening to blow up in his face.

Fighting the enemies of freedom to spread democracy throughout the world.

"Why do they hate us?" It always shocked Daniel to discover that Americans were hated. "Is that what brought the towers down?"

A pre-emptive strike. A fight to remain dominant.

"Sergeant Taylor?" Voices like insect scrapes across the brain, painful and annoying at a low level, but he was trained to ignore such tiny, irritating voices. He was glad they didn't use his first name. Perhaps "Sergeant" had become his new first name. He doubted he would ever use his given name again.

Of course Taylor wasn't his name, either. He'd been misidentified. His face must really be messed up. He'd become the unknown soldier. How much of the rest of him was left?

"What do you think he thinks about?"

"Nothing. How could he? He doesn't move; he barely breathes. Look at his eyes. They don't blink."

"Has anyone on the staff seen him close his eyes? Does he sleep?"

"Look at his eyes, so dry. They should put more drops in them. How could a man stay sane without sleep?"

So they weren't doctors or nurses. Maybe they were orderlies, or maybe cleaning people. Good, he was sick of doctors and nurses. He'd rather talk to the regular guys cleaning up piss and blood. If he could talk.

"I hear he used to talk."

"Yeah, but he didn't answer any of their questions. He only talked about what he wanted to talk about. And then one day he just stopped talking."

Black clouds of smoke drifting with veins of blue. He dropped like a burning cinder, the jungle shooting up around him. Dark wings covered him. Sharp legs and brittle antennae massaged his brain, working their way into his thoughts. The smell of phosphorous so strong it pinched the nostrils. The smell of napalm and the smell of human flesh burning. The evil stench of insect bodies massed for an attack.

AND SUDDENLY DANIEL was out of that soldier, and into another grunt back in Vietnam. Pinkville, up against the border. He skipped through their heads like a stone thrown by a boy across a dark and deceptively still pond. My Lai. Charlie Company. 1st Battalion, 20th Infantry Regiment, 11th Brigade, 23rd Infantry Division.

He'd heard that Captain Medina'd said nothing would be left alive in the village. That wasn't a direct order, but leave it to Lieutenant Calley to try to make it happen. Calley was Medina's bitch, and nothing he could do would please him, but he kept on trying. They all should've just walked away, pretended they didn't hear him that day. Some of them did, and some of them would feel okay about it either way, but for the rest of his life he would wonder if he could have, should have done something.

The film of it was embedded in his head: all those people begging and screaming, and Calley firing into that ditch, and the emotions so high his eyes were burning, the sky in his private film burning, those dying breaths turning into dark plumes of smoke. He had to admit, he used to call them gooks, but not after that. Never after that.

It was your duty, basically, to go to war. He'd even believed in the Domino Theory. But God knows, not that.

SERGEANT TAYLOR WRINKLED his nose, even though he didn't have a nose anymore. The smell of burning shit. That was his first smell of Vietnam—out where there wasn't any plumbing they collected all the human shit in barrels, soaked it in fuel oil and set it on fire. Guys had to stir the barrels to make sure it all burned. Always a bad smell, a bad taste. Pale, bloodless faces. Dark, yellowish, insect-like heads. The salt taste of blood in the mouth. The need to bite, to chew, to rip, to tear tender skin. The need to smash like some rampaging god. To ignite mayhem. Sergeant Taylor used to talk often about the lies of Vietnam. There was little else to do.

Taylor loved the way Alex smiled. He was a good boy. Blond hair, skinny, and eighteen years old. Basketball player, playing now for God and country. He didn't pay much attention to what Taylor said, or at least he didn't act like he did. Still, he was a good boy. But hell, the kid didn't know what they were going to ask him to do. None of them did. Hell, the whole damn country had no idea what it was trying to face.

"Now the way I parse it out," Taylor continued, "is that you first got your big lies. Everybody knows what the big lies are, whether they think of them as lies or not. You know, son, lies about whether we can win or not, or whether we belong here in the first place. The lies that got us into this mess. Then there's the medium sized lies, don't you see, like The Body Count Lie, or the Stupid Math Lie, as I like to call it."

He stared at the boy, who now grinned in embarrassment. Taylor figured the kid was scared to death that some brown bar or the C.O. might walk by. He really shouldn't do this to the boy, he supposed. Damn them all, though. They spend all their time teaching kids in school about being heroic, about being noble and giving your life to something bigger than yourself. They don't teach you about the nights and what to do when you're ass-deep in the dark. These people here in Nam, they've lived in the dark for a long, long time. They know it's got teeth and a belly it needs to fill. They know you have to grow teeth, too, if you're going to survive it. You have to embrace it and become the goddamned God of Mayhem. The number of dead don't matter, except the bodies are just something more you can feed it. What the hell does a body count mean out here anyway?

"You know about the body count, don't you, soldier? Haven't you counted no bodies yet? For shame. You know, twenty here. Sixteen back there—oops—one of them's ours from that not-so-friendly fire so better make that fifteen. Twenty-five over there, but that count includes two cows, three civilians, and a fence post. Out here we use that new Stupid Math. Forty-two in the next county, but then them were all civilians. Now, you got to be careful not to miss the bodies left in the ditches, stacked on the trails like bags of dirty laundry, the bodies in the house, the bodies hanging from the trees, the body fertilizer, the body mayonnaise. How many arms or how many legs or—here's a tough one for you—how many pounds of loose gut equal one body on the C.O.'s body count report?"

Alex wasn't smiling anymore. Sergeant Taylor could dearly appreciate that. Wasn't a damn thing to smile about.

"But, now, it's the little bitty lies that've always interested me, the people lies. Like the lie that said you wouldn't be afraid when you got over here, that you'd be some kind of frigging freedom fighter, or that they'll all be treating you like a fucking hero when you get home. You listen to Sergeant Taylor, boy. Ain't going to happen. Ain't no way. Like the lie that says you'll go back in one piece. Like the lie that says you're a wholesome, all American boy and you're going to stay that way. The lie that says you ain't going to turn into a fucking monster over here."

"Now, wait a minute, Sarge. Pretty personal, aren't you?"

"It's a damn personal war, son."

"I don't intend to change."

"Now I am relieved."

"So, if you hate it so much, why are you here? You already had your tour, you went back for a while, so why'd you sign on for another one?"

Taylor just stared at him. Insect legs scratched along the back of his brain, trying to find the right words for him to say. "My business, son," he finally said. "Go check your gear. Moving out soon." The boy strode off with a little swagger. Probably thinking he'd finally caught his old Sarge on something. Maybe he had.

LIEUTENANT CALLEY WASN'T the only one trotting after the Captain like a little puppy dog. They would have followed Medina anywhere. He gave them those cards, the Ace of Spades, because they were "death dealers," okay? They were supposed to drop those on every gook they killed.

Still, Calley was the worst, always trying to please Medina, and it only made the Captain call the lieutenant a little shit, and that's how he treated him.

If Bill Webber hadn't been killed, maybe things would have been different. He was the first, and that started the dying, and then they went through that mine field. They had one soldier split right up the middle. The villagers could have said something, warned them.

That changed the rules—destroying villages became the standard.

It wouldn't have been wise for the villagers to point out the mines, though. Folks like that, they stayed alive by keeping their mouths shut. It was a bad situation for everybody concerned.

The company set up a perimeter around the village. Those villagers never saw it coming. The older ones had told the younger ones that the Americans were different—they brought candy bars. Not that the Vietnamese didn't resent being occupied, but the Americans could be trusted.

The real problem, though, was there was bad intel. Medina had been told the Cong's 48th Infantry was holed up there around the village. There weren't supposed to be any civilians. And when the company found civilians, Medina wouldn't adjust his thinking. It was going to be all out war.

FOR A LONG time Taylor believed he signed up again because of the way people had treated him back home in the bars, at parties, whenever they found out what he was and where he'd been. But there was more to it than that, and those motherfuckers back home probably saw that part of it written all over his sweating face.

"You're in the service?" His old friends had told him it was a bad idea to wear the uniform, but he hadn't listened. It pissed him off when people said crap like that.

"Yeah. Be out for good soon, I reckon."

"Nam?" The man's tone made Taylor uneasy. The girlfriend just sat there, staring past the man's shoulder, pale lips pouted and eyes blazing.

"Yeah."

"How many did you kill?" And there it was. They always asked that first thing, or after they'd beaten around the bush awhile. Nobody had told Taylor it'd be like that when he got home.

Taylor tried a smile, but it felt too much like the kind of smile you made sometimes back in Nam. You'd have been up for days, strung out on the fighting and running just on fatigue and adrenalin, and there'd be some little hurt kid you're trying to make feel better, so you try to smile, and it's only after you've been making that smile awhile that you realize the muscles in half your face aren't working anymore; they're frozen solid. "Hey, why don't you let me buy you and your girl a drink?" he finally said.

The man almost smiled himself. Then the girlfriend leaned over and with her lips barely moving she said, "So how did it feel, murdering women and babies?"

Taylor had a wife, two kids, a small dog and a couple of cats back home. He'd never lost his temper with any of them. He'd get angry sometimes, and feel pressured, and sometimes they'd box him in. But he never hit any of them, never even thought to. Sometimes he felt he could have been a lot more than he was, if he hadn't gotten married. And that pissed him off some. But he didn't hit anybody for it. He'd get a little agitated, a belly ache sometimes. He went out back sometimes and chopped a month's worth of firewood, or broke every bottle he could find in the trash. But he never hit anybody.

On that first trip home he found he couldn't understand people, not even his family. He had no idea what they were talking about half the time, or why.

It was fucking unbelievable back home. It didn't look anything like what he remembered, or like any of the pictures the wife sent him or he saw in magazines. Somebody had faked it all up, and trying to figure out why they did it made him scared, and dangerous-feeling.

Insects became rampant and joyful, dancing up and down inside his skull.

Most people didn't want to talk about the war. They acted like you had bad breath or were crazy when you tried to talk to them about it.

And something else peculiar. The people walking around in one piece. There'd been so many ways to lose a piece of you in Nam—

satchel charges, punji sticks, grenades, booby traps, swing limbs, little spring-detonated bombs in old C ration cans, Bouncing Betty mines made to cut you in half at the groin. Regular bullets would do as well, zipping by you like supersonic bees. When he got back he expected half the young guys to be missing something. There should have been amputees everywhere. But he hardly ever saw any; where'd they put them all? It made him damned mad—he used to wonder if they had them all down in the cellars or something.

CHARLIE COMPANY OPENED fire on the people running around in the village, because they'd been promised all those folk would be VC. VC only.

Once the first civilians were killed...

There was nothing more to be done. Charlie Company was shooting them all. It became unstoppable. They were angry, they were frustrated, and they'd been told this was the enemy.

Bodies began to accumulate, women and kids. Someone thought they saw Medina himself kick a woman to death, but they couldn't be sure.

TAYLOR TOOK THE second tour because he had changed. He wasn't used to the old way of doing things. In Nam there were only a few ways to get high, to get the adrenalin pumping, to satisfy your spirit. You shot, you killed, you ran for your life, you had cheap sex with the slants or you did dope. You had to get used to dead men's eyes staring right through you, or the awesome sight of a guy's guts hanging outside him, maybe draped up on his chest. You could actually touch his insides, do things to them. It was all hard to understand.

He wasn't a racist when he went in. And in the beginning, the way the others talked about the Vietnamese, it made him damn uncomfortable. But if you don't want a young guy to be a racist, don't put him in a situation where people of another color are always shooting at him trying to kill him. It takes a super amount of will power not to become a racist in that kind of situation. And if you want young men to think independently and question orders and to be good moral decision makers, again, don't put a gun to their heads. Don't put them in a war. Human beings, they just want to live. That shit's imperative.

His first few days in country they'd had him handling body bags and making counts. And playing with the VC bodies. Sometimes a grunt that had been there awhile would decide to initiate a new guy. After a number of months, though, Taylor felt like he'd been there years already.

Taylor got to break in a new guy. A lot like Alex. Sweet boy, shy, good-natured kid. Taylor took the kid out to a rocky outcropping overlooking the Saigon River. They'd had heavy action the past week, and they'd piled the VC bodies up around these rocks. A couple of dozen, maybe more.

"Shoot a couple."

"What?" The boy stared at Taylor as if he'd told him to kill his own mother. "You're kidding."

"Shoot up two of the bodies. That's an order, soldier."

The boy took up his M16, paused, and then fired a burst into one of the dead VC. All the shots in one area. The flesh and the cloth popped, smoked. There was a bad smell. Then, without pause, he did the same to the corpse lying next to it. When he finished he stood with his weapon down, shoulders slightly slumped, staring at Taylor.

"Now see if you can make a few of them dance."

"Sarge, this is crazy."

"Crazy is for civilians, son. I've got my reasons. Commence firing."

The boy turned and began riddling the pile of bodies with bullets. As bodies slipped and fell from the top he was able to get their legs and arms jumping with the force of his fire until it looked as if the whole stack of dead men were seizuring uncontrollably.

"Not bad, kid. You've got a good feel for the weapon. Now pull out your K bar." The boy hesitated. "Pull it out!" He showed Taylor his knife. "Okay... bring me back a finger."

"Sarge!"

"You heard me. Take your time, son. But do it."

It took the boy awhile to get over to the bodies, but he finally did. He then spent the next twenty minutes hacking away with his knife. Taylor hadn't figured it would take him that long, so the boy must not have been using his full strength. And every few minutes he'd choke up a little. Taylor was too far away from him to really see how much. But the boy finally returned, his hands and knife covered with blood.

"Mission accomplished, I see. Now clean off your knife, son. I'll bag this for you. Someday you might ask me for it."

When the boy was ready Taylor helped him throw the bodies into the river, occasionally tossing him a light one so that he'd get used to the smell of a dead body falling all over you. Boat crews didn't like them doing that kind of shit—the bodies fouled the props. But Taylor didn't have to answer to them.

"Did it fine, soldier. Real fine. Maybe later we'll get you a trophy photo, you holding a gook up by the hair maybe, and cutting his throat so's he'll smile real wide for the camera." Taylor chuckled.

Daniel could feel roach heads watching him from the edge of the jungle.

Taylor hadn't meant the chuckle—it was for the boy. And at the time it seemed like the right thing to do. Maybe it was necessary. It was all fake—the swagger, the attitude. The things Taylor was saying, they sickened him. But maybe it would help keep the boy alive later on. Taylor knew that war ran best on that kind of cruelty. Young boys came over to Nam with that young cruelty in them, the cruelty that made them set cats on fire and such shit, and the war brought it back out. Not all of the boys, certainly, maybe just a few, but there were times over there when those few set the tone. In Nam an American soldier had the possibility of becoming a god. He could skin a man alive maybe. He could become a "double veteran"—rape some Vietnamese woman, then kill her, then stomp what was left into the ground if he had a mind to. The thing was, the ones that were inclined to that kind of cruelty, they could get away with crap like that.

You weren't going to fall in love, you weren't going to be seeing your new baby, or go out drinking with your friends. You couldn't get any of that shit in Vietnam. The only way you were going to get your blood up was to kill some folk, mess up a few bodies.

CHARLIE COMPANY WAS pushing people to the center of the village. Some of the guys in Calley's platoon were picking them up, hitting and kicking them, making them move.

One soldier walked away. Another pretended not to see Calley's urgent gestures to get the gooks in line. The platoon moved with the symbolic deliberateness of dream. The ones who were waking up could not figure out what they should do. The ones who walked away figured they could be shot in the back for desertion. Calley, a few others, moved across the village like heroes of the fucking silver screen. It was hard not to be awed by them.

TAYLOR SAW THE boy live long enough to run over an old lady just because some asshole made a dare, fuck some villager's wife in front of the gook then blow his head off, shoot a bunch of old men in a rice paddy for target practice. He was killed when a mine ate him from the chest down.

Taylor didn't initiate Alex into the way of things in Nam, and he wouldn't let anybody else do it, either. Maybe young Alex could stay basically unchanged. Who the hell knew for sure?

Taylor watched Alex get his gear together for the mission. Watched him for a long time. Taylor had been ready and raring for hours. But he'd made that a habit; he'd come to the point where he felt more at ease in combat than he did just waiting for things to happen. Alex was still pretty unsure of himself—you could tell by the way he was stumbling around with his gear. Taylor hoped there wouldn't be any sudden noises; the boy was so jumpy he might kill somebody. But right now Taylor figured Alex could handle himself back home a lot better than he himself could.

Once back home you were asked to keep all that meanness you'd learned in the long Vietnam nights at arm's length. Over here they made you feed it like some kind of junkyard dog—giving it just enough to swell the hunger—because it kept you and your buddies alive. And that boot-black meanness kept you from going crazy from the things they expected you to do here. But there couldn't be any spillover back home. And when you got mad at your kid or the dog was yelping too much or the wife was getting in the way without knowing it, you had to keep that meanness under control.

Taylor'd really tried those few months back home; he knew he had. But after you've been out in the jungle on patrol, and looked too long into the dark, you start seeing things. You start seeing what's out there, and you're ruined for things back home. Sergeant Taylor could feel the changes working on him inside, even now. Roach legs massaged his entrails until his breath tasted like jungle rot.

His squad was pretty far north, and due to go even farther. At the time Taylor had no idea he'd be spending his last days of the war there, deep inside the black heart of Vietnam, so far north it was understood to be okay to shoot anyone on sight, no questions asked. A blank check.

The squad had been assigned to watch an isolated ville. Intelligence had it that it was an important VC way station, or intelligence post, or something. Taylor was soon thinking they must have missed on this one; he'd seen nothing suspicious all the way there, cattle and birds, women and children, a few old men. He didn't think it was the kind of job combat troops should be doing anyway. They must have been low on spy guys that week.

He would never be sure what it was exactly that happened about two klicks out from that village. He ran the film over and over in his head, but it was like large pieces of it had been cut. They were in thick vegetation, on a trail that looked seldom-travelled, and that fact bothered them all. First thing he would remember was seeing Alex's face get real white, white as snow, and Alex's eyes going crazy, looking down, and Taylor saw what Alex was looking at—half his body was blown away.

A lot of screaming, a lot of explosions. Dirt and jungle flying ever which way. Bodies down. Lots of bodies down. Taylor hearing somebody crying, then knowing it was himself crying, bending over all of those bloody pieces that used to be Alex. And thinking maybe this little ville might just be as important as M.I. thought.

CALLEY'S PLATOON HAD gathered a little fewer than 200 villagers. The soldiers herded them to the eastern side of the village near the drainage ditch.

Calley ordered the platoon to start shooting.

THE NEXT THING Taylor would remember would be being in this little dugout cave overlooking the village, then searching through the area where they blew up his buddies, then being back in the cave again. It was all mixed up for days, or maybe years. Goddamn, it could've been years.

Funny how you felt different when Americans were killed. It just didn't seem natural when Americans were killed.

The rest of the squad was dead. Or so he thought. Two or three bodies were still missing but he had to figure they were hid in the jungle somewhere. They'd been separated. Taylor wasn't sure how he'd survived. A couple of bloody face and scalp wounds, but they healed okay. He could feel the puffy scars. The squad had some heavy fire power with them—several pounds of C4 plastique, M 60 machine gun, and an M 79 grenade launcher. He made several trips to get all that up to the little cave he'd dug out of a thickly overgrown hill. And he had all the guys' packs, M 16s and K bars. He should have pulled back once the squad was wiped out. But he hadn't. He was going to take on the mission by himself, maybe even sit out the rest of the war watching that one sleepy little ville.

He watched that village for a very long time. He watched it through the night, when every shadow was a body. He watched it when the sun was overhead and the top of that hill must have been over a hundred degrees. He thought he had killed one, maybe a couple of gooks when they got too close, but he wasn't sure. He didn't see any bodies. Maybe I ate them, he thought, and giggled to himself. He vaguely remembered someone shouting *Chu Hoi*! I surrender, but he might have been dreaming. He wasn't sure if he dreamed at all. Roaches ran amok under his skin. Roach bristles pushed out through his skin, seeking air.

There was a young woman in the village, a beautiful woman with long black hair, almond yellow skin. Eyes seemed a little too red. Dark dress a little too oily. But beautiful. When she walked it was like rustling leaves, vermin crawling under old wallpaper. For a few hours every afternoon she went to a small garden patch at the side of the village, in full view of Taylor, as if she knew he was there. Sometimes a boy came with her. Black, shiny hair. Too-bright eyes. Too-brilliant teeth. Taylor wondered if she had told the boy where he was hiding. The thought scared him. If the boy came too close Taylor was going to have to slit his throat with one of the K bars. See if that wiped the smile away. He wouldn't want to do it, but it would be self-defense.

If he slept, Taylor dreamed of beehive rounds coming in, blowing human bodies to pieces. It made the officers happy, though; it was an old joke that you could get more grunts into one of those trucks if they had all been taken apart first.

But Taylor didn't think he had slept, so maybe it wasn't a dream.

*   *   *

SOME OF THE children hid at the bottom of the ditch beneath the bodies of their parents.

EACH DAY TAYLOR saw fewer villagers around. It worried him. Maybe they had tunneled out, or maybe they were off on a secret mission or something. If something awful happened because of them he'd be blamed for it. He hated them. They were the ones who brought all this dying; they were the ones who'd birthed all those corpses lying out there, fertilizing the jungle. He tasted blood on his teeth. But the woman and her son were still there. They came back to the garden at the village's edge each day.

Some days it got so hot he started scratching at his skin. It seemed every inch of skin had begun to itch, leaving shallow, bloody furrows up his sides and chest. He dug body hair out, roots and all. But there was always more hair. Under the dirt and grime, there was hair even under his skin.

At night his nerves tingled. His nerves rang like hundreds of tiny screeching bells. Roaches crawled inside those bells and kept them ringing. He still didn't think he slept, and the dreams that were not dreams rolled drunkenly through his head.

He thought he must be pretty sick. There were no more villagers, except the dark woman and her evil, grinning son. He'd watched them for days. He tasted blood. He was always rubbing away at his nose because of the awful smell. He burned in every organ in his body. His hair sang.

He had been eating one of the last cans of beans and motherfuckers. His head had drooped, as he would remember it later. Something else drooped, something around his neck, and brushed his raw, burning chest. He looked down.

It was a necklace made of nylon string. Strung along the entire length of the necklace—maybe two dozen or more—were these black, shriveled things. Like dates. They were ears. Some of them were new—the blood was still drying on them—and some of them old. They were usually only good for about four days; after that they started turning sour on you, and then the flies showed up. Eventually they'd just drop off the string.

Sergeant Taylor dreamed he was running, but he never slept, so how could he dream? He was screaming when he entered the village, his nerves exploding from his body, making a copper-colored mane that ran like wildfire over his bare skin, eating its way through muscle and bone. The dark lady and her son stood up from the small garden, their faces dusty in the light falling through the trees. They grinned like old friends. Welcome home… He heard a dog bark. The boy was running toward him, wanting to leap into his daddy's arms.

But Taylor was ready. He had the grenades hanging on his arms like a morning's catch from the old catfish pond. He was throwing his arms forward, ready to swim for safety, his daddy excited and crying from the boat. He didn't want to die, but the dark blue water had such a strong grip, the lady just might have him this particular day. Hard insect wings raked the back of his skull and he looked at the boy again. He remembered something; he was remembering. He remembered going through this a thousand times before. The boy's dying face all too familiar. It stopped him, made him wonder. The boy was running toward him, wanting to leap into his daddy's arms. That stopped him. He looked again. His daddy's arms. And so Sergeant Taylor dived into the ground, the grenades dropping, breaking open like eggs around him, before the boy could reach him.

Black billows of smoke with vague blue highlights. An awful smell of phosphorous in his nose. And Taylor continued to dream, without light or movement, but it wasn't like a dream. Whoever was in the room with him—dark insect faces, hard wings and legs scraping at his brain—would not let him sleep. Taylor didn't think he ever slept, and he knew that those who took care of him weren't able to tell.

He knew the teeth he had grown in the dark never slept. It wasn't like a dream. It was like being alive but still going to Hell. All around him he could hear the other men in the ward moaning in their sleep. They were all still in the jungle, and it was night, and Sergeant Taylor with his brand new teeth was crawling toward them in the dark.

DANIEL STOOD INSIDE the body of the soldier whose name he did not know at the edge of the irrigation ditch—shocked and numb with despair. He wasn't seeing it right. The ditch was full of bodies, and drifts of blood like scarlet oil slicks, and yet he could not quite believe it was real. They had faked it somehow. The special effects in this... memory, were remarkable.

He watched as a lone soldier climbed down inside the lip of the ditch, lowered one arm into the tangle of bloody limbs, and pulled out a small child who had been hiding beneath the bodies of his parents. He gathered the boy into his arms and carried him off to the waiting helicopter.

7

DANIEL FLOATED UP through a rising tide of heat, his face flushed, his eyes burning. He didn't want to open his eyes, imagining the jungle on fire, acres burning beneath sprays of napalm, or maybe the helicopter had exploded, vaporizing everyone inside. None of this was true as long as he kept his eyes closed. Then it could be dream or hallucination, nothing he'd be compelled to feel anything about.

On certain days of his childhood, when he'd been ill, feverish, and kept home from school, he'd lie on the couch and watch TV and his mother would bring him soup and fruit and juice. He would never make it through an entire episode of anything; he'd always nod off and wake up halfway into the next show, so that circus personnel would warp into cowboys and then sailing enthusiasts intent on some mystery, and it struck him then how people were all much the same, scrabbling for a living and being with their family and looking for interesting things to fill their days, hoping to find something beyond themselves. Often some crisis occurred. Often you had to start again from square one.

His mother was at her best during those times of sickness. She'd always been a nervous person, uncomfortable in her skin and with other people, even with her own children. She never knew what to do with him or his sisters. But if your child is sick, you keep him home, you encourage his rest. You bring him food and medicine, and you touch him, you comfort him as much as you can bear. It was pretty clear that she waited for these perfect opportunities to be a good mother.

Perhaps there were parents who really knew what they were doing, but Daniel had not been one of them. He was as a father as he was in the rest of his life—killing time for months, for years, waiting for the event, the phone call, the conversation that would at last make perfect sense of everything.

Now, before he'd even opened his eyes the morning smell of the barracks hit him. An accumulation of terror sweat and the stench of sadness. And there were always those who had fouled themselves as they'd tossed and turned under the grip of some past evil. You adjusted to it just enough to be slightly surprised about how bad it could be.

Nearby, one of the residents struggled to dig something out of the back of his neck. Apparently it was buried deeply, causing the fellow to gouge the skin, his nails breaking, but still cutting flesh, drawing blood.

"Could someone help me! I can't get to it! It needs to come out!"

Falstaff came up behind the man and slapped him on the back. "A button, right? You're looking for a button. You got it! I saw it pop out—it bounced across the floor somewhere over there."

The man visibly relaxed. "Should we go find it? Maybe it's dangerous, just leaving it lying around?"

"I wouldn't. I wouldn't touch it. It's out, it's disconnected, exposed, it won't bother anyone. But still, I wouldn't go near it if I were you."

"Thanks. Oh, thanks."

Falstaff walked over to Daniel and spoke softly. "He's another Charles Whitman. I don't know what the roaches have been doing back there, but there have been four Whitmans so far today. And it's not the first time one of them believed there was a button embedded somewhere on their body, and that someone had secretly pushed it, and that's what turned on the craziness, and that's why he killed all those people."

"I was Whitman," Daniel said, "but I never believed that."

"It's rare. I gather they did find a small tumor in the real Whitman, during the autopsy. But if it was a button, it was a button that turned on nothing. At least that was the consensus of medical opinion. We're full of buttons and switches. And we like to hold them responsible, but most of the time they don't do a thing. They're just these odd bits of scar tissue, unless you make them active, unless you electrify them, because they seem like they're the only thing that will lift you out of the emptiness."

"Why do the roaches keep repeating the same scenarios? Just during my time here I've seen a dozen different Jack the Rippers wake up in this room, not counting my own. A huge number of Hitlers, Green River killers, Albert Fish—"

"I saw two Albert Fishes yesterday. Have you noticed how, the more recently a character lived, the more their character—absorbs you?"

Daniel nodded. "Like with Whitman. At first I was a presence in his head—or at least I was aware of having a presence, of being someone with my own mind, and then I just disappeared into him, and his thoughts were my thoughts, and it was me doing these terrible things."

"I believe what the roaches can do, they can probe through time, and they can detect past brain activity, and they can translate that activity into a recording of a person's consciousness, of varying completeness. Do you believe in ghosts?"

Daniel smiled, laughed. "No, of course not."

"You might want to reconsider that position. Because you've been spending a great deal of time inside these specters, these ghosts. I don't know what else to call them. However their personalities have been recorded and received by us over the centuries, as what we've called ghosts, hauntings, it's a process the roaches have amplified with technology—the superstition has become science."

"So why do they repeat these scenarios?"

"Because naturally the signal must degrade over time—to varying degrees there are the inevitable holes. They need the processing power of your human brain to fill in the gaps—you become part of the software, and of course each person is going to process that information differently. At some point they must balance all of that input to get a fuller picture of a Hitler, a Himmler, and how their brains worked."

"And then what?"

"And then they learn whatever it is they're trying to learn about us. You'll notice they rarely try to make us into a Caligula, or a Genghis Khan. They lived too long ago. There must not be enough signal left to build a reasonable persona out of."

They'd walked to the opening to the hallways. Two giant roaches lounged there staring at them. Something about them emanated disinterest. "And no one's ever tried to escape?"

"Where would you go? At least in here you're fed."

"Still, you'd think some people would take their chances out there, rather than continue to endure this."

"Really, Daniel? Just imagine brushing up against one of the roaches, touching its body, physically struggling with it, as you would have to do. What do you feel when you imagine that?"

Daniel drew a blank. He couldn't imagine it. He just knew it was the last thing he ever wanted to do. He'd sooner peel off his own skin, bite through his tongue and eat it slowly.

"Here." Falstaff grabbed Daniel's hand and thrust it against the shimmering exoskeleton of the nearest roach.

Daniel howled, falling to the floor. It was as if his skin had ruptured, followed by a massive invasion of countless small, dark, wriggling things working their way into all parts of his body. Not that he could actually see them, but he knew they were there, and ravenous.

"That's why we don't rebel," Falstaff said. "That's why we don't even try. And sometime you might notice that the more problematic residents, they don't always come back from a scenario." He turned and walked away.

The roaches had disappeared from the hall. He stared at Falstaff's back, moving away, shimmering. He felt properly punished—Falstaff had made his point. But what troubled him went deeper than the futility of an attempted rebellion—he understood that Falstaff had been here a long time, but still, how did he know so much?

When Daniel rejoined his group in the barracks he found them gathered around Bogart, who apparently had just awakened from another scenario. He was severely shaken, occasionally crying as he attempted to speak, and the confusion Daniel had noticed previously in his speech had become more pronounced.

"Hitler, Jack the Ri—ipper, of course those I—I understand, but Picah—ahsso? I'd always thought of him as just a painter?"

"Even artists can do terrible, monstrous things," Gandhi said. He was hunched over, his narrow shoulders quivering. He always seemed nervous, or cold, a fleshless twig of a figure. "They're, well they're not like the rest of us, are they? They live very different lives. But still, he seems out of place in that list. What did he do, or rather, what did he do in your scenario?"

"Walter, he had all these mistresses..."

"Ha, he loved women," Falstaff said. "Perhaps just too much?"

"Did he love them?" Bogart said. "I know he thought he did, and other people thought he did. That's the leg—gend, isn't it? How much he loved, how much he ob—obsessed over women? He could be quite... pass—ssionate. Dora, one of the mistresses, she'd been young when he met her. He liked to do that, he'd groo—, he'd meet them young. But he beat her; he'd leave her unconscious on the floor. I'm not saying he was any Hitler, or Mussolini, I'm not saying he was anywhere n—near their league, but he still d—did terrible things to them, s—small things on the s—scale of world h—history, but h—huge things on the s—scale of their l—lives. Little evils. I just don't know why the roaches chose *me* for this one!"

"Try to stay calm," Daniel said. "You're not responsible, remember? Just keep going—what happened?"

"Well, and then there w—was Francoise, the one who foll—replaced Dora, he burned her face with—he put a lit cigarette, *out*, on her face. They either had to be goddesses or doormats to him. There seemed, there was no in between."

"Times were different, things were looked at differently," Lenin said. "But the art! You cannot deny he was a wonderful artist!"

A raw-throated howl ripped through the room from somewhere below. It was a telling measure of how accustomed they'd all become to the werewolf's loud protests that Bogart paused only a breath or two, and no one looked around.

Bogart clutched Falstaff's arm, quaking. "You said that the roles they—they have us live here, that they have nothing to do with who we are, who we were back in our old li—ives. Just because we play m—monsters, doesn't mean we are monsters. You meant that."

Daniel, suddenly full of suspicion, watched Falstaff's face. He listened intently to his response.

"The latter part, certainly, is true. Simply because you play one of these roles doesn't mean you *are* them, that you are responsible for what they do. But I won't pretend to know how these roles are selected, or why any one of us was chosen to be here in the first place. What's bothering you, Alan? Are you married, in your other life?"

"I was. I am."

"Is it a good marriage?"

Bogart slowly began rubbing his face up and down, wiggling his fingers slightly, massaging, as if trying to wake himself up, or to cleanse himself of a profound fatigue.

"I used to wonder," he began, "what happiness would look like. I should have been—been happy. I was, am, married to a woman I pursued for years. I knew April from hu—high school, although I was never able to work up the co—courage to speak to her then, and I mus—I admit I used to get furious with her sim—simply because I was too afraid to talk to her.

"I signed up for this biology class in co—college, walked in the first day and there she was. We weren't lab partners, but we were in the same ai—ai—*row*, and now and—and then I was able to strike up a conversation. I eventually asked her out, and of—of course she said no, she was dating someone. But I made sure to be where I thought she would be. I figured out her cla—class schedule and I made sure I was there, somewhere along the pa—path, when she got out, even if it meant missing some classes of my own, just so I could run into her. I really wasn't stalking her—I was ju—just making myself available.

"Then one day she was pretty upset, and it turns out they'd broken up the night before and well, there was my ch—chance. It still took a while, but even—even—fi—finally she agreed to go out with me. It wasn't love at first sight for her then—I had to work for it—but maybe that's best. I mean, that's always the best, isn't it?

"I told her she was the most beautiful woman I'd ever seen. And it embarrassed her that I said it. 'It's just too much,' she would say. 'You always go too far.' But I still think she liked hearing it just the same. I told her I—I loved her on the sec—second or third date. Some would argue tha—that's too soon, but I don't agree.

"She became pregnant, although I think we were pret—pretty careful. So it just seemed a fore—foregone conclusion we'd get married. She didn't seem exactly enthusiastic about it. She seemed, well, she was tired most of the time, so I understood. Now we have two wonderful, two beautiful daughters. I dote on them. She says I spoil them. But they're incredible, the best thing about my life. A father has a special opportunity with—with daughters, I think. Your love for them, it can be like the p—purest statement of affection between a male and a female. B—because there isn't the question of sex, or pride, or competition, to trouble you. There's just this full—fullness of love, and generosity, because you can look at them without all the annoying d—distractions that happen between men and women. You just want them to be e—everything they can be—my g—girls are so smart, so capable—and I can't stand the idea that they m—might miss out on opportunities because of their g—ender, or m—ale expectations. I'm a great fem—feminist in that way, I suppose, even more than my wife and daughters.

"I think per—per—m—maybe April had fallen out of love with me by the day of the wedding. Why do—do they do that, go through with something they don't even f—feel anymore? Is it a p—power thing? Do you know what it's like to f—feel that lack of affection, to know that her at—attitude has changed, but she still won't tell you, she still won't a—admit it? It's dev—devastating. It was clear she didn't want to have s—sex with me anymore, although she still a—agreed to it. At least at first.

"Do you know how to tell a woman's feelings for you have changed? Every little thing you do a—annoys her, everything you say. It's like she can—can't stand you anym—m—more, and you have no clue what you've d—done. She acts like you think you m—must know everything, but that you're stupid and just h—haven't figured it out y—yet. You're the dumbest, most pa—pathetic human being p—possible, incapable of the most n—normal things. You're like this new b—breed of subhuman. You thought you were e—evolved, that you were fully hu-human, but everyone else knew you weren't, so they either l—laughed at you or they p—pitied you, and you were too d—dumb to recognize any of it.

"So this isn't the ma—marriage I was p—promised. Not that she actually promised how it w—would be, but you a—assume, be—because of custom and cu—culture that you're g—going to be p-partners, that she's going to l—love you and be physically attracted to you and just that there's this unbr—breakable b—bond.

"But it hasn't been like that for us at all, except aro—around the girls. Around the g—girls she could pre—pretend we were this ideal c—couple. She's never said a b—bad thing about me in front of the g—girls—I'll have to g—give her that.

"She stopped having sex with m—me. Oh, for a while she m—made the usual la—lame excuses, she had a headache, she was t—tired, she had to get up early in the m—morning. But the last couple of years she's just said 'I don't w—want to.' Just like that. No w—wiggle room at all. Doesn't she re—realize that m—marriage is a *contract*? And like with any co—contract there are ex—expectations and o—obligations?

"I star—started thinking about what I could do. I thought about get-getting nar—narcotics, dropping them into her dr—drinks.

"Still, I n—never hit her. Even when she went w—way out of her way to pro—provoke me. Saying sar—sarcastic cr—crap like 'Everything about you gives me a headache,' or 'You've been lying to yourself so long you don't know how you really feel about anything.'

"And still I didn't hi—hit her because that's n—ot who I am. I'm no Richard Speck or Bl—bluebeard or Jack the R—ripper. I'm not a mo—monster of any k—kind."

Daniel nodded in all the right places, but he felt increasingly anxious and not as sympathetic as he'd thought he would. He no longer wanted to be here listening to this little man's story, feeling himself drawn into his tale of woe. He didn't exactly doubt the man's sincerity, but wondered if he had sufficient self-knowledge to even be sincere.

Some of the very worst things happened at home, in private. It was as if a man going inside his own house was going inside his own skull, where he had freedom to play out his darkest dreams of passion and violence with his wife and children as stand-ins for the primal figures dancing in his brain.

The howling began again, this time rising so quickly and so forcefully Daniel imagined it might start lifting the boards out of the floor. The werewolf sounded as if he were being skinned alive.

"But she pushed me fa—farther than any man should be pu—pushed. And there was such a c—cold de—deliberateness and cr—cruelty about it I couldn't believe this was a—actually the same w—woman I had married. Something had h—happened to her. She'd gone quietly cr—crazy or m—maybe I'd driven her crazy s—somehow. I just wanted a g—gentle, happy life. That's what all of us d—deserve, isn't it? Well, by now that seems pr—pretty much out of r—reach.

"I wasn't actually angry when it st—started, more numb than anything else, and de—determined just that she see m—my point, that she acknowledge I had a legi—legitimate issue. It didn't h—help that I'd been dr—drinking—maybe I wouldn't h—have done it in the first p-place if I hadn't been drinking.

"The lo—longer it went on the ang—angrier I became. I was shocked when I r—realized the anger was actually increasing my a—arousal.

"For just a moment I thought ma—maybe she *w—wanted* to be dominated, she wanted me to take ch—charge. That's what they t—tell you, isn't it? Some people, p—pornography, other m—men. I know a lot of p—people believe that. I—I'd never personally believed it, b—but what if they were r—right? What if that was the element she found l—lacking in me?

"She wasn't dressed all that pro—provocatively. Well, not at all. A b—big loose n—night shirt, all covered up. That's the w—way she always dressed at h—home, and for b—bed. She showed more skin than that when she drove off to w—work every day. Sometimes I think that was just another w—way of sending me a me—message, letting me know that she no longer n—needed or wanted me, putting me d—down.

"She was standing on her side of the b—bed. We have a sma—small bedroom, so she just had a narrow lane over by the w—wall, maybe eight inches wide. I told her I wanted to make love to her that n—night. She just said 'What?' as if I'd completely surprised her.

"'I love you. I want to m—make love. It's been a l—long time,' I sa—said.

"She just looked at me, ob—obviously so sur—surprised by what

I'd said I w—was insulted. That's how b—bad it had gotten, that she'd be surprised at a suggestion of physical a—affection.

"'No, not tonight, Alan,'" she said, and looked a—away from me.I shocked m—myself. I was over there in seconds, holding her wrists t—tightly so that she couldn't r—raise her arms. 'I'm not w—waiting anymore,' I said. 'It's been l—long enough.'

"'What are you?' she shouted, and I s—saw the fear in her f—face as her voice trailed away. She was sca—scared of m—me. I n—never wa—wanted that, but now that I h—had it, it was exciting. She's always had the u—upper hand, and now for once I h—had it. It only seemed f—fair. But still, her fear was n—not what I w—wanted, not what I wa—wanted at all. I knew right then she w—would never trust me again, that our marriage was effect—over.

"I was a-afraid. I knew it was wr-wrong. And I felt like every—like it was all over. How c—could—how could she stay with me af-after that?"

"Did you like hurting her?" Falstaff asked. "Did you enjoy it?" The bluntness of the question made Daniel catch his breath. He didn't want to hear the answer.

"May—maybe for a sec—second. There was a r—rush. I l-liked it, then I didn't. Then I h-hated it. I ha—hated myself. But I kept—I kept d—doing it.

"She started to struggle, but she had no—nowhere to go—there wasn't any r—room to turn or r—run. I pu—pushed her down and I straddled her. She was squirming, k—kicking. I leaned forward, trying to p—pin her fl—flailing arms to the b—bed. 'Stop it!' I shouted, and moved one hand to her thr—throat.

"She stopped then, stopped e—everything and just l—lay there, looking p—past me, above my s—shoulder. I turned my h—head. That's when I r—realized I had my right f—fist cocked, my arm t—trembling, so like an an—angular rock tied to a p—piece of st—stick, a cl—club."

"But you didn't hit her?" Daniel asked.

"I d—don't think so. Or ra—raped her either, I d—don't think I'm ca—capable, but I'm not really s—sure. The next thing I r—remember I was w—waking up here."

8

"Ubo isn't a sentence. Alan didn't come here because of what he did," Falstaff insisted. They were standing by the door that led to the roof. "Besides, we don't know how far it went. Maybe his wife is fine."

"How do you know? How can you?"

"From observation. I've had scientific training. Whatever their method might be, the roaches are apparently able to track brain activity that signals aggression. Human beings often feel aggression without acting on it. Their equipment might not differentiate."

"So, we're here because we were aggressive. The roaches snatched us because of that."

"That's not what I said. Reasonable people feel aggression— but they don't act aggressively unless necessary. Besides, I'm just speculating. I don't really know. I'm sure they have their reasons, and no doubt they're complex."

"You seem to know quite a bit about the roaches." He walked away before Falstaff could reply. Daniel would still ply him for information, even if the information wasn't always reliable. But he'd learned a useful word during his travels through other people's heads. Kapo. In the camps, it was a Jew who cooperated, who supervised the work of other Jews in exchange for privileges.

That was Falstaff, he was almost sure.

He took advantage of the warm day and went up on the roof. So many others had the same idea he wondered if the roof could carry the load. They lounged like refugees waiting to be told where to go, and knowing wherever it was it wouldn't be pleasant.

There were more roaches about than usual. For the most part they kept to the edges of the roof, to prevent escape or suicide or simply to block a clear view of the ground. Today, however, they lingered near the center where large numbers of residents had gathered. They seemed particularly interested in the couples. He had only recently witnessed this kind of pairing off—no doubt it had existed in the past, but the residents seemed to have been more discrete. The roaches still kept their distance, but Daniel could feel them watching. Maybe they considered courtship potential trouble.

A number of men were playing games with pieces of cardboard or plastic they'd written on. Bits of stone were tossed, and men cheered depending on the results. Sometimes pieces were moved across squares and ovals scratched into the dirt.

In other clusters people were singing, a few even dancing, singly or together, the roaches observing nearby. Wherever the roaches positioned themselves, the residents kept several feet away, backs turned.

Daniel searched for the boy he'd met earlier. He'd wondered about him often, thinking how remarkably cruel it was for the roaches to have snatched a child out of his life, away from his parents. There was no justification for it. He doubted they watched this child any closer than the others—certainly he'd been allowed to roam the rooftop free of supervision. He should do something about it, but what? Maybe take the boy to live alongside his group, if the roaches allowed it.

He could always ask Falstaff.

Daniel made his way past several gatherings of men performing exercises. It made perfect sense—you lay on your back most of the day, your mind in another world and another life, the body easily forgotten, simply something to prop up your head. So silent and intent, these men had gathered together for pushups and leg lifts, and weight training with any odd bit of brick or iron from the numerous piles of demolished material like industrial gravesites across the roof.

A large fellow in a rickety chair had set up camp near the center of the roof, surrounded by items he would pick up, examine, and put down again. This activity was casually paced, but constant, repeated over and over again. Now and then he would pause and glower at anyone standing nearby. This big fellow had become a fixture over the weeks Daniel had been visiting the roof. Every time Daniel saw him he looked angrier, particularly if you walked too closely in front of him, as if you had violated his invisible lawn space.

Moving through the more densely populated sections of the roof, Daniel encountered more couples, both mixed and same sex, holding hands, talking intimately, occasionally kissing, using the other residents to shield them from the scrutiny of the roaches. It was all quite risky and appealing to Daniel. He moved past as quickly as possible, but still gathered bits and snippets of conversation.

"Do you love me?" she said, her finger against the tall fellow's chest. "Because I don't believe it."

A man with a deep scar on one cheek, the tattoo on his arm resembling layer upon layer of obsessive writing, grabbed a smaller man by the shoulder. "I can't live without you." He looked angrier than sad.

"If you didn't do those things," another fellow said to a tired-looking older woman, "you wouldn't have to be taught the lesson."

And then a figure chasing another through the crowd. "Sweetheart, don't be so upset. You don't need to be so upset."

It was frustrating, not being able to find the boy. There was always the possibility that something had happened to him down in the barracks. Scuffles were not unheard of—it was a tense environment. Bullying was often a factor. Or perhaps the boy simply hadn't come back from a scenario. That happened with some regularity.

Daniel felt echoes of the heightened alert he'd experienced as Gordon's father. They never knew when their son would have a spell of difficult breathing. More often than not it would be in the middle of the night, and the monitor he'd had since he was a baby picked up his distress. They'd race into his room to find him gray-faced and grunting, his nostrils flaring as his body struggled for air. He'd been born with holes between the heart chambers, abnormalities in the blood vessels and in the aorta. These things made him smaller, paler than other kids.

Daniel's anxiety rose, making him move more swiftly through the crowd. He became careless, running into people, never wise in a population exposed so intensely to violence. Someone shoved back. Others became involved. The roaches moved in, their dark insect limbs grabbing, throwing.

He glimpsed the hunched, sitting form out beyond the edge of the struggling crowd. Daniel made his way through and trotted toward the boy, who was sorting through a variety of small charred bits. The boy looked up, said "Hi," but didn't smile.

"Hello, I was looking for you."

The boy still didn't smile. "Why? Why would you do that?"

"I just wanted to make sure you were safe. What have you got there?"

"Just stuff I found in the building. Nothing you'd want."

"What's yours is yours. I wouldn't take anything that belonged to you. I just want to be your friend, really."

The boy looked at him suspiciously. "If you say so."

"Do the other residents take things from you?"

"Sometimes. But sometimes when they wake up, they're not who they were before. They get confused. And a little, I don't know, grabby?"

"Can you keep yourself safe?"

"I try to hide when they first wake up. Then it's okay."

"I have some friends—they're pretty trustworthy." Daniel hoped that was still true. "Maybe you could move into our section."

The boy studied him nervously. Then he looked away. "Are we on an alien planet?"

Daniel was okay with changing the subject—anything to keep him in the conversation. "I don't know that any of us *really* know where this is." Except perhaps Falstaff, he thought.

"But they want us to think that, right? I mean the dream? The flying dream? The big bugs carrying us here? They want us to think we're out in space somewhere, right?"

"I'm just not sure."

"I've been picking up all kinds of stuff. I've been going through the junk in the rooms, all that broken junk. And the roof?" He held up a small dull metal disk. "I found this. See, it's all rusted and stained." The boy put the circular bit of metal into Daniel's palm. "It's a coin, isn't it?"

Daniel prodded and scraped at it with his fingernail. George Washington. It was an American quarter. "Where—" But the boy stared past him, looking troubled. "Anything wrong?"

"That lady, she's been staring at me all day. I don't—I don't like it."

Daniel turned and saw a woman sitting by herself. She looked away instantly. "Stay here. I'm just going to talk to her for a minute."

The woman, red-faced, weathered skin, looked alarmed when Daniel walked up to her. "Excuse me. My young friend over there says you're making him nervous. Is there anything I can do?"

She shook her head, her eyes cast down. "I didn't mean to scare him, but he—he reminds me of my son Paul. I guess I was staring like some kind of weird-o?"

"He's just scared. I can't imagine a child being here, going through these scenarios."

"Oh, that's bad." She shook her head, bowed as if it weighed a thousand pounds. "Bad enough for an adult." She started to get up, "Won't bother you—anymore."

"I haven't met many women here. Is it the same for you? How often do the women do the scenarios?"

She sat back down, looking tired but not entirely unwelcoming. "Sometimes once a week. For a while most every day, with a break, sometimes."

"Same as it is for the rest of us."

She looked at him with seeming disinterest. But she responded. He believed it was automatic, that she would have responded to anything he said. "Is it?"

"Yes. But I guess I'm not as familiar with the history of violent women. What roles have you played, if you don't mind my asking?"

She stared off past him then, her eyes looking intently at something, some distant event. "Bonnie Parker." She glanced at him quickly, and away. "As in Bonnie and Clyde, you know? Then there was Myra Hindley. And Belle Gunness in America—she killed husbands, kids for the life insurance. A cold woman. I don't think she cared for anyone, including herself. Ilse Koch—the roaches are obsessed with the Nazis, have you noticed? And of course the Countess Elizabeth Bathory—that one was fuzzy, as if they weren't giving me enough information to work with, you know? I just kept killing all these girls, killing after killing, and I was never quite sure why. It became habitual, like the way you snack when you're nervous, you know? Is that an insensitive thing to say? You know it's bad, but you're helpless, you can't stop. And you don't want to stop, not really.

"Most of the others were anonymous women no one ever heard of, the countless, nameless women of history, a lot of them partners, accomplices to their murdering men. Some of them gone crazy, haunted by their own obsessive thoughts. And child-killers, lots of women child-killers. I guess if more men stayed home they'd be the child-killers, but they haven't, in general, so that dirty job has gone to the women. Because you're cooped up with them all day. Some days they're the only human beings you see. So, of course, who else are you going to kill?"

"I'm sorry." He didn't know what else to say.

"Why? How do you know? Am I that obvious?" She looked anything but disinterested now, her eyes dark and shiny as she rose into a crouch as if to spring at him.

"I was talking about the scenarios, how hard it is to get past some of them, to shake them off. Believe me, I know."

"You know, do you?"

"Sorry, I didn't mean to offend—"

"Do you know what it's like to kill your own kids?" She staggered upright, awkwardly, almost falling over until Daniel reached out to grab her arm and steady her. She shook his hand off furiously. "Off! I didn't say you could touch me!"

Both stood silent and shaking. "I'll just go on my way now." Daniel took a step away.

"Do you know how it works?" she asked.

"What? I don't understand?"

"All this." She ran her forefinger in a circle. "How all this works, what the rules are?"

He thought seriously of telling her to talk to Falstaff. "Not really. An insight here and there, but I don't know much at all."

"Can you tell me why they took me away from my kids before I could find out if they were dead or not? Before I could find out if I'd really killed them? Are they sick in the head or something? Who would do that to a mother?"

Daniel didn't want to hear this story. But he couldn't just walk away. "Do you want to tell me about it?"

She shrugged, and her face suddenly distorted, and she looked away, bowed and crying, which left her body off-balance and somewhat grotesque. He kept waiting for her to collapse, but she didn't.

"They'd driven me crazy all day, but they were always driving me crazy, you know?"

He nodded. "Sometimes—they can be a handful. And they go right for your buttons."

"For a long time I didn't think I even wanted kids. I wanted a career, I wanted to feel like I was making some kind of difference in the world. Not that being a mother isn't making a difference, not if you do it right, but I wanted to see what I could be first, without a family, with nobody else but me standing there.

"So I worked my way up, I became a manager. Then I was laid off, and that gave me time to think, and to wonder what it was I had to show for all I'd done. And you know that's a hard question to answer—there are so many intangibles, but what I finally decided was, it didn't feel like nearly enough. I don't care how much logic you throw at it—if it doesn't feel like enough it isn't enough. I was living alone then, and I decided I didn't like living alone. I wanted to have kids. The first guy, Paul's dad, he turned out to be pretty much a disaster. Good riddance, and I'd still say that. Joey's dad, he was very sweet, but we argued about the silliest things. That was me, mostly. I was disappointed, and I know I'm hard to live with when I'm disappointed. He finally couldn't handle it and left.

"And little TJ, well, I'll be honest, I drank a bit after Joey's dad left. I don't know who TJ's father is. Listen to me, I sound like a damn soap opera."

"No, it's okay."

"I sound like I'm just talking about ordinary crap!" She started crying. "I'm talking like nothing terrible happened!"

"Really, you're okay. You're just trying to tell your story. We all sound like that when we're just trying to tell our stories."

She nodded hesitantly, but he could tell by her eyes she didn't really agree. He thought she might even be trying to offer him a smile, but she couldn't quite pull it off. "I don't know why I thought I could be a good mother—I guess I thought once the kids were there it would just come out of me naturally. I kept thinking about how it was going to be with them, how I'd make them happy and content and how appreciative they'd be, and the loving things they'd say. And even when they weren't like that—Paul had such a rotten mouth on him, and Joey was always throwing tantrums and breaking things, and TJ, that baby just couldn't stop crying—I kept telling myself that one day we'd be this unbelievable family I'd imagined, if only I did the right things.

"But I didn't even know what the right things were."

"I know—there's no rule book. You just have to do the best you can." She looked at him again as if surprised he'd spoken, surprised he was even there.

"They'd been driving me crazy all day," she said again. "Paul was in one of his aggravating moods. He was always so bright, so clever. Math was easy for him, and he was always taking things apart, putting them back together again. He could fix pretty much anything. Smarter than me, and he knew it. He only listened to me when it suited him.

"He'd been doing this thing all day. Working up the two little ones, tickling them, then making them cry, then tickling them again. Between the tickling and the crying and the screaming they were so red-faced I thought they were going to pass out. He really knew how to play them, like they were his instruments. And they let him. If he let them rest for just thirty seconds they'd say 'more' or 'again,' so out of breath you could hardly understand them. They loved it. They loved it.

"But I'd had enough. I was ready to scream. All day, you know? All damn day. I told him nicely at first to cut it out, and he did for a little bit. He even said 'sorry.' But he didn't mean it—fifteen minutes later he started up again. I used to spank him when he pulled that crap, when he was smaller. It never stopped him for more than five minutes. Joey too—never did a bit of good. It became a part of their game—it was just part of the story of the day. You scream, you run around, Mom spanks you and you cry and rub your behind, and then you run around screaming even more than before. Joey's eyes would get all puffy from crying, and his face bright red. I swear sometimes he'd be laughing and crying at the same time, like some kind of crazy person. I'd still spank him—I didn't know what else to do. And when they pulled that crap in public—which they often did—I just couldn't take it. I'd just lose it, and spank them as hard as I could. Paul would usually just laugh, but the others would bawl. I never wanted them to be afraid of me, but they have to be a little afraid of me, don't they, if they're going to obey? One time one woman even called the cops on me. Made me furious, but later, I couldn't really blame her."

She stopped then and he looked around. The sun was going down. The distant ruined city glowed red. Most of the residents had gone back down inside the building. It would be feeding time soon, and that was the last thing you wanted to miss. But Daniel didn't believe she was thinking about eating. A few roaches still wandered the edges of the roof, gazing at the residents, gazing at the uneven tear of the horizon.

"By sunset I was exhausted, but Paul was still at it, winding up the other two until they were screeching like they were in pain, and maybe they were. When you're a kid, so much feels like pain, don't you think? I'd had it and I just wanted to lie down for a few minutes. I told Paul to keep a lid on things and I went into the bedroom to lie down.

"I shouldn't have taken that nap for lots of reasons. Most of all because I always feel strange after one of those naps, like I'm not all there. My dreams that afternoon were as high-pitched and jangly as my day had been. When I woke up and walked into the room I wasn't quite sure what I was seeing. They were all three giggling, actually more peaceful than they'd been all day.

"All three of them were sitting in the window. Paul and my two babies. All of them, my babies. More than that, they were straddling the window sill like a horse, one leg in and one leg dangling out. We're three stories up. Paul glanced over at me and smiled, patting Joey on the head, like he was proud of what he'd done.

"'Paul! That's dangerous! Get them off there!' I yelled, but not as loud as I might have. I didn't want to startle them.

"He just looked at me and frowned. And then he said, 'Don't be stupid.' That's what he said to me, his mother.

"All I wanted was to show Paul how dangerous it was so that he wouldn't do it again. Sometimes you have to be creative—that's what some of the other mothers in the building had told me. I don't know. Sometimes you get these ideas and you don't know where they came from but they sound good for some reason. So I ran at him, saying 'You want to fly out of that window? Is that what you want?' Trying to scare him, you know?

"He looked up just as I got there, his eyes so big and his face so white? I had my palm out like I was going to push him. And he just naturally leaned away, and then he was gone, and the babies, and the babies were holding on to him."

Daniel found himself taking a step back from her, as if she were something deadly. But she appeared not to notice. She was too focused on remembering, capturing and conveying every detail.

"I screamed, I guess, although I don't think I ever actually heard the scream. My head went all white inside, like the inside of an explosion. I didn't look out the window. I couldn't. I just turned and ran out into the hall, and down those long flights of steps, my legs pounding like some kind of athlete.

"And on the way down, I kept thinking about how it all might turn out okay. There were some canvas awnings above the first floor, and I remembered how the upholsterer on the block used to leave his waste bin nearby, so they always might land on something soft, and the babies, babies have flexible bones, don't they? That's what people are always saying. But I couldn't remember exactly where all those things were, so I couldn't quite make myself feel better, no matter how hard I tried."

She stopped then. He waited, but she didn't say anything more. And although he didn't want to ask, he finally did ask, "What did you find, when you got to the bottom floor, when you got outside?"

She looked at him with a vaguely puzzled expression, as if he should already know. "I didn't get to the bottom floor. I didn't get off those stairs. I woke up here. I thought maybe I'd fallen, going so fast. I thought maybe I'd fallen off those stairs and died and woke up here in Hell, not knowing, never knowing whether my babies died or not."

Then she was up and running for the edge of the roof. He couldn't stop her. But the roaches closed in, and she screamed when they touched her, wrapped her in their segmented legs, and bore her down.

The boy was nowhere to be seen.

9

THE TIME BETWEEN Daniel's scenarios lengthened from days apart to sometimes a separation of a week or more. He had to wait over three weeks after his last time. He spent a great deal of time in the waiting room, watching as the others were ushered out. Sometimes he was the only one left in the room. Should he stay there or return to his bunk? He was always tired, and he knew that if he lay down on his bunk he would fall asleep, and then he would dream, and he was dreaming enough—his own dreams or someone else's—but enough was enough.

Was he being singled out for some reason? Falstaff had seemed distant lately, reluctant to engage in conversation. Were the roaches suspicious of him now?

Then one morning they grabbed him along with the others. He'd always hated the process, but this time he was strangely excited. Whatever it was going to be, at least it would be different.

Daniel's initial transition into this new consciousness had him confused. The mind he entered felt altered, poisoned or inebriated. A roar of words, the language wet and too much of it, awkward in both his mouth and head. Slavic. Russian perhaps. He thought of Doctor Zhivago, and some old cartoon involving spies. But this oppressive mental space and its linguistic assault were a flood of cold hatred, pouring undiminished into a reservoir hollowed out of the deaths of millions. Koba was the name floated up onto all that hate, but it was one of many this old man had used in his lifetime.

The strange notion that Koba was aware of him produced a sensation like insects marching down his back and suddenly vanishing into his spine.

A softer, dimmer voice lingered in the background, the mind lubricated sufficiently to be heard by the juice, Madzhari, that young Georgian wine.

> *The pinkish bud has opened,*
> *Rushing to the pale-blue violet*
> *And, stirred by a light breeze,*
> *The lily of the valley has bent over the grass.*
>
> *My soul seems happy,*
> *And the heart is tranquil,*
>
> *And yet, will this hope hold true*
> *That overfills me today?*

The poems, sometimes signed Soselo, sometimes J J-shvilli, and sometimes anonymous, were by the same man, this Koba, this man of steel, this Stalin, who now waved his forefinger in anger at the young voice, and of course it dissipated, because Stalin's finger was more powerful than any gun, capable of disappearing millions with a single pointed gesture.

The short legs staggered forward. Despite the immense pain behind his left eye he managed to push his eyes open. He was in pajama trousers, an undershirt, some sort of vest. Daniel probed gently for clues. The body waved his arms in annoyance, as if trying to keep his questions away. Something was wrong here. Daniel wondered if Stalin had any clearer idea than he did what was happening to him.

Я закончил. Я закончил.

The words made rubble in his head until he could make better sense of them. I'm finished. I'm finished. I can trust no one, not even myself.

Я не могу доверять никому, даже себе.

Where was he? The room was large, but modestly furnished. A sofa with rounded bolsters and a high back. A large number of identical windows covered with simple, heavy white drapes. A wainscoting ran the walls, light wood, perhaps birch. Some kind of oriental rug. He walked unsteady as a child, his eyes hazed with pain, into another, smaller room, which seemed slightly more familiar.

He was having to endure the worst headache he could remember, but the answer came quickly enough: the nearer dacha in Kuntsevo. They'd had their usual film at the Kremlin, then travelled here for dinner, music, drinking and the customary foolishness. The others had left early in the morning, leaving Stalin alone with his staff. No one would come find him unless he called for them. They'd be too afraid.

He'd slept on the couch in the small dining room all day, then gotten up that evening and turned on the light. He was confused—he normally didn't sleep this long. He wasn't even sure what day it was.

He felt somewhat dizzy, but he'd been feeling that now and then for weeks. His blood pressure had been high, and yet there were always good reasons for high blood pressure. He had to do everything himself.

Had he had a steambath yesterday? He thought so, a long one. He remembered the way it had melted his thoughts, leaving tired, empty spaces behind. Perhaps the worst of his memories had vanished. They'd warned him it was bad for his heart, but who knew if that was true. He trusted his doctors least of all.

Still he moved forward, but so slowly, as if time itself were on its last legs. His own legs had become so weak, so shaky, he did not recognize them. They appeared to belong to someone else. He could barely struggle across the rug of the small dining room. It was Persian. Was this the one given to him by the Shah? It troubled him that he did not immediately know the answer. In Siberia men older than he was now had been riding horses and starting bar fights, bedding women half as young. The troubles of leadership had sapped his vitality. Once he'd been a cowboy, a bank robber, a Robin Hood robbing the rich and giving to his leader Lenin. He'd been like some highway bandit, his saddlebags full of money.

It had been up to Stalin to keep the revolution financed, and every time he had stepped up to the job. He'd not only been a man of steel, he'd also been a man of action. He'd exerted his considerable personal power over people, and he'd gotten things done.

He still had the power, of course. More now than ever. But it was all at considerable remove. He'd become like Gorky—he wrote the story that made his characters dance. He did nothing himself, and yet he made the orders that did everything. He outlined the plot, and then everywhere mayhem occurred. There was a certain satisfaction in that—it allowed him to be clever.

He remembered that army officer, not that long ago. The fellow had the temerity to visit Stalin himself at his office in the Kremlin. Stalin had been flabbergasted—had the man no friends to warn him against such a plan? He said there had been complaints about him, some dereliction or other, and he wanted Stalin, their great father, to know that these complaints were not true. Stalin had almost laughed in his face—he was too bold—then had him arrested two days later. It amused Stalin to play this way, to create some tragic story out of someone's life, some dark comedy. He actually couldn't remember the officer's name or what the supposed complaints had been about—he'd never even seen them. The man might be perfectly happy today if he hadn't bothered Stalin with his troubles.

Before Stalin had had the great hero D.F. Serdich arrested he had toasted him at a reception. He had pretended to be so impressed by the man. If he hadn't been burdened by the demands of leadership perhaps Stalin could have been a great actor!

And in 1938, he believed, the winter I. A. Akulov, secretary of the central executive committee, had fallen while skating, almost dying from the resulting concussion. Stalin had taken great pains and expense to bring in great surgeons from abroad to save the secretary's life. After a long recovery Akulov returned to work, whereupon Stalin had him arrested and shot.

Stalin had done these things, and he was Stalin, as he was so many other names. People did not understand why he did such things. It was simple. He was at his most powerful when no one felt safe.

He broke them. He broke every one of them. But now perhaps his run had ended. He had had these moments of pain and confusion before during these past few years. But this was different. Never for so long, and this feeling as if he were locked inside himself. A cramped, stinking cell with poor windows.

What had happened? What had happened last night? They'd watched their usual movie—Beria, Khrushchev, Malenkov, Bulganin, the usual bunch—but which movie had it been? Had he already been so drunk he hadn't paid attention? He had been thinking about horses, cowboys, so perhaps it had been one of his John Ford movies, *Stagecoach* perhaps. He hated the ideology of those cowboys, but could not stop watching these films. Even though his sympathies lay with the Indians, who had to struggle against the expansionist policies of the imperialist white settlers. Why hadn't the KGB yet carried out his orders to assassinate John Wayne? Incompetence and betrayal were everywhere. Wayne might be just an actor, but his ideas were a threat to the cause.

But very soon he would drop the bomb on the Americans. That would take care of his John Wayne problem, and all the rest.

Was Comrade Bolshakov still alive, or had he already had him shot? He should know this, and it somewhat frightened him that he did not. And yet it was also a somewhat amusing game. If the man was dead, who was choosing the films? Who was alive and who was dead? It only mattered when he lost track. Who might he order killed today? He would make them all think it could be any one of them, and of course this was true. All they had to do was step the wrong way. This was how a leader leads—no one should know what his next move might be. A great leader was a Lord of Mayhem. *Gospodin Bespredela*. Perhaps that would be his next name.

Whoever was in charge at the Great Kremlin Palace cinema, he would have him put on *Volga Volga* tonight. Stalin needed to sing. Stalin needed to dance, or die trying. He would make sure that Nikita was there. He'd make him perform a Ukranian folk dance for them all, squatting on his fat haunches and kicking out his heels. That fat fool, he reminded him so much of that bureaucratic clown Uncle Byvalov in the movie. Hilarious.

The vague aroma of cooking meat was in the air. He hated the smells of cooking. What were his guards up to? If necessary he would get rid of them all. Death solves all problems-no man, no problem. Svetlana said he had no heart, no gratitude. His own daughter! Her mother had called him a murderer before she'd shot herself. They simply did not understand how a leader must be, what he must do. Gratitude is a sickness suffered by dogs. It made you weak.

Everything was his business, to the kind and number of cars his associates had to the number of urinals on the streets of Moscow.

It had been his own weakness to marry, to have children. So he had to minimize the damage his family could cause him. A true Bolshevik had no business having a family. He'd said this many times. A family distracted, softened you. He should have taken his own advice. His Svetlana, his sparrow. When she was a child in her letters she pretended she was dictator of Russia and Stalin would pretend to obey her orders. And yet however precious she had been to him, she would betray him as they all had. She had visited him when? Yesterday or the day before. He'd been clipping pictures of the happy Russian children from the magazine *Ogonyok*. He'd given her one. "See, they love me," he'd said, and pointed the scissors at her the way he sometimes pointed his finger, as if he might snip snip her out of the air, out of the world.

A smallish figure had entered the room. He tried to raise his head to look, but could only manage a glimpse. A child. But not Svetlana. Svetlana was no longer a child. A boy or a girl? He could not quite make out the face.

"Who is that? Whose child is this?" he said, but he heard no words coming out of his mouth. He had plenty of words—they filled his head, but none could quite make it to his tongue.

Now he could not even lift his head; it had fallen like a boulder against his chest. He felt as if he'd been separated from it. Somehow his mind had travelled to a safer place.

He was staring at his feet. The second and third toes of the left foot were joined, so it was, indeed, his foot he was staring at.

I have more important things to do than look at my feet today!

The legs above those feet were shorter than normal. He would be embarrassed by them, if Stalin could be embarrassed. Because of them he'd had the carpenter cut down the legs on his work chair— had anyone noticed?

He now realized that his right leg, his right arm were tingling strangely, the arm beginning to tighten, to curl into itself, becoming as short as his left. It was the most ridiculous thing. He was turning into an insect! He attempted to open his mouth to protest, but the lip on that side lagged behind, the mouth spitting out "Dzhu... dzhu... dzhu."

He could feel that the child had come closer. He caught a glimpse of the short legs, the torso, the blurred head staring up at him curiously. But he could tell it was a large head, an oversized melon as a child would have. Svetlana? A ridiculous thought; she was a grown woman now. Some child had wandered into the dacha.

"Don't be afraid. Don't be afraid," he told the child. He did not know if this was a girl or boy. "You come to see your Uncle Stalin? Of course you have. I'm still your loving uncle, your loving father, despite what my betrayers say."

Although he was saying the words, he could tell these were not the sounds coming out of his mouth. Coming out of his mouth was garbage, and now he could taste a little bit of blood there, and it made him a little bit frightened, and that made him very angry. He was bleeding somewhere inside himself.

"Go through the doors, child! Tell them your Uncle Stalin needs help!" But he heard something else in his ears. He heard "Dzh... dzhu... dzh."

His tongue was no good, and this child was too stupid to help him. Or perhaps she was in on it. Perhaps she was here as witness, and once he was dead she would report back to the others.

Traumatized children made the best spies. They listened, they stared, and unless they were the rare, talkative type, you never knew how they felt about anything. You seldom knew if they even comprehended what was going on around them, but of course they did. They absorbed everything. It was how they survived.

He would never have said he was traumatized. He was Stalin. But his father, that old drunk, he never knew how much it had benefited him when he beat him for no reason, when he had berated him, embarrassed him. The old cobbler had helped make him. Unfortunately it had not worked with his own sons. For them, Stalin's indifference had only made them weaker. They had not known how to use the gift their father had given them.

When they told him his son Yokov had been killed in the war he'd told them "I have no son Yokov." They thought he had no heart, no compassion. They did not understand what was required of a leader. A leader has no family. Back when he called himself Vassily he had had a son, but not Stalin.

A great leader had to kill his past, he had to eradicate it. His old friends, his fellow bank robbers. Whoever had known anything of Koba in the old days—they could only decrease his legend. They would lose their fingernails, and then they would lose their lives. That drunken cobbler his father, and that old whore his mother— some had the nerve to question his absence from her funeral. Let them say that to Stalin's face. No one understood what was required to be such a leader. You cannot make a revolution with silk gloves, nor can you maintain one. No one understood. No one but he had the grit required to do what needed to be done. The world took Russia seriously now. No one else but Stalin could have done such a thing. He pitied the country in the hands of whoever dared replace him.

But perhaps Russia should not survive him. Russia would be like a dog who'd lost its master—better a bullet in its head to put it out of its misery.

Svetlana's mother, Nadezhda. He'd loved her, perhaps more than anyone. His entire life. But she was a foolish woman, who listened to his enemies and betrayed him. She did not understand what was necessary, what he had to be. And so she'd betrayed him, left him, shot herself. And Svetlana, she would be just like her mother.

All the great rulers had been harsh—they inspired love through fear. So why had his wife, his daughter, all of them, not loved him more?

His head was much worse. It was too wounded to contain his thoughts. His thoughts were spinning around in the air outside his head like little drunken sparrows, like little Svetlanas, chattering away about nothing.

Why had the child not gone for help? She was in on it—she wanted to watch him die. He could have them all killed. He could make up their crimes.

It was important to stay calm and focused. Outside the sky would be wet and overcast with no sun. He would survive this. He would move across the world like a crocodile eating his own.

"Look at my face, child! Look at my face! You must do as your leader tells you!" He heard these words in his head as he spoke them aloud. But he was aware that those were not the sounds coming out of his mouth. That blasted "Dzhu... Dzhu." A crocodile who snores. The child would never understand him.

If she would just look into his face she would see that he meant business. He had a face made out of stone, and a glance of such fierceness he could make the bravest men cower. He used to practice that impressive look in front of a mirror. Its strength, its seeming impassivity, as if nothing could ever affect him, then at the right moment he'd spring the trap and his face would become a terror. His smallpox scars only heightened the effect. His yellow eyes like a tiger's flashing his anger, one eyebrow raised almost vertically, a deeply etched network of wrinkles around his eyes.

His mother had had such a face. She'd already buried three infants by the time he was born.

He'd proved himself through his ruthlessness. He'd made himself a legend, a dozen legends. He'd contained a multitude. Iosif, Chizhikov, Nizheradze, Ryobi, David, Ivanovich, Vassily, Soso, Koba, Stalin—he'd used all these names and more.

Whoever he was, he wasn't even Stalin. Stalin was the unparalleled power of the Soviet Union—the figure in the portraits and on the newsreels. The Great Uncle and the Great Terror.

Ivan the Terrible had been his true teacher. Stalin understood that man as no one else did. When Eisenstein had filmed his masterpiece *Ivan the Terrible* Stalin had advised him well. He'd been the one to point out how in part two Ivan had kissed his wife much too long. Worst, he had made Ivan too indecisive, and his beard too long.

Ivan had been very cruel, but of course he had needed to be cruel. Ivan's only mistake had been that he had killed too few of the boyars.

Stalin did not know how long he had been standing there. He wondered if he might have actually fallen asleep between one step and the next. He could not find the child in the room anymore. Good, perhaps she had gone for help.

He discovered that he was able to steal a few steps now. Right out from under Death's nose. The thought made him smile.

Awkwardly he made his way over to the table. He picked up his copy of *Pravda*. Good, good. It was beginning to feel like a normal day. He felt so thirsty, like one of those desperate soldiers trudging through the desert in Ford's *The Lost Patrol*. He reached for the bottle of *Narzan* mineral water, then stopped himself, suspicious. Some hours before he'd had some, sometime, he wasn't sure when. He wasn't quite sure where it had come from. Where was everyone? What time? He was slowing down. Everything was beginning to feel very peculiar again. He had to order his hand to reach into his vest pocket and bring out his pocket watch, almost dropping it, his hand betraying him. He tried to understand what the numbers were telling him about the time. He had forgotten how to tell time.

The sudden bolt of pain hit him in the left side of the head. He thought he might have been shot or struck by lightning. But he had not given his permission for such things to happen. He stumbled forward. He felt an increased weakness in his legs, and a stab that shot through his shoulders, followed by a profound feeling of loss. His right arm stiffened. He attempted to stretch out the hand. But he lost the borders of himself. He could not be sure where he ended. He fell. He could feel his own piss pooling beneath him, but there was nothing he could do.

For a brief time he forgot who he was, but remembered what he had done and still had to do. There was an increasing coldness in his limbs, but nothing like the cold that, by his own choosing, smothered his heart. He became an infant in an old man's body, possessed of only a vague understanding, but an infant capable of a profound hatred. Hate fueled his determination. But there was nothing he could do with that determination. There was nothing he could do.

He was aware later when someone else came into the room. The man leaned over and looked into his face. One of his guards. He tried to tell the guard what was happening to him, as best he understood it, but again the "Dzu... dzu. Dzu... dzu." The imbecile failed to understand.

Then Stalin could hear himself snoring. His mind was wide awake, and yet here he was snoring. He was aware, too, when others came in, their incomprehensible voices obviously alarmed. They sounded like chickens who've found a dead wolf lying in the coop. They picked him up and carried him to the sofa in the large dining room.

And later, when his subordinates stood over him, talking, he could feel their panic. They were afraid to do anything, and so they did nothing. Beria was alternately kissing his hand then cursing him. Once he stirred and tried to look at this betrayer. Beria dropped to his knees and begged for forgiveness.

Stalin was aware, but he could not respond. Still, it filled him with great satisfaction.

He could hear Nikita weeping in the background. He could not see him, but Stalin was sure he was making a spectacle of himself. A crocodile's tears. Nonsense. Stalin, he was the only crocodile in the room.

He opened his mouth and shouted at them, blood showering his undershirt.

At some point a doctor, perhaps more than one, came in, sounding frightened, unsure. Do not hand me over to these idiots! But the order never reached his lips. He felt someone fiddling with his lips, prying open his mouth with shaking hands, taking out his plates. Careful! They tore his shirt off. They fiddled half-heartedly with his arm. Was his situation boring them?

Finally he could feel them placing leeches behind his ears. This did not disgust him. They were like old, true friends. Perhaps they would bury the leeches with him, suitable companions for the long nights alone.

Later he heard his weak son Vassily in the room, screaming that they had killed his father! But Stalin had no family—he was talking of someone else. Stalin, the real Stalin, would live forever.

At the end his sparrow entered the room. She kept trying to speak to him, but he was too busy choking. Her voice sounded like insects buzzing inside a bag. He was in agony, and yet it was as if it were happening to someone else, Ivanovich perhaps, or Sosa. Finally he opened his eyes and shook his terrible finger at them all. He could not see their faces, but he knew that they were all dead.

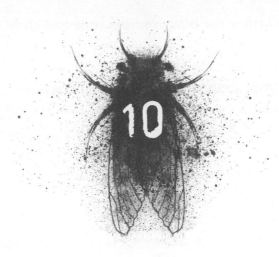

10

DANIEL BELIEVED HE woke up several times during the night. It was difficult to tell, half-awake or half-sleep being so close to the mental state experienced while wandering around inside a scenario. He remembered a great deal of buzzing, as if his nerves had short-circuited.

Was this what dying was like? It seemed entirely possible, the noise memories made as they disintegrated.

His time as Stalin still disturbed him. The lack of human caring always loomed, just on the other side of a fragile membrane. And it didn't require that much effort to cross over—a series of significant losses, disappointments, disillusionment, or maybe just a night of poor, interrupted sleep so that you temporarily forgot how to do the things that good people do.

The werewolf was howling again. It sounded closer, pounding through the floor right under his feet. He wondered if they had moved the werewolf, or if it was some acoustic trick of the architecture.

Again, this howl longer and lower than the rest, as if they were torturing him and he was giving up. But the roaches didn't torture, did they? A matter of definition. Around him the other residents were stirring, rising, talking to themselves as they often did. He wondered whether the boy from the roof had to hide again this morning.

Daniel was the last one of their group to enter the waiting room. He found them arguing, a common occurrence of late. Before joining them he stopped by the large window, thinking of the coin the boy had found. Examining the crumbling horizon line, he felt a mirroring disintegration within himself. What he saw out there would not have seemed alien to certain residents of Detroit or Kosovo.

"The Catholic Inquisition, the Puritan witch hunts, the Mormon massacre at Mountain Meadows—" Gandhi ticked them off on his narrow fingers, bending each back as far as possible and wiggling it for good measure. "—Aztec human sacrifice, the Indian thuggee murders, the Crusades, not to mention all the children molested or abused under the cloak of religion. The greatest crimes in history, all committed in the name of religion."

"Of course, those are terrible, terrible things." Charles/Lenin looked flustered. "But look at Nazi Germany's Jewish Holocaust or Stalin's Great Purge. We all know about those things, right? We've played the roles. Those people were atheists. Certainly atheists have committed more than their fair share of atrocities."

Daniel seldom involved himself in those kinds of discussions. People rarely changed their minds, so what was the point? Especially when there were far more immediate concerns, such as survival, such as the absence from your family.

But if he had said something, he would have told them it was about collective belief. Groups of people believing the same way, in a god, in a cause, in a particular way of life. But perhaps that was too broad—fear made him exaggerate. Belief could be a great thing—people did heroic things because of belief. Belief without generosity, without compassion destroyed people. Daniel didn't go to church—just stepping inside a church filled him with anxiety. But he felt the same way stepping into a filled meeting hall where people planned their perfect world.

The werewolf howled again, and the others stopped what they were doing. "Can't somebody do something about that?" Gandhi was angry. "We should do something about that." No one replied. He scowled, emphasizing the bony, gnome-like quality of his thin face.

"Well, I believe in divine retribution, and punishment for sin," Lenin said, sitting on his bed now. "I don't know why else we'd be here, except for punishment. And those roaches, they look like the very Devil, don't they? And this place, you can't tell me it isn't some kind of Hell where we've been sent to recreate the wicked lives of the damned." He waited, perhaps to see if there would be any objections, and hearing none, went on. "I run a Bible study group, or I did, before I was sent here. It was more than Bible study, actually—we talked about all kinds of things. It was extremely important to me. I used to say it saved me.

"I'd been in and out of jail most of my adult life. Petty theft, mostly, some drugs, and a fair amount of misbehavior following the consumption of alcohol. Sometimes I'd take somebody's car if I needed to go someplace. I don't mean 'borrow,' of course. The way I figured it, you had to survive, and I had this picture of what survival meant—food, clothing, basic supplies and an especially nice meal from time to time as a treat. Treats were important. Treats were a rudimentary human need, I figured, and part of my picture of survival. So I'd get these treats, the meals, some extra nice shoes sometimes, sometimes something electronic. I didn't feel guilty about it, because I didn't think I was asking for much. Just survival stuff, according to my definition, and everybody's entitled to survive, right? Everybody's entitled to their shot at Heaven, and my Heaven was modest—survival was Heaven, that's all it was. And no one was going to get in the way of that."

"No one would deny your right to survive. Many of us have had to struggle with that." Falstaff spoke slowly, deferentially. "But everyone defines survival differently. Some people define it so broadly it becomes an excuse for doing evil."

"Evil? Isn't that a rather extreme term? Who are you to say such a thing?" Gandhi looked unhappy, as did many of the others. "Let him tell his story." Daniel had noticed lately that attitudes toward Falstaff appeared to be shifting.

"Why are you the disciplinarian here?" Lenin was standing, pointing. He made a slashing motion with his other hand to add emphasis. "Why do you always seem to be the one in charge, the one who knows everything? It would seem that no one here understands the roaches better than you do."

Falstaff stared at him. "We're all nervous today. It's understandable. Try to control yourself. What else am I supposed to do when there are problems?"

"We know nothing about you," Gandhi said, "but you seem to know a great deal about us. Why is that?"

Falstaff looked at Daniel then, as if expecting him to say something in his support. But Daniel had no intention of speaking. Falstaff sighed and leaned back on his bunk, but Daniel didn't think he was as relaxed as he seemed. "I listen well, is that a crime? We have to pay attention to the roaches if we're to survive. I pay attention. I try to do what needs to be done. And, yes, I've tried to make myself an expert on the roaches, for the sake of my own survival, and yours. I'd urge you to do the same. But if my telling you more about myself will appease you, then I will oblige.

"I know no more about why I came to be here than the rest of you. The roaches may not be as methodical as we'd like to think. Although I came from a family of financial advantage I took no share in that. It was my grandfather with the money, and we didn't get along. I went to college in the sciences and although I did well, there were no jobs to be had when I got out. It was, it was during a period of serious... shortages."

The other residents listened quietly, respectfully, and Daniel wondered if the others were having the same problems with Falstaff's speech he was. It all seemed so carefully—vague. What science? What shortages? There were never enough details to pin him down. Daniel had always assumed that Falstaff was taken from the same relative time period as the rest of them. But there was something about Falstaff that didn't quite fit for the times Daniel knew.

"I was drinking a great deal in those days. I had not seen my wife in more than a year. She had left me, or she was dead. It was never a very good marriage—I suppose that was mostly my fault. I was always a man of great faults. It was difficult for me to change. I was stubborn. But you said you were trying to change," he said to Lenin. "You said you were trying to turn your life around."

Lenin looked eager, leaning forward. "I was tired of going to jail. Jail wasn't Heaven, far from it. I was too old for jail, too old to survive it. I had to come up with something to keep me on the straight and narrow. But Heaven had to be part of it, you know? I had to have my perfect Heaven. So why not the old-fashioned way? The Bible, I mean. Christianity, all that? I could see it worked for some, so why couldn't it work for me?"

"It doesn't work for a lot of people," Gandhi interjected.

Lenin rounded on him. "Like everything else, you have to give it a chance. You have to take chances in this life, take a leap of faith, or you never get anywhere. And that's a *fact*." Gandhi looked surprised by Lenin's vehemence and scooted back from the edge of his bunk, nodding. "So the last time I got out I started going to church. I went to church after church. I wasn't exactly sure what I was looking for, but I was pretty sure I'd know it when I saw it. It took me awhile to find the church I felt comfortable in. Most of them, well, they were a little vanilla, a little white bread. I'm not talking race here; I'm talking boring. It was hard to sit through the sermons without falling asleep. Not much variety, not much passion. Not much sense that people actually believed what they said.

"Then one day I walked into Reverend Philip's church. True enough, I almost walked back out again, because of the way he was dressed. Light blue suit and shiny white shoes, pink carnation in his buttonhole. Sandy-colored, slicked-back hair. He looked like a high school kid on the way to his prom. But he caught my eye as I walked in, and he grinned like he knew me, so I sat down near the back and listened. And I have to say that although he still looked like the most ridiculous man to me, he spoke with poetry and passion.

"John 14:23. I still remember the first verse I ever heard him talk about. Jesus says, 'Anyone who loves me will obey my teaching. My Father will love them, and we will come to them and make our home with them.' And it looked as if Philips was speaking directly to me. 'Hebrews 13:2—Do not forget to show hospitality to strangers, for by so doing some people have shown hospitality to angels without knowing it.' And he stepped out of the pulpit and walked down into the congregation, grasping hands and patting people on the back, and when he came to me he grabbed my hand and pulled me right out of my seat, and he said to me, 'To be at home with the Lord is to make your home on the heights. There will be no one left to look down upon you because you're way up there dwelling in paradise. Come, come with me, my son, because we're on our way home today. We're on our way to paradise.'"

Lenin was smiling broadly then, remembering. It was the most genuine smile Daniel had seen since he had arrived. And he envied him. But if a minister had pulled Daniel out of his seat in church like that he would have been beyond uncomfortable.

"Paradise would be nice. Paradise would be *great*." Falstaff's voice boomed. And to Daniel's surprise the emotion in it sounded genuine. "Have any of you been hungry, I mean more than for a late dinner? Perhaps you haven't eaten in several days, certainly at least in two days. Nothing but some bad-tasting water that made you sick? My family had money—they could have saved me from that, but they didn't." Then he stopped, looked around, and appeared uncharacteristically unsure of himself. "But I'm interrupting. I apologize. Please continue—you were telling us about this church."

Lenin looked only vaguely annoyed before continuing. "The Reverend made it a point to talk to me after church that day, and every Sunday thereafter, and after Wednesday night services when I started attending those. I told him I had some catching up to do where religion was concerned, but that I was eager to learn. He told me I should start a Bible study group at the church, said the church basement was available to me Monday and Thursday nights.

"With the Bible study happening the day after Sunday and Wednesday services, I began to see those meetings as a kind of debriefing session. We talked about the text covered by the sermons, and any other verses that seemed related—the Reverend would send me notes about those—and we talked about things from our own lives that seemed related. After a few weeks it became clear that the ones in the Bible study—about thirty of us by then—weren't the typical churchgoers. We were stragglers, mostly, wanderers, outsiders with a history of self-control issues, folks who had been to Hell and back. That was partly the Reverend's doing—he was always sending new people down to join the group.

"I didn't ask to be the leader—it just sort of happened that way, like gravity or centrifugal force, something that couldn't be helped and was just understood. They believed in me, and their belief made me believe. The group became everything to me. When I wasn't in the group, I was thinking about the group. They weren't exactly my friends—and one of my regrets in life is that I've never had any close friends—but it's hard to be a leader *and* a friend. It almost never works. I took the responsibility seriously, and I embraced modesty. I made myself obedient to the Lord. I was only going to follow God's instructions. Of course, there've been killers who have said the same thing—we all know that now. But I trusted myself. I trusted I would hear God accurately. I knew about Jim Jones and the People's Temple. The dangers of an arrogant leader who believes himself divinely inspired. But I knew I wasn't going to be any kind of Jim Jones. Not even close. God would guide me."

"Have any of you done the Jim Jones scenario?" Falstaff was standing again. Several of the men looked annoyed. The conversation must have hit a nerve in Falstaff—Daniel had never seen him look this agitated. No one responded. "Suicide as a social event—it's almost unheard of. That was the charismatic power he had over these people. He abused them psychologically, blackmailed them, and still they revered him. Sometimes we underestimate how vulnerable people are."

"But like I said," Lenin continued, "I was no Jim Jones. There were vulnerable people in that group, troubled people. and every new member seemed to have a different kind of trouble. We had our alcoholics, our addicts, our thieves, wife beaters, gamblers, and adulterers. There were folks into pornography and all manner of sins of the flesh, and we had individuals who were just sad, almost too sad to live.

"I kept painting them this picture of the Heaven I wanted them to see. I wanted to convince them how wonderful it was going to be. The ultimate location! If they strayed, if they started veering into beliefs and speech that didn't contribute to my vision of Heaven, then I'd tell them, 'my Bible doesn't say that. You must have gotten hold of the wrong Bible.'

"I didn't try to cover up any of the hard truths. I talked about Noah, and all the people that had to die. I talked about Lot's wife. They had to know that the stakes were high. Their immortal souls! The stakes don't get much higher than that! This was serious business, and I had no tolerance when they weren't serious about it.

"I'd give them verse after verse to say with me. I wanted to get the words embedded so far into their heads they wouldn't be able to tell the difference between a Bible verse and their own thoughts. 'Repeat after me,' I'd say, again and again, 'repeat after me.'

"I convinced them all to tithe. Sometimes I shamed them into giving more than they planned to, and doing more. Maybe you don't approve of that, and maybe you're right. But I saw it as just winning more souls to Christ. Sometimes the ends *do* justify the means."

"But it always comes down to the money, doesn't it?" Some of the men were trying to get Falstaff to sit down but he appeared oblivious to them. "The church needs it to get their message out, to convert people to their way of thinking. The rich man needs it to shield himself from death, or so he thinks. My grandfather was a rich man; he could have prevented everything that happened to me. I don't know, maybe he wanted me to learn my lesson. Rich people are all for poor people learning their lessons, pulling themselves up by their bootstraps and all that. My grandfather was one of those people who make money even in the hard times. Like they say, 'the rich get richer while the poor only get poorer,' something like that. He was always on top. Perhaps he sent people to look for me, perhaps not. I would have been difficult to find.

"But so much could have been prevented if we'd all just agreed to get along with just a little less. If all of us had made that sacrifice— accepted a lower standard of living, fewer things, less expensive foods, a smaller footprint on the planet. Maybe we could have sustained things better. In the part of the city where I lived things had gotten pretty hopeless. There were just too many people and not enough good housing, not enough food. The New England summers had gotten hotter every year. Augusts were unbearable— it drove people crazy.

"The neighborhoods were full of strangers-immigrants from Mexico, South America, and down from New York. Of course they came because they thought they had to. People have to eat somehow. But if you don't want people to be racists, don't let them get into situations where they have to compete with people from another culture for food."

"The money was for *good works*!" Lenin shouted. "Sometimes you have to feed the spirit while you feed the body, otherwise people forget *what life is for*. I was going to tell you about Malcolm before you interrupted me. One day the Reverend Philips brought

Malcolm down to the basement and introduced me to him. He certainly looked troubled—his eyes buried in his face and never once did that young man look at me directly. The Reverend said, 'I'm delivering our young Malcolm here into your care and to the ministrations of the group.' What can I say? I took on Malcolm as part of my holy mission.

"I admit I didn't like him. Oh, I tried to like him, but you're never going to like everybody, now are you? Most of the time you don't need to take care of that—God will take care of them, God will adjudicate, but sometimes it's God's will that you take action."

Even the residents not part of their intimate little group had turned their heads to listen. Some had moved to closer bunks. Only Falstaff appeared nervous and restless. In the windows a red sky had fallen over the crumbling city. The distant shadows appeared smoky, on fire.

"… abandoned by his parents to wander the streets begging, the addiction, the aggressive theft and other crimes. Obviously this young man was in considerable pain. But some of the things he would say about God, Jesus, and religion! I started to think he actually might be some kind of demon sent to test me. So defiant. So unreasonable. Maybe God let him in the door just to test me. God has all kinds of tests—you never know when you're going to be tested.

"'A belief in God's worse than heroin!' He'd blurt out something like that right in the middle of a serious discussion. 'More people have prostituted themselves in the name of Christianity than have ever whored for drugs!' That kind of thing. It made some of the group furious. A couple even jumped out of their chairs and went after him. I had to break up more than a few fights, something I never expected to do in Bible study. Still, I kept telling the rest of them to have patience with 'Brother Malcom,' that his soul was wounded, but eventually we would win that soul for Christ and wouldn't that be a triumph!"

"People would riot over the smallest thing." Daniel turned his head. The voice—he recognized Falstaff's voice—had come from the corner. He could see Bogart and a few others sitting there, listening. Perhaps they'd been turned off by Lenin's religious rhetoric. Or perhaps they simply found Falstaff's pre- or post-apocalyptic narrative more intriguing, or in fact, more relevant. Daniel moved closer so that he was between the two groups.

"The police rarely interfered. They generally stayed away from our part of the city—I suppose they found it too dangerous, and the local residents had too little power to influence them. The fire fighters still came—there were a large number of fires in those days, but I guess there are always fires—it's one of the ways people vent their anger while still remaining largely anonymous. But in our neighborhood people didn't shoot at the firefighters. It was a point of pride, I think.

"But buildings still burned, and they were torn down, and everybody looted, sometimes in the middle of a fire. When you think you're starving, and your family is starving, you'll risk pretty much anything."

"So why did this Malcolm come?" Gandhi was asking Lenin. "How did you hold him there?"

"We didn't. And that's why I didn't kick him out when, to be honest, I used to kick people out for less—showing up intoxicated, for example, or when, say, one man's wife divorced him for having an affair. I couldn't *abide* that kind of hidden sin, that kind of hypocrisy. But Malcolm, even with all the trouble he gave us, the blasphemous interruptions of our discussions, he still came there voluntarily. No one was forcing him to come, so obviously he was desperately reaching out for our help. I just couldn't turn my back on that. The Lord was testing me, and I wasn't about to fail him. So I let that boy have it. Every meeting I gave him a double shotgun blast of the Lord! Winning souls to Christ, that's what I was all about. I was even keeping a notebook listing all the souls I'd won, and I was determined to add Brother Malcolm's name to my list.

"I'd get right up in his face. 'God told me to tell you,' I'd say, 'that he wants you to be one of his soldiers! God wanted me to tell you that you're alone no longer!'

"I'd talk to the others, and once a week I'd arrange for the group to plant a 'lovebomb' on him. Even the ones who hated the fellow did that for me! We'd surround him and we'd hug him, we'd pat him on the back and tell him we loved him, God loved him, everybody loved him. We were all on his side so he had nothing else to fear.

"And I tell you he began to come around, even to participate a little. He still didn't say much in the meetings, but those blasphemous declarations pretty much stopped. I gave him little chores, little assignments, and he did them well. He proved to have some real skills with words, so when the Reverend would give me some text to go over for him, some plea for money to keep the church's message on the radio or on TV, I'd pass it to Malcolm, and he'd almost always improve it. Of course I gave him credit for it, and the Reverend Philips was *so* pleased with the both of us—I won some important points for the way I handled that, I gotta tell you.

"And when we were looking for support for the new building program or the missions in Africa, he found some great pictures on the internet for us. That black child with the flies on his face? A *huge* increase in donations after we put that one up on the website!"

"I hadn't had much to eat that week," Falstaff continued. "I could say that's why I did what I did, but I'm not going to use that as an excuse. That night I didn't think I was risking much. It was some rich man's food storage. The fire had been put out, the firefighters were gone, the looters were gone, I was tired and on my way to this little room I shared with eight other people. I was thinking I'd just check it out, see if they'd missed some little thing I could eat."

Lenin, apparently aware of the distraction in the corner, raised his voice. "In no time at all Malcolm was handling some of our key initiatives—the prayer requests, the brochure for our Spring tour of the Holy Land, the special pleas for unexpected expenses, the lists recognizing the members who had contributed the most to the cause. He could have had quite a career in advertising if he only applied himself.

"But it became clear after a while, I'm afraid, that our young friend Malcolm still clung to another life, a life outside the church. I gotta admit it was the other members of the group who saw it before I did—of course, they'd always been pretty suspicious of him. I suppose I just didn't want to lose a soul. I'd been adding up all the souls I'd saved, and I was feeling pretty good about the number.

"He started missing the Thursday night meetings. Now, they didn't *have* to go to all the meetings, but it was pretty much expected. I just wanted them to attend voluntarily. So I asked Malcolm about it, and Malcolm, he said 'I've been going to therapy,' he said. 'I still have problems, all kinds of problems. I still need help,' he said.

"I was a little shocked. 'You don't need that,' I told him. 'Jesus will provide for all your needs.'

"'It's not enough,' he said. 'I still hear this little voice inside, telling me that things are wrong.'

"'That's the Devil's voice,' I told him. 'The Devil's just trying to steal you away from us, your family. We're your family now, Malcolm. You have to trust in Jesus—he'll take care of you. You mustn't listen to the devils and demons trying to keep you away from faith.'

"He looked like he might hit me! 'Don't be angry, Malcolm,' I said. 'Anger is a sin. You don't want to end up in Hell, do you, Malcolm? The angry people—they'll all end up in Hell, burning for all of eternity.'"

In the corner, Falstaff was increasingly emotional. "But I wasn't alone, as it turns out. I was going in just as another fellow was leaving. He had a loaf of bread and a couple of cans of tuna in his arms. I figured that must be the last of it, otherwise he'd be carrying more.

"He was a young guy, but a big guy. But he looked scared. A big muscular fellow like that, and he looked frightened. I suppose it was the stakes. He *needed* that food."

Lenin, too, appeared increasingly upset. "I told Malcolm, 'at least now you're a part of something. But you have to do the right things if you're going to stay part of this group. You can't be selfish—you have to give of yourself, you have to help us meet our goals. You have to be a good example to the others. We all do. If you fail, then you leave. God sets a certain standard you have to strive to meet. It's a job, just like any other job, and when you disappoint your boss he makes you leave, right?'

"I could tell he wanted to confess, but I'm not a priest, and besides that isn't part of my beliefs. He didn't say anything. I guess he thought that was the end of the conversation. Later on I heard that he was seeing other people, that there were people waiting for him a couple of blocks away, and he'd go there after the Bible meetings. So one night I followed him. A couple of blocks, then three. And I saw something that greatly disturbed me.

"In the distance there were these men, at least I thought they were men, their shapes distorted, blocky bodies and oh-so-skinny legs, and heads like what you get if you twisted up one corner of a handkerchief. He went right up to them, and then they all turned and walked away. I have to say I had no idea what to make of that."

Falstaff had lowered his voice. Daniel had to lean in more closely in order to hear. "'Just let me pass, okay?' this big fellow said to me. 'I have a wife and three small kids at home. I *need* this food. No trouble, just let me pass.' He was desperate."

"We all had relationships outside the group. Well, I didn't, but most of them did. But I encouraged them not to let their kids play with the children of nonmembers. And I always asked in detail about the acquaintances of those attending the Bible study. We had to make sure those relationships didn't disrupt the group, otherwise we'd have to say goodbye to those relationships, however painful it might be. Oh, God understands pain. Pain is God's currency.

"Sometimes to get right with God you just have to hide yourself away from the world. Sometimes there's no other way.

"But I was thinking that what Malcolm was doing outside the church was more than just having other relationships. Those people he met up with, those distorted shapes, well, they had a sinister aspect to them. After thinking on it I became pretty frightened. I came to the conclusion that Malcolm was also part of some other church, some church that had nothing to do with God. Maybe that sounds far-fetched, but I could come to no other conclusion based on the evidence."

Somewhere beneath their feet the werewolf howled again, desperate to get out of his incarceration, forever trapped in his own head. The residents shifted uneasily on their feet, on their bunks. Both men paused in telling their stories. Falstaff was the first to resume his tale, and in that way some of the men became aware that he'd been speaking, telling his own story off to the side. Some grumbled over his rudeness. But others wandered over to see what he had to say.

"He could have pulverized me if he'd wanted to, a big young guy like that. He could have killed me. But that little bit of food might have been scattered and lost in the process. He couldn't take the chance.

"I kept thinking about all those little, petty battles you get into in your life, you know? Obsessive, nasty little conflicts when the stakes are nothing, just nothing at all. A better position at work, school competitions, winning some random argument with friends. I used to act quite badly in those situations. The smaller the issue the worse I behaved.

"But here the stakes were important. It was one of the few times in my life the stakes were vital."

"The argument broke out before the next Bible study meeting. I don't know how it started—I hadn't yet arrived. Some of the regulars, the ones who always got there early, they said that Malcolm had gone back to his old habits. Blaspheming. 'Backsliding' is the word one of them kept using. I'd taught them that word. All I'd ever wanted was to encourage them along their path toward Heaven, whatever Heaven might be for them."

"Here the stakes were absolute, probably more important for this man, because he had kids. But I'm embarrassed to say that his plea for his family didn't sway me in the least. I told the man sure, go ahead, take the food. 'Go feed your children,' I said. And when he turned his back I hit him over the head with a board, shattered it over his skull. I picked the food off the floor and ran away with it."

"Malcolm was on the floor writhing. I don't know which one of them hit him, if more than one hit him, or what they hit him with. But he was delirious. He was spitting. He was cursing us all and he was cursing the Lord. I honestly thought he was possessed. I honestly did. I made them all back away from him. I made them create a circle of safety around his struggling, distorted body."

Falstaff was actually crying. "I didn't even bother to see if the man was okay. I was hungry. If he hadn't looked scared, and especially if he hadn't mentioned his family I would have let it go, I would have walked away. He was just too damn big, you know? But he showed me his weakness. He made me take the risk."

"I thumbed through my Bible. Proverbs 20:30," Lenin proclaimed. "'The blueness of a wound cleanseth away evil: so do stripes the inward parts of the belly,' I read to them aloud.

"'And it shall be, if the wicked man be worthy to be beaten, that the judge shall cause him to lie down, and to be beaten.'

"'Judgments are prepared for scorners, and stripes for the back of fools.' Again from Proverbs. I didn't see the stick until too late. I think it might have been a broken-off broom handle. Or a mop handle, not that there's any difference. But I didn't see it. I was too busy thumbing through my Bible, and finding the verses I'd found before, the ones about punishment."

Some of the men surrounding Falstaff commiserated, some of them said they might have done the same thing. The others kept quiet, maybe because they didn't approve or maybe because now they were frightened of him, of what he could do, or perhaps, as with Daniel, they were wondering which world and which time he was actually talking about.

"'He that spareth his rod hateth his son: but he that loveth him chasteneth him betimes.' Proverbs is just full of punishment. And advice for those who feel they need to dish it out.

"'Chasten thy son while there is hope, and let not thy soul spare for his crying.' And Malcolm *was* crying then, although weakly.

"I just stared at the one holding the stick. He was one of the newer members of the group. To tell the truth I couldn't even remember his name. The stick had all these red stains on it. And there was red stain on the man's hand gripping the stick. I was telling myself he'd gotten into some paint, that he'd made a mess.

"'If thy hand or thy foot offend thee, cut them off, and cast them from thee,' he said. 'That's from Matthew, ain't it?'

"But I was thinking that was a poor choice of verse. It wasn't apropos. They hadn't cut Malcolm—they'd only beaten him." Lenin looked around at the residents still listening. "And then the roaches brought me here. Tell me now this isn't my punishment. Tell me this isn't Hell."

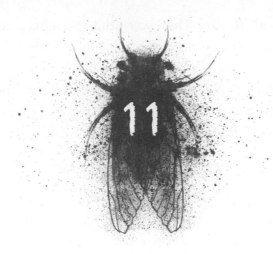

11

SHE HAS OVERSLEPT and she is going to be late for school.

This one didn't feel like all the others, and almost immediately Daniel knew that something had gone wrong.

He floated through a windy place, unmoored, the gusts battering and pushing him at random intervals, although it wasn't his body, exactly, that was being pushed—he had no sense of his body. It was his mind, or rather, some complex of desires and fears and memories, some cluster of roots and nerves driven along the cold streams of time, surrounded by the voices of the lost, all those who had drowned in history never to be remembered.

She has overslept and she is going to be late for school.

There must have been a short in the system, a break in the connection between who he was and the dead whom the scientists had sent him to occupy, some sort of guesstimation of how that person used to be. Instead of a well-insulated trip directly into another life, he'd gone off floating through pools of personality, random bits of lives cut short, meaningless squibbles of biography.

She has overslept and she is going to be late for school.

He became aware of intimations of language, staccato rhythms and harsh vowels, not fluid like French, but simply meant to communicate, to say a thing and then leave it lying there on the table for all to see. They were the thoughts and dreams of German children, he realized, Jews and non-Jews alike struggling to make sense and stave away fear. Somehow they'd captured that, recorded that, extrapolated that, and perhaps not knowing what else to do with it the roaches had just left it lying around in their data banks, for atmosphere or insulation. It was during the war and that anxious time preceding it, that terrible war when all the rules changed.

She has overslept and she is going to be late for school. Her father is in a panic and is now speaking harshly to her, something he almost never does.

"Lazy, foolish girl, what is wrong with you? You've slept late again and now the entire family must pay!" And then he slaps her across the face. But she doesn't cry out. She is too busy examining his face, trying to decide if this is some imposter who has taken her father's place.

Her mother comes in and roughly strips her out of her bedclothes. Then her mother tries to dress her in her school uniform, but she is struggling, trying to explain to her mother that this is the wrong uniform—it is completely different from the one she is supposed to wear. But her mother speaks a different language from her and cannot understand. "Dakka dakka dakka," her mother says. "Dakka dakka dakka."

Her parents drag her into the school and up the stairs to her classroom. They stand in the doorway waiting for her to find her seat. The other students stare at her in her strange uniform. She says hello to several of her friends but they pretend they don't know her. She is sure it is her strange uniform that is the problem and she tries to take it off.

"Wicked girl!" the schoolmaster shouts. "Only a sad whore takes off all her clothes!" In the doorway her parents cry out in shame.

She stops undressing, because of course the schoolmaster must be correct. She remembers that she is wearing nothing under the uniform.

Another girl is sitting in her assigned seat wearing the proper uniform. She doesn't bother to ask her, but she knows she also has her name.

"Sit down! Sit down!" her father shouts from the doorway. "You have to find your place!" Her mother weeps and wrings her hands.

It is no use. There are no empty seats, and no one will get up to offer her one. She leaves the classroom in despair and walks out of the school with her parents.

Her family returns to their neighborhood, but when she starts up the walk to their home her father stops her. "It's no use," he says. "Now there's no place for us here."

"No, Father. It will be all right," she says, but when she knocks on the door to their home a stranger answers. The rest of his family soon gathers behind him, gazing angrily at her.

"There must be some mistake," she tells them. "My family and I live here."

"No, no," the father of the strange family tells her. "It is you who has made the mistake, Jew."

They wander all night looking for a new place to live. Finally there is nothing more to do than to go to another neighborhood which was recently destroyed by fire. After much searching they finally find one wall still standing, and a soot-covered door in the middle of it.

She can feel her family standing behind her, anxiously waiting as she pushes and pushes on the edge of the door.

Finally it swings open, but there is nothing on the other side but wind and a distant light. "That's all right," she tells them. "It doesn't matter," she says. One by one they follow her in.

Abruptly Daniel felt himself snatched, pushed along so quickly and so far from any previous context he had no chance to gather himself. He had an odd notion of something failing, falling back and lost in the crevices between years, and then he'd landed.

Initially Daniel thought he might be playing a German schoolmaster this time, as in this mind's idle play the most prevalent

149

themes were discipline and pedagogy. Or perhaps he was a kind of administrator, as this was a mind filled with statistics, movements, logistics.

Die Weisen Könige wurden von einer Vereinigung von Asen abstammen und Vanir.

And a touch of madness, or at least a deep eccentricity. Irminenschaft. Wiligut had explained to Heinrich in meticulous detail how the Bible had been Germanic in its original state, how that ancient German god Krist had been stolen by the Christians for their own purposes. Wiligut claimed that German culture reached back at least as far as 228,000 BC, an idea that thrilled him and confirmed his own notions of the profound antiquity of the Aryan race.

It was simply undeniable that the inhabitants of Atlantis were Aryans who had descended from the heavens and settled on the continent. After the deluge they established a mythical city in a subterranean world below Tibet somewhere in the Himalayas.

This consciousness was flooded with these visions of color and light and dramatic gestures. The mouth became brutally dry as his excitement grew. It was the physical response to imaginative wonder typical of adolescent boys.

He had carefully filed notes from Wiligut elaborating on this buried city. He'd received the relevant letter in March, so it would be there. He could not recall the time the letter had been delivered into his hands, but that information would be noted on the front. And such a letter was significant enough that there should be a corresponding entry in his diary from that time.

In his diary he had precisely recorded everything he'd ever given anyone, how long he'd slept on any particular day, when he bathed, how many plums he ate, how many soldiers had been killed so far in this great war.

All they needed was additional proof, substantial evidence from more expeditions like the one he'd sent to Tibet. It was crucial to have something to show the Führer, something that would persuade him, and perhaps renew his hopes.

The Führer had not been the same of late. But Heinrich had hopes that this insidious deterioration in their savior would reverse itself. If not, perhaps they could persuade him to take a quieter role. Of course Heinrich was torn—his loyalty was pure—surely Hitler was ordained by the Karma of the Germanic world to lead them! Hitler was one of those brilliant figures who always appeared in Germany when it had reached a final crisis in body, mind, and soul.

But he could not bear the thought of anything lessening the reputation of their deliverer, even the Führer's own actions.

Heinrich hoped he might persuade the Führer to see both the Germanic far past and far future as the endless unbroken stream that Heinrich Himmler—reincarnation of that pre-Christian Saxon, Henry the Fowler—had seen for himself.

"Pardon, Herr Reichsführer. Are you ill?"

In that ancient time there had been three suns and the Earth had been inhabited by giants, dwarfs, and the other creatures of legend. Truly there had been gods walking the earth in those days, and there would be again. He knew he was no god, but with the right breeding, the correct policies carried through by his SS, some day there would be.

"Reichsführer? Should I summon your doctor?"

Heinrich gazed up at the handsome blond officer and smiled faintly. He wondered if the man had fathered children. Perhaps the children, too, would be gloriously blond and handsome. If a man like that had multiple partners he might father many, many Aryan children. Heinrich would have a friendly chat with him after the speech was over. "Thank you for your concern. Dr. Kersten is in Sweden, I'm afraid. Felix cannot help me today. My stomach is bothering me, but I will be fine without his help, I assure you. I simply need a few minutes to collect my thoughts. Has the podium been inspected?" The Poznan town hall had not been his first choice for the speech—he had some security concerns. But it would do.

"Ja, Herr Reichsführer. Twice."

"Then inspect it again."

He should never have permitted Felix to go to Sweden. He needed him here. His belly had been much worse the past few days, and Felix's massages were the only thing that brought him relief.

An unpleasant beer smell was in the room. Beer upset his stomach. There also seemed to be... a corpse smell. He did not know how else to describe it.

He picked up his handwritten notes off the table beside him. They were terse and informational, but they arranged themselves in his head into a kind of formula, an architecture, a prescription. He had his list of attendees—33 Obergruppenführers, 51 Gruppenführers, and eight Brigadeführers from key areas of the SS. He would acknowledge the setbacks—to do otherwise would be to undermine their trust. Then he would build their confidence, he would remind them of the inferiority of their enemies, get them to recommit themselves to the challenges ahead. He had not yet decided if he would address that other issue. It was a delicate matter, an unpleasant bit of housekeeping. But these were good men whose consciences needed to be salved.

It was for himself as much as for them—it had been a difficult year. The *Tausendjahriges Reich* was inevitable, but of course there would be setbacks along the way. If they could only reach some sort of agreement with the British and the Americans, then they might concentrate on the Slavs.

He gazed down at his slender, pale hands, their delicate blue veins. They'd always been too girlish, but if he kept them still they seemed to keep the rest of him calm.

He removed his pince-nez and cleaned it again. It wouldn't do to misread a figure because of some speck on the glass. He'd had some trouble with that recently, blurred objects appearing along the edge of his field of vision, vague disturbances in the air. Perhaps these were the harbingers of some immanent vision, but probably that was too much to hope for. Although it embarrassed him, he considered that his eyes might be weakening further.

Minutes later he walked out into the hall. Something bothered him about the crowd, something that did not fit, some disturbance. Something stirred there on his left, skin paler even than his own, eyes which did not blink, as if there were no eyelids, and dark holes in the milky eyeballs where the pupils should have been. But he had a task to perform and his men were waiting. He scanned the crowd again but could find nothing more.

Daniel could tell that he was less into this part than normal, his consciousness only partially absorbed. Certainly this mind was a twitchy, uncomfortable place to be. But part of the issue, he thought, was that Himmler was so difficult to pin down exactly, his mouth always saying one thing while his mind was thinking another, and more. Himmler was like a robot with more than one program running inside.

Among the SS higher-ups in their stiff uniforms and feigned expressions of attention, a dirty young boy in striped pajamas drifted in and out between the seats, floated along the floor, insinuated his stick thick arms and legs among the chair legs and uniformed legs, pushed his twig-like fingers upwards in a reach for the sky.

Had Himmler noticed? Yes, but only vaguely. He was not yet quite ready to see.

Heinrich climbed the podium. He looked about to see who was in the high-backed chairs, how many were empty. The town hall was not as impressive as he would have liked, but at least there were the vaulted arches, a Teutonic feel to the stone work.

"In the months which have passed since we last met in June of 1942, many comrades have fallen and given their lives for Germany and for the Führer. Before them, in the forefront—I ask you to stand in their honor, and in the honor of all our dead SS men and dead German soldiers, men and women—in the forefront, from our ranks, let us honor our old comrade and friend, SS Obergruppenführer Eicke."

They rose from their seats. Eicke had been a difficult loss for him personally. He'd taken the man out of an asylum and made him commandant at Dachau. If nothing else he would make sure Eicke was remembered as a hero. He gazed at the men assembled before him, seeking some sign of the disturbance he'd sensed earlier. There—a bit of ragged cloth, a filthy foot, but he could not see what they were attached to. His men shifted their weight impatiently. Some boy had gotten in. Someone would pay. But for now Himmler said, "I ask you to sit."

Heinrich usually felt in control in these situations, speaking authoritatively, those he commanded hanging on to his every word. At times like these he thought of his father and all those years he'd stood in front of a classroom. His father must be proud of him, but the old man had no idea how far Heinrich might take this. No one did. He had to rid himself of that filthy intruder. A brutal bit of housekeeping was called for.

"I have considered it necessary to call you all together, the High Leadership Corps of the SS and Police, now at the beginning of the fifth year of the war, which will be a very difficult year..."

Heinrich had his fears, more than he would name. Throughout the year he had utilized his control over the courts and civil service to advance the racial reordering of Europe, paying particular attention to the fates of the 600,000 Jews he estimated to be in France. Earlier last month one thousand Jews had been deported from Paris to Auschwitz.

This Autumn there had been the Allied air raids on Hamburg in early August, followed by the destruction of the armament center of Peenemünde at mid-month. The Allies were calling for Germany's unconditional surrender.

Some days, they seemed much further away than others from the supermen they would one day become.

Heinrich heard his own voice continue on and on, and it seemed to him he was putting parts of himself to sleep. His men continued to sit bolt upright in their chairs, but here and there he could detect some glassiness in the eyes, some strain in the necks. They would all let him down eventually, and he would become the commander of an army of corpses. They needed stirring. They needed a bit of mayhem.

But the future still lay before him. In the years ahead he would expand Wewelsberg into an SS kingdom. It would be his great city, his SS Vatican, the center of the new world. An 18-meter-high wall with 18 towers. The whole of the complex would be in the shape of a spear pointing north. Part of him focused on this and nothing else. He liked to imagine all his brave knights gathered together in the castle dining hall, sitting in their pig leather chairs and eating from silver plates with their names engraved on them. This would be just the beginning of the next phase of human evolution.

Daniel wasn't always sure which Himmler to pay attention to— the officious accountant of the dead or the dreamer who had lost his head. Both were frightening, and equally dangerous.

"The Bolshevik system, and therefore Stalin, had made one of its most serious mistakes…"

He kept hearing a murmuring, a clanging of pots and laughter. That boy in the audience, was he causing the trouble? There—part of the boy's face—so blue, as if the flesh had lain on frozen ground.

"… the total loss of approximately 500 km of front.

This loss required the withdrawal of the German front, in order to be able to close it again at all. This loss made the sacrifice of Stalingrad necessary from the point of view of Fate."

There it was again. Heinrich turned. Who? Were they listening? He marked his place in the notes and stopped his speech. "Hold on. Koppe!" The men stirred anxiously. "Down there! It's so noisy! Does a shaft lead to the kitchen?"

There were service people in the kitchen who might listen. He had to shut off the possibility.

He looked back into the audience. He didn't see the boy. Perhaps he was still sneaking around, attempting to sabotage Heinrich's speech? "We are going to wait for a moment," he announced. "Because what I say isn't for everyone's ears, right?"

He left the microphone. His men were scattering, moving rapidly, much to his satisfaction. Now there would be action! He followed two of his staff down into the kitchen. They began to question the workers. He pulled one of his men closer, yanking on his elbow. "Are there Jews here?"

The young man looked alarmed. "Oh no, Herr Reichsführer. Everyone was checked beforehand."

"Make sure," he whispered. "Shoot them if necessary."

Peering around them, Heinrich saw something on one of the counters that made him gasp: a bloody rabbit carcass, waiting patiently to be fully butchered. He shuddered, his belly twisting in knots. Vaguely, he heard one of his men explaining how they could not close the door to the kitchen, but they had found a mattress in one of the rooms. They would stuff it in front of the door.

He scurried back toward the podium, trying to leave the image of the butchered animal behind him. He had no tolerance for such things—for him a meal was ruined if he was reminded that animals had been slaughtered.

He could never understand how a hunter received pleasure from shooting an innocent creature. Every animal had a right to live. The Buddhist monks had the right idea. They carried a bell with them to keep the woodland animals away so that no harm might come to them.

He was rattled, but he went on to discuss the evacuation of Kharkov, still hearing things out in the crowd and glimpsing movement. Why couldn't the child at least lie still until Heinrich was finished?

"An element basic to an overall evaluation is the question of Russian population figures. That is the great riddle... 400 times 10,000 men, or 400 new divisions. I calculate this in approximately the following manner: the Russians have already drafted all men born in 1926, and some of the men born in 1927..."

The man clearly loved his dates and figures, his theories of population. But those thoughts were not music—they were like sharp rocks rolling around inside Daniel's head. "… amount to 1.5 and 1.8 men respectively, while our men born in the same years amount to only 500,000 to 600,000 respectively, that is, that is… the subhumans …"

They took a break. It was very warm in the room, "Could someone open the windows?"

He took a few steps away. He could smell the boy—that's what he had smelled earlier. That Jew flesh, that dead Jew flesh. He would never be able to get the smell completely scrubbed off. He should stop the speech. He should send his men out into the audience to find the dead Jew boy and drag him outside. It was the only way to be sure. But what if the boy had friends, collaborators? It was a sad thing, but Heinrich could trust no one.

He calmed himself. He began again. "America is waging a war on two fronts, even more than England: the Pacific…"

What was that? He turned his head. "What's going on?" he asked. "America is waging…" He stopped and repeated himself again.

He fell back into his notes, his speech. He tried to keep his eyes down. But he kept looking up, and finding the boy's eyes burning like twin stars in the shadows, hiding behind the men, his men.

"The Slav is never able to build anything himself. In the long run, he's not capable of it… with the exception, therefore, of an Attila, a Genghis Khan, a Tamerlane, a Lenin, a Stalin—the mixed race of the Slavs is based on a sub-race with a few drops of blood of our blood, blood of a leading race…"

He was disturbed to see more of the striped pajamas in the gaps between his brave Aryan men. Had the boy brought his friends? There on a pale hand, draped across the shoulder of one of his finest, a gleaming drop of blood. Heinrich was disgusted.

"It's just as true that he is an uninhibited beast, who can torture and torment other people in ways the Devil would never permit himself to think of. It's just as true that the Russian, high or low, is inclined to the most perverse of things, even devouring his comrades or keeping his neighbor's liver in his lunch bag."

Skinny arms were coming out between the seats. A paleness beyond pale. And yet his men did nothing. They simply sat there.

"It is basically wrong for us to infuse all our inoffensive soul and spirit, our good nature, and our idealism into foreign peoples."

He could not tell even whether they were male or female. In death all Jews became the same. He was appalled when one pale sexless head placed its lips on the mouth of one of his finest...

"One basic principle must be the absolute rule for the SS man: we must be honest, decent, loyal, and comradely to members of our own blood and to nobody else. What happens to a Russian, to a Czech does not interest me in the slightest."

At least he had attempted to be efficient.

"Our concern, our duty is our people and our blood."

The problem was that ordinary men had no appreciation for the larger demands of history.

He read off statistic after statistic. The numbers were spell-binding, possessed of magic. He could tell that his men were uncomfortable. There was nothing more important to him than his men, his brave SS men. They all had some very difficult work to do.

"Ich will auch ein ganz schweres Kapitel will ich
hier vor Ihnen in aller Offenheit nennen. I also want to talk to you, quite frankly, on a very grave matter. Among ourselves it should be mentioned quite frankly, and yet we will never speak of it publicly. Just as we did not hesitate on June 30th, 1934, to do the duty we were bidden, and stand comrades who had lapsed up against the wall and shoot them, so we have never spoken about it and will never speak of it... It appalled everyone, and yet everyone was certain that he would do it the next time if such orders are issued and if it is necessary."

Ausrottung? Was that the word he wanted to use? Look at them—the way they all sat up, their attention renewed. Yes. *Ausrottung.*

"I mean the clearing out of the Jews, the extermination of the Jewish race. It's one of those things it is easy to talk about—'The Jewish race is being exterminated,' says one party member, 'that's quite clear, it's in our program—elimination of the Jews, and we're doing it, exterminating them.' And then they come, 80 million worthy Germans, and each one has his decent Jew. Of course the others are vermin, but this one is an A-1 Jew... Most of you must know what it means when 100 corpses are lying side by side, or 500 or 1000. To have stuck it out and at the same time—apart from exceptions caused by human weakness—to have remained decent fellows, that is what has made us hard. This is a page of glory in our history which has never been written and is never to be written."

Heinrich hoped they understood the gift he was attempting to give them. A way for them to look at what he'd asked them to do, this unpleasant yet necessary task, but without guilt or blame. These were good men, SS men of fine character. Hadn't he always been concerned about their emotional health?

Two years before while visiting Minsk he'd asked to see a shooting operation. Originally it had seemed the simplest way to handle their Jewish problem. Just shoot them. Commander Nebe arranged the execution of 98 men and two women by an *einsatzgruppe* unit for his benefit.

Before the execution he'd walked up to one of them. He'd asked him point blank, "Are you a Jew?"

The man had stared at him as if trying to think of a good reply. Finally he'd said "yes."

"Are both your parents Jews?"

Again he'd replied, "yes."

"Do you have any ancestors who were not Jews?"

"No."

"Then I can't help you."

The Jews had to jump into an open grave like an upside down triangle and lie face down along the apex. One or two rows of Jews would be shot, and then the next group would have to lie down on top of the dead ones in order to be shot by the soldiers standing along the grave's edge.

He'd made the mistake of stepping right up to the edge and peering in.

After one particular shot a bit of flesh made a high arc from the ditch into the air and landed on him, some on his coat and some on his face. He could see that it was a bit of brain. He immediately felt ill and began heaving. He felt dizzy and one of the men had to lead him away. He was quite embarrassed for his men to see him this way.

Later he gave a brief speech letting them know how much he appreciated the difficult things they had to do. Unfortunately there was no help for it. They were SS men, they had to stand firm.

But almost immediately he began his search for a better way. His SS men should not have to endure such a thing. That was what had led him, finally, to the gas.

The previous Fall he had seen a gassing at Auschwitz. He had watched the selection process. Then he had stood at a small window and gazed at the Jews dying inside. He had said nothing, but there was an interesting effect. The Jews had been packed into the room with admirable efficiency—there was no wasted space. The light was very dim, so their bodies, all heights and sexes, shapes, were these soft gray pieces fitted together against a background of a darker gray with occasional patches of blue. As they began to die there was no space for them to fall, but they moved, frantically at first, but then more slowly, the patterns their bodies made one against the other changing shape, flowing, a kind of slowly moving painting that was beautiful in its way with all its shades of gray and blue.

One of the Jews looked straight at the window. Heinrich could not tell if she saw him. There was nothing in her eyes. A spot of dazzling red appeared on her lip where she had bitten herself during her final moments.

He observed the attitudes of the SS men through every step of this process. He still said nothing, but he was very concerned about their emotional well-being having to perform such a necessary but onerous task.

Finally he watched the labor crews take away the bodies for burial. He spoke up then because he had a suggestion. "You should burn the bodies instead," he told Hoess.

Daniel forced himself into a very tiny place inside Himmler's mind. Then he tried to make himself go to sleep.

"We have taken from them what wealth they had. I have issued a strict order, which SS-Obergruppenführer Pohl has carried out, that this wealth should, as a matter of course, be handed over to the Reich without reserve."

Some in his SS would let their personal greed make a travesty of his own code of ethics. The anger built in Heinrich until the internal volume of his moral outrage shook Daniel from his little hiding place.

Heinrich began to explain the punishment that would be delivered, and by the end of that explanation he was growling. "He who takes even one Reich Mark of it, that's his death! A number of SS Men—not very many—have violated that order, and that will be their death, without mercy. We had the moral right, we had the duty to our own Folk, to kill this Folk which wanted to kill us. But we don't have the right to enrich ourselves even with one fur, one watch, one mark, one cigarette, or anything else!"

Himmler seemed to blink more than the average person, or perhaps Daniel was simply intensely aware of it. Between the blinks Daniel saw the Jews in the audience moving again, but whether to get closer to Himmler and the podium or to make their own escape he could not tell.

"Again and again we have sifted out and cast aside what was worthless, what did not suit us. Just as long as we have strength to do this will this organization remain healthy. The moment we forget the law which is the foundation of our race, and the law of selection and austerity towards ourselves, we shall have the germ of death in us, and will perish…"

Heinrich could feel them slipping away. What would become of him if he lost his command?

"We shall colonize. We shall indoctrinate our boys with the laws of the SS-organization. I consider it to be absolutely necessary to the life of our peoples, that we should not only impart the meaning of ancestry, grandchildren and future, but feel these to be a part of our being. Without there being any talk about it, without our needing to make use of rewards and similar material things, it must be a matter of course that we have children. It must be a matter of course that the most copious breeding should be from this racial super-stratum of the Germanic people."

Heinrich had spent his childhood staring up at the stone castle at Burg Trusnitiz on the high hill. He'd fantasized about a brotherhood of Teutonic knights who gave their blood defending the sacred soil of their homeland from invaders who had no notion of the necessity for honor, duty, and purity. Now he had his own brotherhood of dark knights who he hoped might one day thrill the world with their power. Without his SS he would be less than nothing.

"We want to be worthy of being permitted to be the first SS-men of the Führer, Adolf Hitler, in the long history of the Germanic people, which stretches before us. Now let us remember the Fuehrer, Adolf Hitler, who will create the Germanic Reich and will lead us into the Germanic future.

"Our Führer Adolf Hitler.

"Sieg Heil!

"Sieg Heil!

"Sieg Heil!"

They all stood, saluting. Heinrich could see how the ragged child who had first intruded upon his speech now lay beneath their polished boots, falling into bits too fine, he hoped, for history to hold them.

It was the curse of the great to have to walk over corpses.

And deep inside, Daniel prayed *let me out let me out let me out.*

STRIPED PAJAMAS. GORDON had had a couple of pairs. His favorites, with the red stripes. Not like the blue stripes on the uniforms the Jews wore. His stripes had been narrower. And of course they hadn't had the two superimposed yellow triangles making the Star of David. Still, Daniel wished now he hadn't bought them for his son. Now he couldn't think of them as anything but uniforms for the sleep walkers, for the walking dreamers, the soon-to-be-dead.

Daniel and Elena had recognized that something was wrong, although they rarely put that worry into words. Gordon was less active than his classmates, more reticent to enter into the almost mindless, almost violent play of other boys his age. Although he clearly wanted to—Daniel could see it in his dark eyes, the vague shininess they took on when he saw the other boys playing. Daniel recognized the desire to be a "real" boy, all boy, the kind of boy everybody loved.

Before the diagnosis Daniel had taken Gordon's reticence for shyness. He saw it as his job to draw his son out of his shell. For about six months when Gordon had been six or seven, the normally affectionate boy had become squirmy, stubborn, and reluctant to be held.

"It's natural," Elena had said. "My sister's kids went through the exact same thing."

"Maybe. I'm not so sure." Daniel's strategy had been to rough-house with his son, wrestling, grabbing, pretending to be a cowboy astride his horse. Daniel as the bull had been an angry force of nature.

Gordon waved the giant beach towel in Daniel's face. Elena had sewn a picture of an enormous frog on it. Daniel aimed his head with its imaginary horns at the frog's round belly.

"Here, Daddy-bull! Come get me!"

Daniel crawled on all fours as fast as he could beneath the towel, shoulders and butt thrashing. "Snort! Snort!"

"Daddy-bull's got a cold!" Gordon leaped onto Daniel's back, clutching his T-shirt at the shoulders, digging his small hands into Daniel's sides, giggling. "I'm beatin up Daddy! Hey, I'm beatin him up!" Gordon liked the game more and more as he grew older, playing his part even more aggressively.

And Daniel encouraged it. He was even rougher in his play, as if to demonstrate to his small son how much the boy could actually handle, that there was no reason to be afraid.

"Wrestle, Daddy! Wrestle!" Daniel pulled Gordon off his back, laughing, put him on the floor beneath him, straddled him and began tickling. Gordon squirmed with uncontrollable laughter.

"That's probably enough, Dan," Elena said from the kitchen. "You're getting him all worked up."

It was a guy thing, he supposed. Not that girls couldn't play as aggressively as boys, but it seemed that more frequently they knew when to stop. A father and his son, that was just two boys playing together, not knowing when to stop. And sometimes the games lasted a lifetime.

Daniel tickled more insistently, then bent over, wrapping his arms around Gordon, trying to hold him more tightly, kissing him on the cheek, clutching him with a strange sort of desperation, kissing the boy's small hands, and before he knew it he had taken his son's upper arm into his mouth, as he had at other times--playing "lion" or "monster," and Gordon was giggling so, and Daniel thought about biting him, thinking how adults were always telling kids "I could just eat you," and he tasted the salt, and stopped.

Gordon's giggles faded, and he stared at Daniel with those shiny black eyes as if waiting to see what Daniel was going to do next. Daniel didn't know himself. He loved this little boy so much he just had to step away before he ate him all up.

After the heart diagnosis Daniel would think back to this little wrestling match and shudder. He would remember the grunting sounds his son used to make, and his puffy eyes, and how he used to think Gordon must have allergies, terrible, persistent allergies. Later he and Elena would work out their shifts so that one of them could be with Gordon at all times. It all accumulated, there was so much to think about, and they became estranged. They hardly knew each other anymore. If only Gordon hadn't gotten sick, but he'd always been sick, hadn't he, since the day he was born? They just hadn't known. And Daniel, and Daniel could have just eaten him up, eaten him up.

Later, in another life, in a scenario in which he floated in and out of the mind of Albert Fish, apprehended 1934, who had killed-- and oftentimes eaten--a dozen or so children, he would think how the desperation, the hunger, was all-pervasive and inescapable.

ONE MORNING DANIEL woke up to discover Gandhi sitting on the edge of his bunk. From this angle he looked as small and fragile as a child. "We let you sleep in. You've been having a particularly hard time of it lately, I think," he said. "Alan didn't come back from his last scenario."

Daniel sat up quickly, blinking. Alan? Bogart. He had no idea what to say. But it wasn't as if they were actually friends, any of them. "Are you sure, Walter? Maybe he's just late. Sometimes we're late coming back."

Gandhi shook his head. "Never this late. If you're this late you're not coming back." He looked down, closed his eyes as if offering up a prayer. "Well, I just thought you'd like to know, for when you didn't see him." He started to get up.

"What do you think happens to them, Walter, when they don't come back?"

Gandhi shrugged. "Some of the fellows, they say the roaches execute them, that it's like a trial, and then they're executed." He shook his head. "In our situation, people believe anything. I think sometimes they have heart attacks. It's a lot of stress. I've always wondered if the roaches screened for high blood pressure before they took us. Probably not. And sometimes I think they go crazy, afterwards. Not hard to believe, is it? That's what happened to the werewolf, I suppose. Maybe there's a ward full of them someplace, unless the roaches put them out of their misery, unless they want to study them, like with the werewolf. That would be the humane thing, under the circumstances. Not an execution, exactly. Euthanasia."

Gandhi got up and walked toward some of the others gathered nearby. His small bare feet made no sound. He seemed to barely have a presence. That slight, tentative profile, made Daniel ache for Gordon.

Unexplained disappearances had happened several times since he'd been in Ubo, but never to anyone Daniel actually knew. Joining the others, talking to them—however little it might do—was the decent thing.

He had reached the group, taking his position beside Falstaff, when a peculiar thing occurred. The lights blinked. He might have thought it was just his own eyes blinking, but from the look on the others' faces he knew that wasn't the case.

Except for Falstaff. Falstaff looked thunderstruck, appalled.

But the truly peculiar thing was the momentary hallucination or crazy notion he had during that blink. He saw skin melted away, and something not bone underneath. And metal prostheses of some sort, as if they'd all been maimed. He couldn't be sure if the others had seen the same thing, but they all looked uncomfortable. And Falstaff, Falstaff looked sick.

It would be impossible to say whether the interruption in power had anything to do with it, but there were no scenarios for the rest of the day. Daniel had never seen so many men in the barracks or in the waiting room, and they all acted as if they weren't quite sure what to do with themselves. There was much staring off into space, staring at each other, visual and hands-on inspection of their own bodies. Daniel himself felt compelled to wave his own hand in front of his face, fingers spread, moving it fast, then slow, trying to make himself aware of the point at which it blurred and whether that matched experiences he'd had of similar actions on earth. Maybe this was related to the slight shimmer he'd noticed around the roaches, like the visible distortions of air on a hot summer day.

The roaches themselves were scarce. None had appeared in the observation windows all day, and Daniel had had only a brief glimpse of a guard in the outside corridor. Some crisis must have occurred—he just hoped it wouldn't make life for the residents more difficult.

By afternoon nervous energies were spilling over into small quarrels and shoving matches, usually because someone had been staring too long or chosen to extend his physical examinations beyond his own body. Usually it was Falstaff who broke these quarrels up.

FOR SEVERAL NIGHTS in a row the werewolf howled incessantly, his voice transitioning from a low, dream-entrapped groan to an ear-splitting hysteria. Periodically Daniel would climb out of bed and find Lenin or Gandhi sitting on the edges of their bunks, hanging their heads wearily, or walking around in the gray-dark, listening, not knowing what to do. The next day they'd all be groggy and staggering, except for Falstaff, who apparently refused to let it bother him.

They rarely spoke about it during the day. He supposed they all just hoped it would get better.

But on the sixth night of the howling, the raw-throated screams, Gandhi and Lenin and Daniel were standing, staring at each other, with occasional glances at Falstaff's snoring and immobile mass. "Let's put a stop to it," Lenin said. "Let's go find the beast."

"How are we going to stop it?" Daniel sat back down on his bed.

"Who knows? Give him what he wants, maybe." Gandhi sounded spent, aggravated. "Sometimes at night when I can't sleep I wander around. It's strange, but I almost never encounter the roaches that late anymore. Maybe they're short-handed."

"Or they're hiding, waiting for us to overstep our bounds." Lenin threw up his hands. "Not that it matters. I'd try anything at this point." He started off toward the wide door at one end of the barracks, the "roach door." "Be bold, gentlemen," he called back.

Gandhi glanced at Falstaff's sleeping mass. "Should we wake him?" But Lenin was almost to the dim outline of doorway. Daniel and Gandhi stumbled into each other, then hurried after him and into a series of increasingly damaged hallways, down neglected staircases, Daniel fought to keep his nerve. At least the spaces they travelled through were generally, if dimly, lit. The walls throughout the structure had been equipped with shallow baseboards that glowed in the dark, casting the surfaces with a pale blue. Some of the larger rooms had matching parallel ceiling borders in white. The resulting light showcased wall after wall of damage and corruption.

Navigation was inexact, based on whatever directional clues the werewolf's cries provided. They let Lenin take the lead. Daniel didn't know that Lenin possessed any more understanding of the building than the rest of them, but at least he showed confidence. The werewolf continued to moan and whimper, scream and howl, the perceivable origins of these sounds complicated by the echoing emptiness in this part of the building.

For a time they shuffled their way across floors inches deep in wall and ceiling fragments that rattled and clacked against their shoes. "Who knew concrete would turn out to be a universal building material?" Gandhi said at one point, underlining a detail that had been nagging Daniel. For all their alienness, the roaches appeared to have problem-solved in a way not that different from human beings.

They descended several floors, but to Daniel's ears they were no closer to the werewolf, who now alternated whining complaints with a rhythmic shrieking as if he were being stabbed. It increasingly troubled Daniel that they hadn't seen a single roach, and he wondered if perhaps they were going where the roaches wanted them to go.

But then they saw one asleep in a far corner, surrounded by empty brown drink bottles. They walked slowly, watching where they put their feet, until they were past.

They came into a large area lined on one wall with broken windows. Encroaching vegetation had covered part of the floor and traced the walls. "Perhaps we should go back," Lenin said softly.

"I want to finish this," Daniel said, and no one disagreed.

The fractured window frames allowed moonlight to flood the space, providing a different view of the city than any he had had before. He was immediately drawn there, walking over a floor dotted with shrapnel pits and larger sections where the tile appeared to have been completely scraped to the subfloor. The wall beside and under the window frame looked unstable so he kept a couple of steps back. When he peered down through the frame he could see a great pile of debris several stories in height banking the base of the building. More ruins spilled out of a huge hole caved in the outer wall. Thick, woody vines had pushed their way into the hole and webbed the exterior, some tendrils snaking into the destroyed windows in front of him.

In the distance he could see a few standing structures within the rubble at the edge of the tumbledown city, and beyond that the red of fires and boiling black smoke. Faint traces of shouts or maybe screams floated in the air, but he might have imagined them.

"Someone's done a mural," Gandhi said behind him.

Daniel turned and moved toward the back wall, the mural revealing itself gradually in the unobstructed moonlight. Bullet holes speckled parts of it, and one portion nearest the door had been heavily damaged by fire. "It's religious, I think," he said, although he wasn't sure why he thought so. "And it's crude—I don't think anyone professional did this."

It was a city scape, ill-proportioned or from a severely distorted perspective. Central to the painting were the rooftops, seen from above, squares and rectangles distorted, with tiny human forms clinging desperately. It was a mix of paints and drawing media, markers, anything that might register on the wall, so some parts had faded to near invisibility while other portions were still quite vivid, as if an observer had precisely recalled only certain details and allowed the others to recede into a blur of forgetfulness.

"What are those larger beings?" Gandhi pointed at several figures, glowing and unrecognizable, floating above the rooftops.

"I believe they're meant to be angels, the way they observe everything," Lenin said.

Daniel thought they were meant to represent people, or what people someday hoped to be, but he might be wrong. They all might be wrong.

The buildings in the mural were bent, wobbly, snaky things, more like giant square hoses with windows than proper rigid architecture. Down at the base of these surreally twisted high rises lay—'pandemonium' was the word that came to mind. Dark figures danced in joy or agony, their bodies shiny and broken like those of insects, vehicles smashed and fires spreading as a frightful mania travelled through the streets.

"It's an unhappy picture painted by an unhappy person," Gandhi said.

The howl beneath their feet shook the floor. Gandhi stamped his foot. Even though the gesture made but a small sound, another howl returned. "Just one level down, I'd say."

They moved on. Daniel lingered to touch the art piece. The lines and colors had been rubbed and gouged in, as if drawn with great passion, with a need for the mural to last. At the bottom of the images, just above the floor, was a border of larger figures in panicked poses, as if desperate to escape the destruction. They were humanoid for the most part, but the occasional stick figure had gears, pinions, pulleys—it was some sort of mechanical creature. All of them looked panicked, all of them persecuted in this strangely detailed Hell. Who would have drawn this, and when? Had there always been residents? This experiment, or study, whatever it was, might have been going on for decades. He looked through the window at the shambling sprawl beyond, and wondered if something out there had inspired this.

As he turned back, his shoes kicked up rubble on the floor. Something white and shiny, torn, lettered. "... *Psych*..."

"*This world is grown old.*" Shakespeare's Falstaff had said that, but Daniel could imagine those words coming out of his large acquaintance's mouth. It seemed an appropriate title for a painting such as this. Perhaps they had made a mistake in not awakening Falstaff and dragging him down here.

The howls gained force and volume again as the men moved through the next level down. The werewolf must have heard their approach and wanted to make sure he could be located. But the howls didn't feel like cries for help exactly, more like some mindless complaint. Finally, off a long and empty corridor, they found the door with the sound of intense scratching on the other side.

The small glass window in the solid door was broken out. A thin bar had been bolted over the opening. A low moan issued from the room. Daniel pressed forward. A pale face suddenly filled the opening, wide-eyed, multiply scratched, some of the scratches scabbed over, others fresh with blood.

"At last!" the face sobbed. "Human beings! I never thought..." His skinny hand came up and one fingernail clawed deeply into the flesh on the left side of his nose, tearing down with a fresh stream of blood.

"Stop that!" Daniel cried.

"I can't help it! It itches unbearably! It's growing inside my skin. It's trying to tear its way through!"

"The hair?" Gandhi said. "The hair of the wolf?"

"My *rage*!" the face screamed. "There's more of it every day! It wants to cover me!" And he disappeared.

Daniel walked slowly to the window. The stench was like a punch in the face. The man had moved to the center of the room, naked and gesturing frantically at the hundreds of scars, old and new, layering his body. "See, see how it's trying to get out?" The man had a starved appearance, but it was hard to tell how emaciated he really was, given the confused mess of torn flesh and dried blood.

The cell was unfurnished. But floor and ceiling and all four walls were covered with severely stained, worn padding, soiled foam innards protruding like yellowed fat from a deep wound. One corner was thick with the prisoner's waste.

"Look at me!" the werewolf shouted. "No one has looked at me in—no one *sees* me anymore!" The prisoner tore at his face, yanked his long matted hair, contorted his mouth. His teeth were yellowed and blood-stained, and looked incredibly long although that might be an illusion. Daniel backed away from the window, unable to look at the man anymore. The werewolf screamed, and Lenin jumped in to take his place at the door.

"Hush!" Lenin ordered. "That won't help you!"

The werewolf stopped, struggled to control his voice. "I was once… like you. A prisoner."

"We wouldn't call ourselves that," Lenin said.

"Then you are foo—oo—ools!" The werewolf's voice went high into a howl on the last word before he managed to cut it off. "You did not volunteer, I know this," the werewolf continued. "No one would volunteer for this. You were snatched right out of your lives, just as I was. My wife in bed beside me, my twin babies in the other bedroom, at last asleep, their aimless, maddening energy spent. Like most nights, I was unable to sleep. My mind raced with the most insane impulses. I should have been a happy man, but apparently happiness simply will not thrive in a creature like me.

"So they brought me here, those… insects. They strapped me into their torture chamber, and sent me off into that faraway place, that mad space inside an evil man's skull, and I had to watch from inside that space as he raped, as he tortured and killed, as he dismembered child after innocent child, and I was unable to return, and as you can tell I still live in that hateful room inside the monster's skull!"

"Ask him if he means de Rais," Gandhi said. "He is speaking of Gilles de Rais, isn't he?"

"You mean Gilles de Rais," Lenin said.

There was a pause. "Who gave you permission to use my name?" The shredded voice was quite different, heavily accented and somewhat musical, but as if the music were coming out of a torn and battered instrument.

Lenin took a half-step back. Daniel quickly took his place. The werewolf looked different, his eyes dark and piercing, his posture erect. Daniel tried to be formal. "We did not mean to offend, Sir. We are at your service."

The werewolf blinked, then appeared to relax a bit. "It is no bother, you could not know. It is a difficult thing, understanding how a person should behave. I never knew how to behave. I never understood the power. I could do anything I wanted. I could kill a peasant like you, just on a whim, particularly during war time. But of course you do not understand the problem. When you can do anything you want, how then do you know what you should do?"

"Listen to God, perhaps? Is that what you did?"

The werewolf threw his head back, and Daniel did not think he could bear to hear the howl again. But the werewolf laughed instead. "I did that. I spoke to Our Lord God for years. I was good, I was pious, I was the most devout. I was the very best of men. But in the end it did not get me where I wanted, not that I could have told anyone what I wanted. Nor could I now. It's maddening!"

He revolved suddenly on one foot, his laugh a rumble deep in his throat. When he came back around he looked embarrassed. "I took the family to church every weekend, the wife, my babies—we did it as a family. But my babies didn't understand what they were hearing, of course. And I knew I was a hypocrite, even as I tried to be a good man. Maybe if I'd really been a good man I would have gained some joy from it, but I was so full of need and dissatisfaction. I think my wife got some strength out of it. Maybe it helped her deal with the likes of me."

He spat on the floor and a bit of blood trailed down his chin.

He lunged toward the door. Daniel had an urge to retreat, but held fast. "Tell me," the werewolf said. "Are you angel, or are you human? No, do not tell me. Let me hope. Let me at last have a voice that will tell me what I should do. That bitch Jeanne d'Arc, she had her voices, all her mad voices. When we served together at Orléans I had to suffer that bitch's voices. They would command her what to do, and then she would command us what to do. Charles demanded that it be this way, and we obeyed. And then she became the saint and I became the monster! Where is the justice?"

The more the werewolf spoke the faster the raw quality in his voice faded, so that at some point Daniel could see him as more or less a typical human being, and then there came a point beyond that when a certain serenity bled through, a calmness in the eyes and a reverence in posture, that made Daniel think of portraits of saints.

"Not that I am doubting her miracles. I would never deny them. She believed in God. She listened, answered and obeyed. 'Here I am Lord!' she said. 'I come to do Your will!' She recognized the Dauphin, Charles the VII, on sight, although she had never seen him before—she picked him out even when he was dressed as an ordinary man and attempted to blend with the rest of us. She changed the direction of the wind at Orléans so we could cross the river. The men loved her! Even I was not immune to her charms! The way she rode across the field in her white armor, waving her standard with a field sown with lilies, Christ holding the world with an angel on each side! She survived an arrow to the breast that would have killed a vigorous man. She won a battle no man could win! The vision of her will forever haunt me, that maid, that bitch, that whore! I tell you we all loved her!

"But I grew weary of her voices, always her voices! What about mine? No one wanted to know of the things speaking to me!

"I had followers of my own, of course, but I had to pay them for their loyalty. For a time everywhere I went I was preceded by royal escort, accompanied by an ecclesiastical assembly and two hundred armed men and trumpeters, all on my payroll. I wanted to fascinate the crowd, I wanted to dazzle them! I discovered I could do *anything* I wanted—the peasants could not object for fear of their lives—can you even imagine how frightening that was for me?"

The werewolf closed his eyes and sighed, growled, and then began to speak again. "My wife told me she was going to leave and take the babies. Not that I wanted the babies. Oh, I loved them, even though they hadn't much in the way of personalities, but clearly I wasn't the nurturing one—I could never have taken care of them by myself.

"But to be rejected that way by the person who had promised to love me forever—how humiliating! I was nothing!" His voice fell deeper with the last few words, and the eyes told Daniel this was the wolf again.

"No one could understand how a man could spend his wealth this way. Certainly not my family, certainly not my old bastard of a grandfather. He was an indifferent guardian—he let us do as we liked. Our nurse raised us, but of course she could not control us. In only a short time we realized we were above the law, or the law was applied differently to those of our position in society. But I must say it did not make us feel safer in the world.

"When you have such resources, does it not compel you to use them in the most creative, most dramatic way? I cared nothing for the riches. I wanted to be an artist who would be remembered for all time. So wealth was like my paint, and the world the background where I could create anything I desired. My *Le mistère du Siège d'Orléans*, surely no one before or since has mounted so grand a production! If wealth had been my prime motivator, would I have staged such an elaborate and expensive spectacle? One hundred forty speaking parts and over five hundred extras. In an attempt to preserve the purity of my vision the six hundred costumes were worn once, discarded, then recreated for each new performance. The grand scaffolding erected and taken down and then erected again. And of course we had to feed our audience, otherwise they might not have come! My family was livid over the expenditures, but they were not possessed of my vision! Should I apologize because I was driven by my imagination? In order to create something grand, something everyone will remember, you have to be willing to sacrifice yourself to extravagance!"

Daniel decided to try a different tactic. "You hold an innocent man inside you." He wasn't sure if this was exactly true, but he had no proof otherwise. "His name is Henry. You have *no right* to keep him prisoner. Please, won't you release him?"

But the werewolf acted as if Daniel hadn't spoken at all. "Eventually, of course, they had their way. They appealed to the king and I was allowed to sell no more of my property in order to finance such magnificence. Never mind that it was no business of theirs. Never mind that I had created something that had never existed before!"

Suddenly he stopped speaking. "My mouth is like a desert cave. Could I have some water, please?"

Daniel looked questioningly at the others. "There's no water here." Lenin shrugged.

"I'm sorry," Daniel said. "We have none."

The werewolf winced, and there was movement along the inside of the cheek. When he next opened his mouth blood spilled from the corners. "I needed moisture, to speak.

"Still, I attempted to find my satisfaction in religion. I became creative in my devotion. I constructed my *Chapel of the Holy Innocents* where I officiated in robes of my own design.

"But it was not enough. Nothing is *ever* enough!"

The werewolf sobbed. But when he lifted his head it was clearly Henry who was crying. "He's not going to let me go." Then the face distorted again and the werewolf shook his head and flashed his teeth.

"I turned my back on my religion and set out to pursue my own demons, the demon Barron, specifically. My learned accomplices assisted me in my alchemical and demon-summoning activities at my castle at Tiffauges. Am I to blame that the ceremony required the parts of a child?

"I loved my beautiful children! They were my angels! They were poor, they had never had anything to speak of, and I dressed them in the finest clothing they had ever known. And then when we led them upstairs, we told them what was going to happen to them. I am not ashamed to say that that was the initial part of my pleasure. Their reactions. Have you never wanted to tell someone some terrible truth and then observe the drama of their reaction? It is an experience far better than any play by the greatest of our playwrights! It is a creative act! As the children cried and screamed, as they begged to be returned to their parents, I am not embarrassed to say that I wept with them. And when finally I broke their necks and removed their parts I kissed their flesh and I wept!

"I loved my children, my babies! I just wasn't capable of taking care of them! Is that so difficult to understand? I wondered, I… speculated, if I killed them, and killed my wife, I could be a good human being again. I know that sounds insane. But think, who could be more sympathetic, more admired than a grieving husband and father?"

He was panting, hot and raw.

"I have no idea how many I killed—I may have exaggerated. I wanted it to be a very large number in my final confession, because if I had to play the monster, I wanted to be the greatest monster who had ever lived!

"I burned the bodies whenever possible in my fireplace. It was a large and grand fireplace, I must say. And I made a grand play about doing so."

Daniel stepped away from the door, unable to stand there anymore, not wanting to listen to one more word and yet not wanting to miss any piece of this confession.

Gandhi came forward. "There, there. We understand. It has been difficult for all of us."

"The children, they were as beautiful as angels. My two, my twins, when they weren't crying, I could imagine them as angels. I could almost imagine myself happy with that life, that wife and those children, with nothing more to show for all my remaining years. No pageantry, no spectacle, no special accomplishment, simply an ordinary life. Why couldn't that be enough? Why couldn't I make myself feel that would be enough?"

"You're talking of your real life now? Not the one you played as de Rais? What was your name? Henry, wasn't it? Try to hold onto your name." Gandhi kept pressing. Daniel waited for some kind of explosion.

"Again, should I apologize because I was driven by my superior imagination?

"I should be ashamed to say that I have eaten a variety of human flesh and that I know that babies taste the best of all. I understand there are some things a human being should never know, but there is the fact of it and should I deny it now?"

"Wait, wait, are you the werewolf now? Are you de Rais?" Gandhi cried. "I don't want to hear this story anymore! I really can't!"

Gandhi stepped away and Daniel gestured for Lenin to step up to the door. But Lenin shook his head. Reluctantly, Daniel returned to the window.

"But those are the facts of it!" the werewolf shouted. "What kind of man is it who cannot or will not deal with the facts?"

The werewolf stopped speaking suddenly and stared into Daniel's face. "Am I frightening you, Sir?"

"No, not really," Daniel lied.

"Well, there's no need for armor, so why do you wear it?"

"I don't understand…"

"I cannot abide a metal face during polite conversation. I show you who I am, so please, Sir, permit me to see your eyes!"

Daniel didn't know what to say. The werewolf blinked a few times, then his body convulsed in a series of muscle spasms. His arms suddenly looked crooked. His eyes swayed in their sockets. He jutted his chin forward and his ears appeared to flow back against his skull.

The werewolf rambled on for another ten minutes or so. The more Daniel listened to the man's confession the more his vicious acts sounded like those of a young boy prodding and pulling the guts from a frog. Except these frogs had been children. And this creature seemed unable to tell the difference between the two. In the end pure evil was a banal and stupid thing.

"He's crazy, but it's not right that he is locked up like this," Gandhi said. "Obviously this only makes him worse. We have to get him out of there."

Lenin stepped between Gandhi and the door. "Are you sure that is wise—look what he's done to himself!"

"To himself—that is the point. I did not hear him threaten any of us, however paranoid he might be. It is himself he damages. This isn't right, to hold him like this. We've got to get him out of there!"

"I suppose. What more can they do to us? He is right, Daniel— now and then you must stand up for what is right, if you want to call yourself a decent human being."

Daniel knew he'd feel unsafe with this monster running about, but he didn't want to make any important decisions out of fear. He helped the others hunt for anything that could be used as a pry bar.

Lenin came up with a two-foot piece of ridged metal rod under a pile of crumbling concrete at one end of the corridor. It was rusted brown but still appeared strong. Daniel recognized it as what they called rebar, or reinforcing bar used to support concrete. *Where have they brought us?*

Lenin jabbed into the door frame with the end of the bar. The werewolf bobbed back and forth inside the cell making a high yipping sound, like a dog overly excited that its owner has come home. Finally Lenin managed to get the bar wedged into the frame and wiggled the bar back and forth; it chewed into the frame. He stopped and put his weight onto the bar, trying to pry the door open. Gandhi ran over and pressed his own small shoulder against the bar, his feet slipping futilely on the tile as he pushed. Although Daniel was conflicted, it embarrassed him to see Gandhi applying so much pointless effort. He came up behind the small man and placed his hands on either side of his trembling shoulder and pushed.

"Stop it! Don't let him out!" Falstaff was at the end of the hall running toward them. "Get away from him!"

"He doesn't belong in there! It's not right!" Gandhi shouted back.

"You don't know what you're doing!" Falstaff slammed into them and all three went sprawling. The bar clattered to the floor. The werewolf's throat made a painful huffing noise.

Lenin clambered to his feet and picked up the bar, swinging it about furiously.

"Stop it!" Daniel cried.

"He doesn't get to make all our decisions! We're going to get this man out of there!"

Falstaff was standing, bent over and breathless. "You... under... est... imate him. Henry... Henry come to the window."

The werewolf's face appeared, wide-eyed and panting. "Yes yes yes..."

"Would you hurt us if we let you out?"

The werewolf rolled his eyes. "Noooo... but I might eat you. You might taste good. If you tasted good I might not stop. Do you taste good? And that one?" He glanced in Gandhi's direction. "Would he taste as good as a child?"

"We can't, we can't just leave him like this!" Gandhi cried.

"You can visit him, talk to him. As I do. You just can't let him out. We won't leave him alone, we'll visit him more often, but we won't let him out."

The werewolf pushed his head as far into the opening as he could, his lips pressed and distorted under the metal rod. "I was alone at school, when they weren't harassing me. My wife didn't know me back then, or else I'm sure she never would have married me. She would never have been able to get that image out of her head. I was so pitiful, so humiliated. I knew I was a weakling, but sometimes I tried to pretend it wasn't true. I tried to pretend I was a great warrior who hadn't yet discovered the secret that would unlock his power." Henry spoke weepily, a child caught with his hand where it should not have been. Daniel came up to the opening as three tears came out of the man's right eye and streaked his dirty cheek as precisely and cleanly as a set of invisible claws. "I used to have dreams I destroyed the world on a whim, with no reason." Then the voice changed, thickening into de Rais' coarsely musical tongue, "But the power to transform a living man into a corpse." He tilted his head back and sniffed the air with a scowl. "I can think of no greater *léger de main*."

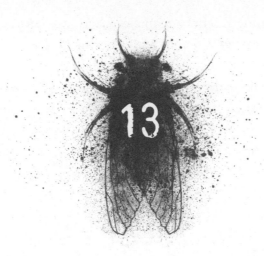

THE GROUP LINGERED for some time around Henry's cell. As unpleasant as his situation was, they felt guilty about leaving him, and Daniel could tell that both Gandhi and Lenin were as distrustful of Falstaff's reassurances as he was. But eventually they moved on, promising Henry they would visit him regularly, and promising each other to refer to him as Henry, not as the werewolf. Daniel couldn't tell if Henry understood anything they said to him, or if he even heard the words, but there was nothing more they could do.

Lenin had grown sullen over the encounter, and when he insisted they find a place to rest before going back upstairs to the barracks, they agreed. But it took some time to find a resting place he was satisfied with, until he discovered another room with a broken exterior wall providing an open view of the distant city. Lenin glanced once at that panoramic pre-dawn view, but then he turned his back on it and took them further into the space, around a corner into an empty room with no window. He plopped down against a wall and the rest of them joined him.

No one said anything for several minutes. Curious about the view they had passed, another glimpse onto an outside world they knew nothing about, Daniel stood and wandered out to the empty windows, keeping safely back in case there was more collapse. The first thing he noticed was that a number of fires were burning deep in the city's interior. They flickered and changed, some appearing to wave, like things dying and attempting to get his attention. The farthest one looked huge, probably covering a number of blocks, a molten balloon rubbing against the black drop of sky. Again he heard distant shouts, perhaps, or screams, but no motor or vehicle sounds as far as he could tell. It all might be his imagination; he might be mistaking ordinary reflections, a distortion of distant noise, for some ongoing disaster, but he didn't think so. Elsewhere in the darkened metropolis, tiny pockets of light flickered. He thought of candles or camp fires, or maybe some small intermittent source of power.

If he crept just a little closer and looked down at a sharp angle he caught a glimpse of another ruined part of their building. Several large holes in the outer walls, a giant ramp of rubble leading up to low windows, scattered signs of repair, and shining in the moonlight some sort of metal bracing spider webbing the raw edges of the worst areas of collapse. It was particularly thick around the lower foundations.

He couldn't quite figure it out. There had been no attempt to do a legitimate repair—the walls hadn't been restored, so the open holes allowed the weather or vegetation or anything else to invade the building's interior. Certainly it made those rooms immediately adjacent to the holes unusable. The metal webbing— he'd just assumed it was metal but it very well could be something stronger—kept everything intact and probably stable. But anyone seeing the building from the outside might think it was going to collapse at any moment. As stable and as inhabited as it was, it would still look like an empty ruin from some distance away.

He looked back out at the fires, and listened to the distant sounds that might or might not have been a distorted chorus of panic. *Whoever they are,* he thought, *they probably don't even know we are here.*

"I don't always expect good sense from the others," Falstaff said beside him. "But I would have thought you of all people would have awakened me before trying to come down here." Falstaff could be a supercilious prick.

"Maybe if you weren't so secretive, maybe if you'd taken us down here earlier and explained things, we wouldn't have gone without you, and they wouldn't have tried to let Henry out."

There was a long pause before Falstaff spoke again. "Of course you have a point. I've been here longer—I suppose sometimes I don't want to say too much. Life here... it's hard enough. And it rarely changes."

But Daniel didn't want to hear it. "Have you seen the fires out there? Does that happen often?"

"I have. Someone is having a very bad day. We all know about bad days—in here we re-live some of the worst days in history."

"That doesn't sound very empathetic."

Falstaff sighed. "It's not that I don't care. But we're here, trapped in this building. They—whoever or whatever they might be—are out there. There's nothing we can do for them."

"That's very reasonable." Daniel peered down at the base of the building. The stones looked wet, even though it wasn't raining. "But it's too easy. Maybe it should be unbearable that those people are suffering. Maybe that's what we need, to make more truths unbearable." A small wave of water splashed over the stones. "Is it flooding down there?"

Falstaff stepped past him, and Daniel held his breath as the big man leaned over the broken window wall. *He knows it won't collapse,* Daniel thought. Obviously the webbing did its job.

"I've seen it before. We're not too far from the ocean, apparently, and sometimes at high tide there's some flooding. Nothing to worry about, though." He was still hiding something.

"This is a coastal city?"

Falstaff shrugged. "Perhaps, but I wouldn't know. I don't know any more than—"

Frustrated, Daniel approached him. "We're somewhere on Earth. You know, have known that, of course. This building. I didn't see it for the longest time—maybe the roaches have done something to our heads so that we don't question it, or even think about it. But creatures like that, they would have never come up with this sort of architecture, something so unreflective of their anatomy. We're still on Earth, and wherever this city is, they've reduced it to rubble, they've destroyed—"

"Have you talked to the others about this?" Falstaff looked at him intently.

"No, answer me. Did you know, or have you at least suspected? If you want me to trust you, tell me, stop hiding things."

"I don't know where we are, and neither do you. Maybe they want us to believe we're still on Earth—maybe their intention is for you to have this realization—"

"Stop, just stop lying!" Daniel shoved the torn piece of plastic band into Falstaff's hand.

"What's this?"

"It's an old bit of medical wrist band. Look at it! It says 'Psych' on it. A psychiatric ward, or a psychiatric hospital—it must be what this building used to be. That's English. This is Earth. New England maybe, although I hope not. Our families may still be out there. We've got to get out of here and go find them."

Falstaff put up his broad hand. "Wait, just wait. Do you really think you're the first person to have figured this out?"

"Well, normally I wouldn't think so. But no one's let on. And if you knew this, it only proves that you've been lying and can't be trusted."

Falstaff turned his face away and began to pace. "I don't know for sure where we are. Maybe we're on Earth, maybe not. Maybe some other planet, I have no idea. Do you recognize anything out there?"

"No, the city's been mostly destroyed."

"Exactly. I've heard these ideas before, Daniel. Maybe they're close to the truth, maybe not. But it never goes anywhere because the men who come up with these ideas are always gone within a few days. They don't come back from their scenarios, or maybe they just aren't there when the rest of us wake up one morning."

"Is that a threat?"

"I'm one of you. How could I threat—"

"If we could only get out of here we might find out more. Don't you *want* to know?"

"Come closer, Daniel. You showed me that piece of wrist band. Let me show *you* something."

Any new information at all seemed worth taking risks for. He stood beside Falstaff, who could toss him out that window with the flick of a wrist. "What is it?"

"Grab my hand and lean out the window. You'll see some letters spray painted on the outside of the building just above. You won't have to lean far—they're big and easy to see. And I'll be holding on the whole time. I won't let you fall."

"Just tell me what it is."

"You might not believe. You have to see for yourself. Someone else showed me, now I'm showing you."

It didn't matter that he didn't trust Falstaff at all. He just needed to know anything he could find out. He grabbed the big man's hand, leaned out, and looked up. Spray painted in black over the window opening: U B O in huge black letters. "Okay. Please haul me in." And Falstaff did.

"You saw them."

"I did, but I guess I don't get it. Ubo, it's the name of this place, or what the roaches want us to think is the name of this place— they implanted the word when we came here. We thought, or were led to think, that Ubo was the name of the world. But people are gullible—they believe whatever is presented to them. Apparently it's just the name of this one building. So what? What difference does it make?"

"Does that look like an official name to you? Spray painted like that?"

"Maybe not, but still—"

"Have you ever seen news coverage of disaster areas, how the responders spray paint body locations and numbers on buildings? And warnings? DANGEROUS? DO NOT ENTER? That kind of thing?"

"But it's so high."

"It has to be high enough that people can see it from far enough away that they know not to get too close to the building. And look out there—see how there's nothing for hundreds of yards between us and the rest of the city? As if the whole area has been cleared into a kind of No Man's Land?"

Daniel looked out. It was quiet out here, the building out by itself away from everything else. And there was a great deal of scarring in that empty space, so if structures had been demolished and removed, you might see those traces, a kind of ghosting. He could still hear the waves hitting the foundation. "An old resident here, he said he'd figured it out. He said we'd probably find it written on other buildings in that ruined city, if we ever got close enough. Unidentified Biological Organisms. UBO."

"But what does that mean?"

"We'd talk about that, he and I, a couple of others. There were theories. Before he and the others started disappearing, not coming back from scenarios, not there when I woke up. Maybe a plague, certainly something dangerous. It doesn't sound welcoming, does it? An infection maybe? Certainly not anything you'd want to take out of here and carry back to the people you love."

"But why jump to that conclusion based on three letters? They could mean anything."

"It just makes sense. It fits. Do you have a better explanation, and would you want to gamble on it?"

Daniel did not.

* * *

FALSTAFF LEFT HIM alone. Daniel couldn't help but imagine his family out there somewhere, struggling, no doubt in danger. But he wasn't going anywhere. Was he infected with something? There was no way of knowing. But he couldn't say he felt well, certainly not that he felt normal. He hadn't felt normal since he'd been here. He was so far from normal he might as well have been on another world.

"You fellows were out here a long time. Were you discussing the—Henry?" It was Gandhi. Daniel hadn't even heard him come up. The fellow was beyond light on his feet—he was as weightless as a ghost.

"Oh, Walter. Yes. That, and odds and ends." Daniel had some inkling how lies might have come easily to Falstaff.

"Can you see much of the city from up here?"

"A bit. See for yourself." Daniel moved to the side.

"No, no. I'm fine here. I don't like tall, open areas, to tell you the truth. I'm always afraid, I have this fantasy—" He looked down at his feet. "That I might jump off."

"Are you feeling suicidal?"

"Well, no, at least, no, I'm not. Now poor Henry, he's someone who'd be justified, thinking about suicide. I can't even imagine. Compared to the rest of us, well, it would be an insult to him, I think, for me to contemplate suicide."

Daniel studied him. "I don't think of it that way. There's no shame in it, to have those urges. Not that you should act on them—there's always a better path. But there's that quote from Thoreau, you know it? 'The mass of men lead lives of quiet desperation.' We seldom adequately understand what the other feels, so how can we judge the quality of their pain? And this place, who could blame you for feeling desperate?"

"If I just had something else to do," Gandhi said. "Besides the scenarios. Anything to take my mind away from them."

"Can I ask you, what was your life like before? Did you have a family?"

Gandhi looked up with a vaguely grateful expression. "There was never anything particularly special or interesting about my life. And I suppose that would be the point of anything I'd have to tell you about myself." Daniel began to object. "No, it's alright. Just let me say it. When I was a boy I dreamed that I was going to be someone special, someone with some elevating sort of talent which would raise me above the everyday and the run-of-the-mill. Good parents encourage that sort of thing, don't they? They tell you you're special, you have the capability of doing something wonderful someday. They say they're proud of you even when you haven't done anything yet to particularly make them proud.

"They tell you you'll do great things, even when you're smaller than the other children and skinny, no matter how hard you try to add muscle or even fat to that slight presence you have in the world.

"That's all well and good and positive, and it does build confidence. But at some point you have to deliver, don't you, otherwise it's all a bit meaningless?

"I believe I had reasonable expectations—I knew that any such talent required singular focus, years of practice, and obsessive devotion. So anytime I perceived even a hint of talent I…"

He stopped then, as if he'd forgotten what he was going to say. He looked as if he had stage fright. Some people, when they had to speak to others, it was as if they were actors on stage. They had to figure out what they were going to say, otherwise they were too shy to speak. "Take your time, we're friends, aren't we?" Daniel patted Gandhi on the arm. "I'm interested in anything you have to say. But you sound as if—it just seems like you're unnecessarily hard on yourself."

Gandhi smiled. "I know, I know. But I've always thought that a life should have meaning, otherwise it's as if you didn't even exist. It's like trying to make a mark with a pen that has no ink in it, or drawing a brush across the canvas and nothing shows because you didn't load the brush with paint. The gesture means nothing. It was pretense. It wasn't even practice.

"For a while I wanted to be a musician. Guitar, then clarinet. I practiced hours every day, and the music finally got to be pleasant enough, but there was nothing special in the way I played, and I realized I didn't love it that much anyway, and you have to love it to be good at it. So I tried out for sports, and I was a pretty good runner, and I exercised myself to exhaustion, and I was pretty good, but never the best. And I kept waiting for that euphoria some runners get, at least I could have that, but it never came for me, or I didn't recognize it when it came.

"I used to get *so* angry. I trembled, Daniel, I actually trembled. I tried to express that anger in some way, to let it go, but I failed in that endeavor as well.

"I learned computer programming, and some companies hired me, and I was competent enough, but never inspired. I implemented, but I didn't create. Believe me, I worked with creative programmers, and there's a difference. Maybe it should have been enough. At least it provided me with a good living, and it paid for various avocations, some creative writing instruction, dance lessons, art classes, woodworking tools. But nothing quite stuck. Once or twice I accidentally cut myself on a wood chisel or a scraper. I discovered that it was vaguely, strangely soothing. I found new ways to accidentally cut myself after that. It was quite embarrassing, I was always afraid I might be found out, but after a time, I have to admit, it was deeply satisfying. I'd have these wounds on my hands, my arms. People must have thought I was really absorbed by my craft, or maybe they thought I was simply clumsy. And when the wounds started to heal, then I'd interfere with that healing. I couldn't control the world, but I could control that. At least to a point. Ultimately, if I had decided to stop scarring my body, I don't think I could have.

"I would have weeks I'd be so depressed I couldn't get out of bed, or if I forced myself out of bed I'd spend my time sitting, staring at nothing. It was as if I were inside a dark closet that no one else could see, and sometimes the weight of it, well, my shoulders would become so painful, as if I were carrying some huge piece of furniture

I could never put down, because if I put it down it would ruin everything.

"I knew I didn't belong in the world, but I didn't exactly know what I should do about it. Sometimes I would sit in my window, my feet dangling outside, four floors up, terrifying myself, wondering if I could just let myself slip out.

"I say that now, and it sounds illogical. But logic has nothing to do with you when you are in that dark world. Everything becomes a matter of belief and, I don't know, a kind of dark, a so very dark, faith."

"You sound like you were an interesting person—with all that background, I'm sure you could have talked knowledgably in a number of areas. You must have had friends, and women must have—I don't want to be too nosy, but if there are people who love you, then to my mind, you're definitely a success."

Gandhi smiled at this, but there was something in his eyes that made Daniel feel so sad he thought he might weep. "You're a very kind man," Gandhi said, "and I'm sure you were loved, and you've told us you had a wife and child, so I know that must be true." Daniel nodded, but did not want this line of conversation to continue. "But the key thing about love, I believe, is that you have to recognize that it's happening. You have to recognize that someone is loving you, otherwise it's no good to you. You miss it, so it might as well not be there. I'd like to think now that someone might have loved me, and that I just didn't recognize it. That would at least be something. But since I didn't see it then, I'll never know.

"I never knew love, Daniel. Wouldn't that have been something if I had? But I couldn't quite make it happen."

Daniel let his eyes wander. Off in the distance there appeared to be more fires than before, a line of them, it must have been miles long. He wondered if the entire city, what was left of it, was going to burn. He wondered if their building, even surrounded with its dead zone, would survive it.

"I did keep trying. I don't think I really gave up until a year or so ago. Obviously, I wasn't going to achieve my goals, and I wasn't going to be satisfied with anything less. I could not let myself remain colorless, anonymous, never to have left a mark on the world. I had to do *something*. I needed to be thought about, to be remembered. And no, I didn't do what some of the men in our scenarios have done. I didn't carry guns into a school and murder children, or try to assassinate some important person or other. I could never have done something like that.

"I did decide to commit an act of violence, but against the sole person responsible for all the disappointments, for all the negative things that had happened to me during my life. Myself. I decided to commit suicide.

"But even after coming to that decision I was at least somewhat hopeful, I suppose. What if no one knew what happened to me? What if I disappeared? I'd be a mystery, a mystery for a lot of people. Nothing nags at the human mind more than a mystery, am I correct? They wouldn't be able to help themselves, thinking about me. Maybe for years.

"And if they found the body a certain way, well it would make the news, would it not? People would be curious. I'd give people something to talk about. You know, like when they found Richard III's body under that parking lot in central England?"

"Or maybe you wouldn't be found at all?"

"Oh, I thought about that. But if I were inside a concrete building like this, I figured it would last two or three hundred years. But practically speaking, they would probably tear it down after forty, don't you think? Technology progresses faster and faster, and even buildings become obsolete, the heating and plumbing systems, the features, the expectation of new innovations. It becomes cheaper to tear them down than to retrofit them.

"I'd been watching them building a large municipal government complex downtown. They'd build these forms with a framework of rebar inside them. Then starting early in the morning they'd fill them with concrete.

"I'm extraordinarily skinny. And small in stature. A small human being. I always have been. I realize it doesn't make me the most attractive person. In fact I sometimes wonder if knowing that has contributed to my lack of success. But I was small enough to slip naked through the spaces between the bars one night in one particular form. Barely, even with my body well-oiled, and I bloodied myself pretty thoroughly in the process, as well as breaking a rib or two. It was a rather deep form, but I made it almost to the bottom. At least deep enough that I was pretty sure they wouldn't notice me all the way down there when they poured the concrete. They might, and they might pull out my body and I wouldn't be buried inside the building as I'd planned, and then discovered a century or so later when they finally tore it all down, but I was quite willing to take the risk.

"But all that exertion and I didn't break the cyanide capsule in my mouth, until then. I was very pleased to have obtained such a poison. A splendid detail. Very international spy and all that. But I slipped and twisted my arm, popping my shoulder out of its socket. I inadvertently bit down on the capsule. I was in so much pain, you see. Not just physically, but I was cursing the world and everything in it, how existence itself had betrayed me." He stopped and once again smiled at Daniel with that dreamy, almost unworldly smile.

Daniel stared at him. It had begun to rain, and the drops blown in through the window were softly beating the side of his face. The sensation was soothing, so he didn't move. He had a vague notion that the sounds of the waves against the foundations below were even louder, and there was a kind of churning noise under it all. "Wait. When did the roaches come into this?"

"I first saw the roaches when I woke up here. In Ubo."

"I mean before that. What's the last thing you remember in your old life?"

"I told you. That terrible pain, and then the raging. And I must have fallen unconscious, because I had that dream about the roaches we've all had."

"Well, no, I don't think that's a dream," Daniel said. "As far as I know that's a memory, however unreliable, of how we were kidnapped, how we were physically carried away."

"Yes, and then the next thing I woke up in Ubo."

"But that makes no sense."

"I'm sorry, but that's the way it happened."

"But how did they retrieve you? How did the roaches get to your body before you would have died? The rest of us, everyone I've talked to, we were taken from our beds, or out in the street, after we'd done something, or thought of something. The trigger seems to be different for everybody. They snatched us. How could they snatch you, deep inside a concrete form, trapped inside a cage of iron bars, and presumably seconds away from death by cyanide?"

Gandhi blinked, looking stricken. Then he began to weep.

"I knew it!" he cried. "None of it makes any sense! I really must be in Hell!"

14

It was just past dawn when they arrived back at the barracks. Falstaff grabbed him by the shoulder and pointed at Gandhi. "What's wrong with him? He's almost catatonic."

Daniel trusted Falstaff even less than before. "We're all exhausted," he said. "And him more than the rest of us, I think. All that drama with Henry, it really upset him."

Falstaff nodded and let go. Daniel crawled under the blanket on his bunk. He'd hardly shut his eyes when the roaches invaded the barracks. He woke up to giant insect parts on his face, black mandibles hovering only an inch or two above his eyes. Huge roach legs churned eagerly, leg hairs the size of drinking straws snagging his blanket and tearing it off the bunk. He panicked, raising his fists to knock them away. Something sharp pinned his arms and his vision went slightly blurred. He was jerked to his feet. All around him the roaches were pulling residents from their bunks and herding them out of the room.

The roaches seemed more numerous than they had the past several weeks, but still there were far fewer of them than when he'd first arrived. They were agitated, antennae waving and wiry legs scrabbling over the broken tiles as they shoved and carried the residents rapidly back into the labs.

Daniel was in the corridor now, several roaches surrounding him. Normally he would have been in the waiting room and they would have come for him, and then there would be this gradual loss of consciousness as he was taken into the labs where they induced the scenarios. Although he wasn't aware of them giving him anything he'd steadily fall toward sleep until he was almost unconscious by the time they reached the final door. As they pushed him through the door it would feel as if they'd just pushed him out of an airplane without a parachute, his face exploding with light and air, his eyes registering no more than a vague impression of the room itself: shiny metal and glass, fragments of mirror and a distant babble of musical voices. But this time he was fully aware when they hit the lab's double doors. Had they simply forgotten to do what they had always done before, or was there a problem with the drugs they normally used?

He was fully into the room and they were hurriedly strapping him onto a flat surface suspended within a mountain of spiraling glass, great crystalline stalagmites piercing a shadowy net of webbing and blinking nodes, claws and, if he wasn't mistaken, human hands making a blur of tunings about him, adjusting something around his skull, tubes the size and shape of prescription bottles attached and humming on his head, then something slipping into his mouth, pinpricks along his breastbone and underneath it all a layering of near and far voices in English and French and German and languages he did not recognize, weeping and angrily spitting out their complaints and ecstasies, their life stories uncleansed and uncensored.

Suddenly there was a rapid blinking. The brilliance collapsed into a complete blackness, as if they'd been swallowed up by the earth, and then there was a hum and everything lit up again. The voices around him were frantic, unintelligible. Then the smell of something burning, a whine, and again a profound darkness. A chitter of voices in the night, the sounds of a frenetic exodus, or was it an invasion? They jostled him, but he couldn't tell if he was being moved. A weight on his chest and then the room blazed again painfully, as if his eyes were on fire. Shouted commands and fast-moving hands.

With a slap to his head he was gone then, and came out of it swallowed up inside the core of someone else's life, so deeply embedded he could not detect the sound of his own thoughts, as if he were all receiver with no ability to transmit at all.

The God of Mayhem woke to a new kind of stench. It happened all the time now, and for no reason that he could tell. He stepped outside to see if anything had changed since the day before. The world was an unpredictable place. He sniffed the air. The world was a foul place.

Fires burned in the neighborhood, and fires still burned in the old suburbs stretching far behind him. Some of those were his fires, and some were fires set by others. Some of the fires had a practical purpose. Maybe somebody tried to clean up the trash that lay everywhere. Maybe somebody tried to burn the body of someone they loved who had just died. Murder was everywhere. Burning was the decent thing, with no decent place to bury.

Some were for worship—there were a thousand gods and Mayhem was just one of them. And some were probably just for fun. An explosion went off in his head. He wanted to run as far as he could, run right out of this trash heap city.

Barbed, narrow legs played with his thoughts, hard shell and claw and bodies torn and leaking.

The human rats who worked through the trash every day were always uncovering new stink, a constant clatter and rattle of noise as they picked and traded. He could hear the wild dog packs howling on the other side of that collapsed row of houses, and it was all he could do not to howl back. Sometimes the sourness went so deep he could feel it in his lungs.

They'd made the world a terrible place, God damn them, his moms and his pops and all the ones that came before. The air was full of black bits and all the little kiddies were dying. Even the drinking water stank.

The early morning sky blazed red with the sun peeking through a curtain of black boiling clouds. Down below a paler smoke wrapped the buildings and wandered lost as a ghost through the alleys and streets. Roofs and ceilings fell into wavy stacks with trees growing through. Out front was a bus half-filled with dirt. A churn of filth decorated the rooftops. A fuzzy green border hung from the eaves. Beyond the broken backs of roofs and a scatter of walls was one edge of the flooded and foul Boston Harbor. Three tanker ships sat low in the water on the near side, slowly leaking their dark shadows to wander the harbor. He'd had a notion to set those ships on fire, but didn't like starting a fire he knew he could not control.

He couldn't control the weather. He couldn't control starvation or the invasion of disease. But he could control who he killed and how. The first time he'd killed—a shovel to the back of another boy's head—it was just to see how it felt. But it hadn't been an impulse—they were always saying he was impulsive when he was a kid—but he'd been planning it forever.

He could control his fires by how he placed the fuel, and where he started them, and pretty much how they spread. And sometimes who they burned.

Farther south and near the old docks was the quarantine area. "Unidentified Biological Organisms" was the name they used. UBO painted on all the buildings. It meant "If you come here, you will die." So even if you couldn't read, you recognized those three letters, and you stayed away. The worst kind of diseases, if they were telling the truth, which was rare. Whole neighborhoods flattened to the ground, and in the middle that big building like a castle on a hill. He remembered it had been a mental hospital for a long time. Rumors were that years ago they kept the worst of the plague victims there. No problem—creepy thing like that, who'd want to go there? What a world. A world that could make something like him deserved to be killed.

The God didn't think he'd been born to do evil, but it had been too long ago for him to remember for sure.

He let some ash fall on his tongue. He tasted it but couldn't identify it. One day if he got good enough at what he did he'd be able to figure out the sex, the race, maybe even the nationality of the body they'd burned.

Sharp insect legs and brittle antennae massaged his brain, working their way into his plans. He thought of dead bodies underground shedding their underwear. He wobbled his head to shake the crap out. He'd always been part bug. He had bug needs and bug appetite. That was part of what made him a god.

The trash and the waste was always talking about him, what he had done. But when they saw him they had no idea he was the one. They talked about the fires, and they talked about the murders, but they weren't smart enough to tell that the same one did both. He thought maybe he was almost as old as time. The bug who would inherit the earth.

He went back inside and stood in his living room with what he had saved over the years. The walls were covered with photographs, none of them of people he knew. Some were of adults he had killed, not that he liked collecting trophies, but just because he thought they should be in his collection. Many were family pictures he'd taken from the abandoned homes he looted: people on vacation, young men in their graduation gowns, couples at dances, family picnics and barbeques, nameless people straining to grin into the camera lens.

All night long the savage shadow people had rioted, beating on their non-working appliances, their motionless automobiles, drinking their poisonous hooch, screaming out their lungs, setting their pitiful fires and dancing until their brains shut down. He'd waited, listening from his thin pad of a bed, thinking about what he'd charge them for his loss of sleep.

Somebody new was inside him, but it was afraid, and had no voice. It made him grin. He'd finally begun to scare his own demons.

Each morning the God of Mayhem rose with the sleepless insect chatter eating its way through his brain. Each morning he could feel the heat spreading through his blood. Each morning the God of Mayhem stepped out into his backyard to see a tumble and a collision of houses falling down the slope behind his home, a collection of closed-down, boarded-up, scribbled-over buildings sitting in mounds of garbage and discarded furniture, housewares, the worn-out and the broken, the last sorry pieces of America.

The ground near the bottom of the hill was soggy with a dark and poisonous-looking liquid. People didn't live in the houses there. What was left of the police never came around.

Sometimes swastikas appeared on walls, but it was hard to tell what people meant by them. Sometimes it was just a complaint about everything. He'd seen both the whites and the brownskins painting them.

He pulled on his overcoat and hid his insect eyes under a hat and trundled out the door, jogging down the street narrowed between piles of rubble until he reached the backside of a row of low shacks. He found the one that had made the loudest screaming the night before. Five bodies were sleeping under a window propped open for air. He reached in and grabbed a clump of black hair at random, yanked the head back and drew his knife across the throat. The blade was gratifyingly sharp and the new opening in the body quickly filled with blood. No one even stirred. He jogged back to his house, whistling.

Buried inside the God of Mayhem, Daniel was only occasionally aware that he had ever had his own life. At best his self-awareness was muted—this was a scenario unlike any he had experienced. He'd been swallowed whole and digested.

The God's gray beard softened his face, made him look less fierce, less brutal. He drew no one's notice when he moved through the Boston ruin. He'd stoop and limp to exaggerate his age. If anyone did think he was weak, well, he'd just kill them.

But this morning he needed to take care of things at home. He heard the scream close by and ran out into his backyard. He could see the top of the boy's head above the fence next to the alley. "You! I told you not to come around here anymore!"

He could hear the boy laughing in the alley. Then there was a whining noise, and then another scream. It sounded like a child or a wounded animal. The God of Mayhem moved to his back gate, flung it open, and stepped into the lane. He saw the boy about ten yards down, waving the leash with the empty collar.

"I said stay away!" the God of Mayhem shouted. The boy smirked and turned his back, walked away.

The bloody mess of dog lay in the middle of the pavement. At least the boy didn't set the animal on fire this time. After considering whether to take care of the corpse or not, the God of Mayhem went back into his house. If this was a message he had no idea what the boy was trying to say.

He had never killed a child, but if the boy came back he would have to reconsider. Clearly the boy must know who, what the God of Mayhem was. So why wasn't he frightened?

The God of Mayhem was bothered by vivid memories of the first creatures he had ever killed—an assortment of pets and countless birds, a few snakes, dozens of frogs. When he was just a boy he had called them his experiments. They had been good practice, so he didn't understand why the memories were so troublesome, but they embarrassed him.

He'd discovered the pleasures of fire when he was a boy, too. The beauty of it, the shape of the flames, and how efficiently it consumed and transformed. It calmed him, filling him with undeniable pleasure as he watched. So pleasurable the fires had been that for a while he didn't feel the need to kill anything at all.

Once he killed an entire family of adults, planted them around the circular kitchen table, soaked their heads in oil and set them on fire. He'd called it "his birthday cake."

Daniel had brief moments of self-awareness when the God of Mayhem entered more deeply into a ruminative mode. So compartmentalized was the man, so disconnected from the voices that drove him, Daniel discovered he was able to ride quietly inside this monster for some time.

The God of Mayhem had come to understand that his was a religion best practiced at night, when not so many curious eyes were watching.But the terrain was treacherous—he had to scout things out during the day. Broken building facades were typical in most neighborhoods, wall sheathings sloughed off, timbers rotted and fragile décor disintegrated and liquefied, spilling out of empty windows and past ruptured doors hanging from their shattered frames. That didn't necessarily mean no one lived there.

This particular night he would invade a shopping district several miles north of his home. The overcoat came on, hiding an arsenal of guns and knives and other deadly devices. By the time the God of Mayhem exploded out his back door he was in full adrenaline mode, his feet propelled into a dance of constant movement, his palms itchy with the need to grab, smash, and tear. He burst through the front door of a house a few blocks away, for no particular reason other than its proximity to his planned trajectory. He swung a hammer into the skull of a man sitting in his kitchen sucking something out of a green bottle. He paused only long enough to pry the hammer from shards of bone before flattening the two younger men screaming into his face, then through the back door and another yard and down a broken sidewalk where he sliced a piece off a figure walking with its head down. His victim tumbled into the tall weeds crying weakly.

Daniel was fully aware then, drunk on whatever chemicals raced through the blood of this outrageous psychopath. Peeking into this head was like the mortals who dared look into the eyes of the most terrible deities—it was impossible without pain and you risked losing your mind.

Feel this! Can you feel this? Like a fire the God of Mayhem had set at the center of Daniel's mind.It was impossible to say how many were killed or maimed during the God's venture north. Nor did the God care in the least. When they reached the vast parking lot, a sea of metal vehicles frozen within a sheen of rust and filth, Daniel felt the God's body pulsing with even more energy.

He roamed through the parking lot on his way to the buildings beyond, the vehicles missing tires, batteries, windows, seats. Now and then the God would stop at a car and peer inside. Most of them were empty but occasionally he'd spy a sleeping form stretched across the upholstery, and sometimes two or three people who looked terrified when the God tapped on their window. He always wondered if they could tell by the look of him that he was skilled at turning living things into dead things.

The building ahead appeared to have been some sort of department store. The front of it had fallen onto the sidewalk, an enormous G, a twisted S rising out of the rubble. As he came closer he saw that several floors of the building had been exposed.

A man with a yellow bottle was standing by the entrance. He staggered, holding the bottle out as an offering. "You find something... maybe we can trade." The God of Mayhem reached inside his coat, stepped up to the drunk and stuck him below the waistline with a hunter's curved gut hook, then dragged it up quickly while stepping back. The drunk stared at him blankly, then fell back with a spray of blood. Some splashed on the God's coat, but he didn't mind. It was dark and besides he wanted a little blood on his coat. The thought made him slightly light-headed. He breathed in sharply and licked his lips.

He had not yet tried tasting any of his kills, although he'd thought about it. Once he'd killed four in a one day frenzy, with gun and knife and holding one fellow under his bath water and bludgeoning another to death—he'd put his nose against the dead flesh, and his open mouth, and breathed in whatever aromas he could, and licked one corpse along the small of the back, and found it to be unusually salty but not unusually foul. *Why...* Daniel said from somewhere lost within the God's tangle of hunger, rage, and passion.

The fellow asked me a question, the God of Mayhem thought,

at Daniel. Daniel, shocked to be spoken to directly by the God like this, was desperate to hide. The God's inner voice roared with astonishment and laughter. My conscience, you nag me!

This had never happened before. Daniel hadn't thought it possible. He was supposed to be a silent passenger, a listener, not a participant.

The God muddied his coat on the damp ground to obscure some of the blood, not wanting to telegraph his intentions to the crowd. Swaddled in a rainbow of rags covering everything but his eyes he strolled inside.

The sheer number of squatters surprised him. As he went room to room and floor to floor he was overwhelmed by the mass of them, filling every available space except for a few cleared pathways, and with entire families jammed even into the spaces under the stairs. And the stairs and frozen escalators had people sitting to one side of each step. Had they noticed the rust flaking off the beams? And the crumbling concrete, the borders of each room layered in gray chips of the stuff? It wasn't safe to live here.

Violent young men and lazy females, sprawling families, orphans, criminals, all jammed together with their limited belongings, bodies on top of bodies, acts of theft and violence and degradation seeping out between layers upon layers of human stink.

He didn't care who he killed, as long as they weren't children. It was hardly his fault that people had become furniture. The God of Mayhem wasn't obligated to feel guilt over the death of furniture.

Several potential targets of his rage became obvious. There was the thin man wearing the high collar that hid his mouth. His eyes constantly scanned the crowd as he rubbed up against one female after another, particularly the young frightened ones, the exhausted ones, reminding the God that even during the lean times there were predators of different appetite.

Another candidate was that fellow with the bushy black beard that had been half burnt from his face (one of the God of Mayhem's own fires, perhaps?). It appeared that no beard would be growing anytime soon on that side, but the fellow had made no attempt to modify the damage to his appearance by trimming the beard. As far as the God was concerned that was in his favor. But he didn't like the way the fellow stared. He noticed too much.

Off in a corner a crazy looking fellow did comical impressions of anyone who passed. He'd suck in his belly and bloat his belly, allow his tongue to loll and cross his eyes.

An old man sat by one of the many fires up on raised bricks. Now and then he would toss a burning stick at a child and laugh. The old man was layered in burn scars up and down his arms and on his face.

Others were guilty of some simpler form of rudeness. A woman who insisted on her right to public defecation, and who did not hesitate to demonstrate; a fellow who enjoyed showing his rotted teeth to strangers; a fellow whose constant monologue mourned everything lost to time and society's poor choices. Everything he said was true, of course, but it brought those around him no peace.

All no more than rude behaviors, but a desperate and overcrowded world had no place for the rude. The toilet-rights lady received an iron bar across the base of the skull while everyone's head was turned in disgust. A large rag stuffed into the rotted maw of the dentally-impaired, his jaws held shut by the God's powerful hands, the two of them huddled against the wall like lovers: the man's eyes fixed on the face of his new deity until the light burned out of them. A quick shove sent the body out an open window.

The God of Mayhem decided to take his time with his next subject—that vocal mourner of all things lost to the world. "Here, I want to show you something," he said to the mourner, his arm around the man's shoulders, squeezing them. "I hear what you've been saying, and I am deeply in tune with it. You, my friend, are the voice of a generation.

"I have a gift for you and I think you will find that it greatly clarifies your situation. I think, in fact, that you will find this quite healing."

At first the man quivered, looking up at the God of Mayhem as if he were the monster that he was, but the God had a way of making his eyes soft and welcoming. The man actually smiled and looked surprisingly eager.

"Yes," he replied, and the God led him out of that crowd, and down the stairs, and outside. He walked around the exterior of the building, his arm still over the man's shoulders, which had started trembling again. "What—what is it exactly we're looking for?" the man asked.

"I think we will find him, ah, here," the God said, and pulled the tremulous man closer, and made him sit down with him on the ground in front of the fallen corpse. He increased his grip on the man. "So, you see, all those things you have mourned, all that we have lost in the city—art and culture, beautiful parks, a sense of safety—those are nothing compared to a human life. Because as long as there is life we can hope that things might change, even though they probably won't."

"Wait, just wait—"

"No, no, have some patience," the God of Mayhem said. "You have to be patient. Tell me, do you believe in God?"

"I don't, I don't know. In times like these, with all that has happened to us—"

"No, the times shouldn't matter. Either there is a god or there isn't."

"I can't believe a god would be so cruel—"

The God of Mayhem laughed. "Sometimes it's part of the job. I'm a god, and I'm right here in front of you." He took the man's chin and turned the head to face him. "Can you believe in me?"

The man looked terrified. Hesitantly he nodded. "Just please don't kill me."

The God of Mayhem made his sad face then. "I'll be honest with you. I'll consider it, but once I start to kill someone I don't stop until the job is done. It's one of my rules. Hesitating, having second thoughts, that's how I might get myself caught or killed."

"How ... how?" He tried to kick his feet. The God raised a finger and wagged it in warning.

"I do have some ideas as to what I'm going to do, unless I change my mind, which I'll just say again, is highly unlikely. Although I prefer the quickness and efficiency of a gunshot to the heart, or into the back of the head, or under the chin, ammunition has become much harder to come by. Have you ever tried it? Do you own a gun?"

"N-no."

"I believe you. Now if I didn't believe you, or you had answered yes, I would have made you take me to your home and I'd take that gun and all your ammunition. Hell, I might just leave the gun behind, if it's one I already have, and I have plenty, and just take all your ammunition, because that's what's really important. A gun without ammo is just another piece of iron to beat somebody with, you dig?" The man nodded shakily. "Oh, and then I would kill you, of course.

"Now I use a shotgun from time to time, but I don't really care for them. I shot a man in the head once with a sawed-off and the man's head just completely disintegrated. Imagine my surprise! I thought that just happened in those old movies. Hey—when you talked about things you missed, things that had been lost from the culture, you didn't mention movies! I used to love movies! Anyway, I'd lured this fellow into my house and did it there—always a mistake but at the time I felt I needed to seize the opportunity. The clean-up took most of a day and the house stank for weeks!"

"I—" The man looked sick. He started to cough and choke up.

"Don't you vomit on me! You vomit on me and I'll be beyond angry!"

The man's eyes went red and he kept licking his lips. Finally he didn't look sick anymore. "I avoid poisons—they never really work for me. Sometimes they will vomit when you feed them poison, and I hate vomit. If I happen to find the right amount of cyanide that's okay—I know how to use cyanide. Everything else is too unpredictable and likely to have a messy, drawn-out, and generally unpleasing outcome."

The man's nodding looked strangely eager. The God assumed by that he didn't want to be poisoned.

"But stabbing always works out pretty well, if you have a pretty good sense of anatomy, which I do. I know just where to stick it in. Just like I know how hard and where to club someone in order to kill them, as opposed to stun them, depending on what I club them with. It's all about knowing the job, understanding the craft. It's good to know a craft, but it doesn't come easy.

"Of course it's hard to make a precise strike if there's a lot of frantic wrestling around. It's best to blindside them, catch them unawares. Otherwise you're exhausted and covered with someone else's bodily fluids by the time the job is done.

"So, should I club you, or stab you?"

Daniel squirmed, if squirming meant anything without a body to squirm with. Aware that Daniel had risen back into consciousness, the God of Mayhem swatted Daniel's self-awareness away. *I'm busy.*

"No!" his victim cried explosively.

The God covered the victim's mouth with his hand and brought a finger up to his own lips. "Shhh. If someone hears I'll just have to kill you and leave. You're not ready for that, are you?" The victim shook his head. "I didn't think so. And by the way, that wasn't a Yes or No question. So, no stabbing, no clubbing. For now. So what else can we do?" He scratched his head in an exaggerated fashion. "Let's use our imagination. Not a good thing in general, by the way, but I'll get to that later. But when you have a specific problem to solve, an imagination can be useful. Simply for variety's sake if for no other reason experimenting with your killing methods is a pretty good thing. You don't want to get stale—and that applies to any line of work.

"I once shot an arrow into a fellow's eye at close range. He died eventually, but not without making a lot of fuss—so you'll be happy to hear I won't be using that method again anytime soon. I also once set a couple on fire while they were sleeping."

The victim began to sob. "Please, I have a child. Please let me go!"

"I won't warn you again—not so loud. Don't make me rush this, okay? And if you really have a child, I'm curious why you didn't mention it before. Anyway, I hadn't planned on using fire—don't make me change my mind." The fellow nodded. Daniel wanted to weep for him, but as soon as he thought that his self-consciousness evaporated. "I once killed a man who lived in a shack, a real eyesore, simply by pushing the shack over on him. It was that easy. People should take better care of their property. Hey, lie down. I'm getting a cramp sitting this way."

The man wavered, but finally lay down in a slightly fetal position but with his face skyward, because the God of Mayhem had him firmly by his shoulders, and then when he was at last still, by his neck. "You c—could let me go," he said to the god hanging over him. "I won't tell anyone."

"To be frank, what are you going to tell them? I'll tell you what, if you happen to get out of this, which you won't, but if you did, tell them God did this to you. Is this too tight, what I'm doing with my hands?"

"G—guess not."

"I knew that it wasn't—I know what I'm doing. I just wanted to see if you'd be honest about it. I know how to create the right amount of pressure with my hands, how to support, how to caress, how to kill. See, you can feel my palms on either side of your neck, and the fingertips, they're near the base of your skull, just below the ears? That's your sternocleidomastoids. They hold a lot of tension, and I have to say yours are really tight right now. When's the last time you had a good massage? Never mind, I realize people are too busy just surviving anymore to get massages, but they really should—it would improve their quality of life. There, doesn't that feel good?

"Once I let some rats eat a fellow down in an old abandoned cellar. No, don't tense up again. I'm just telling you a story. It was hard to get the both of us down in there, and that in itself was a little exciting. Dragging him through narrow spaces, and climbing down a shaft. At least it was different, kind of an adventure like you fantasize about when you're a kid, you know? It ended up being just too much trouble, too much of a time investment. But it was an experiment. Not all experiments are bad." He paused, and grinned. "Well, depending on who's the scientist, and who's the lab rat. But I brought all of these spreads with me—mayonnaise, mustard, peanut butter, whatever I could think of. And I spread them on different parts of his body. He was tied up, of course, otherwise he might have eaten everything." He stopped. "That was just a joke. Anyway, see, I wanted to see which parts the rats went for first. What they liked, what they didn't like. What they wanted to eat most. When he was all done up I just stepped back as far away as I could and watched. But the screaming went on way too long for my tastes."

The God of Mayhem leaned in closer and almost whispered, "I like my hands on your bare skin this way. It's a little more personal, as this kind of thing, well, as it should be. There's always a kind of... charge, when it's skin on skin. Much more intimate than a rope, or a chain, or a wire attached to handles." The man began to struggle, and the God tightened his hands just enough to still him. The man's eyes kept moving around. The God could tell what he was thinking.

"No, no you can't get away. I'm too strong. Whatever fantasies you might have about getting away from me are lies. Your imagination, you should have learned to control it better. Your complaints about what we have lost from our past are quite accurate, but that is past—all that you can do now is imagine it—it is no longer real. Now we are in this world—that other is lost forever. It will not return." He tightened his hands a bit—the man went rigid with fear.

"We always imagine we can have things we cannot have, be things we cannot be. That is the human tragedy. Our imagination is both a cruel bastard and a liar." He squeezed a bit more and tears rolled out of the desperate man's eyes. "We should be angry about that. We should make some noise." Tighter still, and the man began to squirm and kick. "We should tear down some walls and kill whoever we can. Heaven or Hell, is there really that much of a difference?

"Listen to me, little man. You are here, now. You have to take care of the problems we have now. Don't worry about the past, or make assumptions about the future. You have to knuckle down now. Do you think this is all about us, that we're the only ones hurting? Why, I hear there isn't even a Brussels anymore!" The God of Mayhem squeezed harder still, and he began to see veins in the man's face. "And by the way, I found out that rats will eat anything. I mean anything." The man began to convulse, his hips thrusting up into the air. "But they especially seemed to like the molasses." He stopped, looked around. "Do you hear that? I swear it sounds like running water."

But the fellow was done, and the God of Mayhem was exhausted. People did not appreciate the effort required to strangle a human being by hand, the strength, the focus. He had others to kill here, people who were far more deserving to die, but they would have to wait until another evening. It was strangely quiet, except for that vague sound of bubbling underground.

Somewhere down in the dark of the God of Mayhem's soul, Daniel felt himself losing hope. He'd never been in a scenario that had lasted this long before, or that had been so aggressively consuming.

A flame flickered in the darkness. "A little fire always makes it better." The boy held the flame closer to his head, illuminating his face.

"Not tonight, boy. I'm too tired." But the God hesitated. Much to his surprise, Daniel realized the God feared the boy. "I don't need to set a fire every day."

The boy laughed. "You are such a liar! Who do you think you're talking to? I've been with you since the beginning!"

The God shook his head as if trying to rid himself of an annoying insect. "There's too much trash around. Always too much trash."

"But you're an expert!" the boy cried. "You can set a fire anywhere you want. You're the master fireman!"

"Just because I can set it doesn't mean I can always control its spread or its volume. I could burn down the whole neighborhood, maybe even the whole city."

"So? And what would be so bad about that?"

The God thought seriously about it. "I don't believe it's time."

"There's nothing more wonderful than a beautiful fire. What's that you're always thinking? There's a *purity* in the way it cleanses things? It greatly simplifies a complicated world?"

"It does. It does all that."

"Then see what I've found."

The boy led the way into the darkness carrying his small torch in front of him. They were in an area of collapsing houses, porches sliding into yards, rubbish piles everywhere. Again the God heard the burble of water. He watched the ground, careful of where he placed his feet. "Is this far? I have things to do. Is any of this occupied?"

"Oh, nobody's lived here in years. Come on, you have nothing better to do. Do you have your propellant on you?"

"A little, I have a little." He always carried some in a small bottle in his coat pocket. The boy led him to a place where two tall houses had fallen against each other. A shower of siding and shingles covered the piles of junk which looked to have been layering the yards for many years. The God of Mayhem wet his lips. A narrow goat path of a trail ran between the houses. Recklessly he followed it until he was standing beneath where the two collapsed houses connected. He raised his arms over his head, suddenly thrilled, giddy. He looked up—he couldn't see much, but the available moonlight revealed shadowed angles and daggers and spears of collapse, ready to fall and pierce and crush him. It made him breathless with excitement.

Daniel wanted to scream as he looked up into wreckage hanging over them. The scenarios had taken him into dangerous regions before, but this time he was half-convinced that if the God of Mayhem died he might take Daniel with him.

The God pulled out his bottle and dribbled the contents onto the rubbish on both sides of the pathway, now and then climbing onto the piles in the yards and wetting certain areas. He did it all quickly, at a jog, but he had a pattern in mind, a complex design. Once that pattern was laid down, he ran back around lighting it, activating his scheme as the boy cheered. He wasn't sure if he'd used the boy's torch or his own lighter, but in either case it worked, everything started, and over the next couple of hours the fiery forms evolved, and like a machine the fire rose and proceeded to dance with grace and nuanced expression.

The boy jumped and shouted, at times his excitement rising into a hysterical screech. The flames climbed into two swirling, ambitious towers, and then the towers descended, the houses enveloped in hot streamers of crimson, yellow, and blue, the streamers combining and recombining, and between recombinations pockets and tunnels of the deepest black opening up the God was eager to see through to their ends, but they closed much too quickly, and the great shutters of heat drove the tears out of his eyes. Daniel could not deny the raw power of it—the destruction was so fast and devastating that the excitement racing through his body far outpaced any coherent emotional response. The God began to giggle like a brain-damaged ape, and then hysteria swallowed both the God and Daniel.

The fire burned another hour or so. As the geometry of the night dissolved into burning color, trailing smoke, and invisible waves of heat, the God of Mayhem felt calmed and quieted for the first time in weeks. He walked away from there, slowly picking up speed toward morning and home.

Even this early the garbage pickers were out in force, picking up bits, tossing bits away, trading and arguing. Some of them had turned their faces into masks by pasting odd pieces of plastic and other materials onto their skin. This made the scavengers look like burn victims, or atomic bomb survivors. He found them an annoyance, and over the years had killed one or two, but not lately. They weren't worth the trouble.

Daniel floated out of the God's consciousness. The God had allowed it, had made it happen. It was as if Daniel was the God's newly adopted pet.

The God of Mayhem turned and stared at the coastline. He put up to his eye the telescope he'd fashioned out of salvaged metal tubing and lenses. The water was higher than it had been in years. There were areas under water he'd never seen under water before, including much of the quarantine zone, and standing like an island the battered hulk of the old mental hospital. It had the U B O lettering sprayed across the top. Quarantined. Stay away at all costs. Then something shifted along the side of the building, and pieces slid off and into the water, and black smoke boiled out…

DANIEL BOLTED UPRIGHT on the platform. He'd dreamed of drowning, and flying through the air at such speed he couldn't catch his breath. His head felt swollen. He reached up and discovered a series of cylindrical protrusions pushed through his hair and making a tight seal against his skull. He pressed and pulled on them, but they wouldn't be budged.

At least half the room had been destroyed. Fragments of glass and cracked appliances, spilled liquids, fried components. Still, portions of instruments glowed and buzzed, and a few digital readouts measured… something. He stared. Ghostly images of past trauma and high emotion overlaid the room. It was as if he were in the middle of a scenario but he was awake, fully aware and moving around. Whatever was welded to his head still kept him connected to their machines. He watched as the train rolled in. As they unlocked each livestock car they herded out the Jews. He was part of the crew assigned to drag out the dead bodies left behind, the ones who hadn't survived the trip. But he wouldn't touch the dead babies abandoned by their terrified mothers. He'd rather be shot. This time he'd traded the task to another Jew but what would he do next time? The image swept away as his eyes grew wet.

Daniel pushed open the fractured double doors and stumbled down the corridor to the waiting room. Smoke and debris were everywhere. He could hardly see anything above waist height. Contoured lengths of metal, tubing and hydraulics, electronics, littered the floor, and in one spot a metal contraption resembling a rib cage. The lights flashed painfully—he wanted to cover his eyes. His head felt unwieldy. He didn't understand. The cylindrical things attached to his skull felt fragile, insubstantial to the touch, and yet he felt he might fall over from their weight.

"Here, let's get this off you!" Falstaff suddenly shouted into his ear. The alarm was going off, the volume rising with each repetition. It seemed needlessly hysterical.

Falstaff struggled with the apparatus on his head for some time. "It's no use!" he shouted. "It's welded to your skull!"

Daniel wobbled his head to shake all the Jews from his skull. They lay everywhere. They had drifted into the corners of the room.

"The character I played, this killer." Daniel panted. "He *knew* I was there. He knew I was a *witness*!"

"There's a peculiar thing with the scenarios that are more or less in real-time," Falstaff said, working to remove the head gear. "A kind of feedback occurs. Damnit! It won't budge! The character feels the observer's presence. They become paranoid."

"But it wasn't contemporary! It was set in the future. Something bad happens in Boston, in the future!"

Falstaff hesitated, hands on Daniel's shoulders. "Probably not.

You're probably mistaken, Daniel. The future doesn't exist yet, so there's nothing for the roaches' system to read and record. The farthest they can go is to this moment, *today*."

15

"I'll see if I can find something to get this off you." Falstaff went away.

Daniel couldn't quite interpret the frantic activity, the destruction, and the fleeting suggestions of old dramas surrounding him. Unsteadily he made his way to a chair and sat down. The constant movement of the residents made him nervous—too many legs. He focused on the floor, now littered with bits of circuitry, metal, plaster and ceiling tile. He looked at the walls—spider web cracks and small gaps that hadn't been there before. Sections of the ceiling hinged back and forth exposing the wiring above.

Residents were milling around, going to each other, waving their hands, staring at each other in shock. *Fewer of us*, he thought. By at least a third. He didn't see Gandhi anywhere, but Lenin walked by. Daniel grabbed his arm. "Where's..." For a second he couldn't think of Gandhi's real name. "Walter?"

Lenin acted impatiently. "He didn't come back from his last session. A lot of us didn't. You heard the explosions, didn't you? Someone said there was a surge and an overload, then part of the structure failed."

Daniel nodded. "We have to find him."

"Maybe. Maybe we can search, if they let us." The roaches in the room moved around aimlessly, seemingly as confused as the residents. "But I'll keep asking around, find out if anybody's seen him." Lenin left. Daniel heard him shouting Walter's name, saw shaking heads. There was a blur of ghostly shapes both in front of and behind them. Transparent, insubstantial bits of scenarios.

Most of the residents were on their feet and moving about, but a few were sitting like him, preoccupied. Someone walked in front of him and their scissoring legs tore the air. The figure now across from him was sitting on a different kind of bunk, a dull, greenish wall behind him, bent over, his nose against a broken piece of tile he held on his knees. He snorted, jerked up, white powder caking his upper lip. He rubbed at his nose furiously, grinned, and wiped his finger over his gums.

Then Daniel saw the girlish haircut, or was it a wig? The man had breasts, not fully developed but on their way. The man laughed, winked in Daniel's direction, looking familiar. It was Richard Speck, the student nurse killer, in prison, his face recognizable even under that wig. The Speck scenario was the one that had disturbed Bogart so much.

Eight student nurses. He'd slept in a nearby park the night before. Tied them up at gunpoint, strangled them. *Quieter that way.* The knife was just there to scare them. "It just wasn't their night." Tearing the bed sheets into strips to bind them. He felt nothing. *Born To Raise Hell* tattoo. Later he slashed his wrists. But he survived to be this person, whoever this person was.

Daniel was right there inside Speck's head, so high, so fuzzy, but he was outside the scenario, outside the lab. He wanted to warn everyone that Speck had escaped. But Daniel also had escaped. He was outside his head.

Speck looked right at him. "They sent me in here, and look how I'm living. Like a queen in here. This is me laughing now!"

The room began to strobe. Daniel closed his eyes—he had a flowering headache. He made himself get up. It was one thing to be forced while lying strapped to a bed, another when they followed you into your world.

He walked around the room slowly. Voices echoed from somewhere outside the range he was able to understand. People stared at him. Then he saw his shadow with the swollen head from all the cylinders affixed to his scalp. "What happened to *you?*" someone asked, but he didn't answer. He started searching faces, seeking familiar ones. A few he had a nodding acquaintance with, none he knew very well. Where was Gandhi? He couldn't believe he was gone.

That fellow in the old-fashioned suit with his back turned, talking and joking with the others. He looked completely out of place. The suit looked worn, sun-damaged, as if he had travelled a great distance. They either laughed or nodded at everything he said, but offered up nothing of their own. The man turned his head slightly to the side. Daniel stared. The man apparently felt the stare, turned his head a bit more and nodded slightly in Daniel's direction. It was Adolf Hitler.

As Hitler turned his head back toward the other men, Daniel could see that they were enveloped by transparent mountain and valley views. The Bavarian Alps. Berghof. Hitler tapped a cane impatiently on the stone floor. There was a woman on the other side of the men, smiling, blinking into the sun, and fading out briefly with each blink. She carried a basket of food. It was a semi-formal sort of meeting, Daniel thought, a summer gathering outside in the fresh mountain air. Eva was laughing now, their dogs barking. It was a typical afternoon at home.

A couple introduced their young daughter to the führer. He smiled, put his palm against her cheek.

Hitler stopped, stood erect. He turned his head toward Daniel again, his nose wrinkling as if he'd smelled a bad smell. The führer's pupils were like black beads, his face pale as a sheet. Around him the buildings were on fire, the blasted streets. A burn spot grew slowly on Hitler's cheek, like a spot on a piece of film stuck over a hot projector bulb. The führer's lips curled. He started to speak. The others leaned forward, mesmerized. The German cities had been bombed, but *nein*, he would not be visiting. He wore the same look he'd had when he'd ordered the generals to be hung on meat hooks in 1944. An expression of mild distaste. Something rotten had been hidden in the room. *Alle meine Frauen Selbstmordversuch*, he was thinking. *All my women attempted suicide.*

Hitler's large pale-blue eyes were shining. Certain and cold.

Certainty is boring. Certainty means the mind is dead, Daniel thought at the fuehrer. But if Hitler heard him he did not react.

"I submit to fate," Hitler said. Daniel couldn't tell if that was directed at him personally. *"Ich lege das Schicksal."*

He'd come from ordinary stock, and he'd grown up an ordinary man until history had given him his opportunity.

The führer's eyes widened. Something brushed Daniel's arms on both sides. He backed away, but they were all around him, running into him, packed so closely together he could not breathe, all the thin men in their blue-striped pajamas, all those Jewish *Muselmänner*, starved and exhausted, and Daniel could not tell if they were staring at Hitler or if they were staring at him. He squirmed back through the crowd trying desperately not to scream, because if he screamed the rest of the building would come down with the power of his distress. In the distance he saw the windows, and although every emaciated hand seemed to be upon him, every mouth whispering in his ear their truncated story of a life cut short, he managed to reach that singular view of an outside world.

The sky was a silver color streaked with gray. Their usual view of other parts of the building had changed. It was difficult to say how exactly, given that much of that wing had been in ruins ever since he had arrived in Ubo. Daniel tried to make sense of it, then realized that parts of the structure were simply gone. He peered down toward the base of the building and saw the flood waters swirling past, eating at the foundations.

"How are you feeling, Daniel?"

Lenin was standing beside him. The group of men Daniel had interacted with since his arrival had been relatively small, and even among those he would hardly have called any of them friends, although Falstaff had come closest, despite Daniel's many misgivings. Lenin had probably been the one he had talked to least. "A bit better, I think. Still somewhat fuzzy."

"Do those—" He pointed at the cylinders attached to Daniel's scalp. "Does all that hurt?"

"Not exactly. But they make my head feel bigger... heavier. Although I wouldn't think they'd weigh that much. But it feels as if my neck is likely to snap if I don't balance things correctly. I feel like the Elephant Man, afraid to lie down normally, my head about to crush my spinal cord. John said he was going to go find something. I don't know where."

"How are they attached?" He reached to touch one of the cylinders.

Daniel pulled away. "Better not—I don't know if it's safe. I don't know how—I assume they're stuck to the scalp."

"I don't see any burn marks or—sorry—melted skin. But the truly strange thing is the way they go right through your hair. Your hair isn't flattened, cut, messed up in any way. In fact it looks perfectly combed. Don't you even get—what is it they call it?— 'bed head'? What are these things anyway?"

The state of his hair seemed a trivial concern, but it strangely disturbed him to think about it. "The cylinders appear to be part of the equipment transferring the scenarios into our heads. I don't understand much about it, but I think they place them on our skulls, and they're the devices that deliver the information. But they're not supposed to be attached. They're wireless."

"Was that a result of the explosion?"

"I have no idea. I didn't really hear the explosion—I just woke up to the results. Were you in one of the labs?"

"No—they didn't take me this time. They took Walter, and I

guess they took John—at least I didn't see him around for awhile. I'm sure John will figure out something to help you." He sounded less than convinced. "Or maybe the roaches will just remove them when they send us all home."

Daniel was shocked. "You really believe we're going home?"

"I had a dream I went home. And I have faith. You have to have faith, Daniel—it's too hard to live without it. Didn't you say you have family? You have to have faith you're going to see them again."

"We don't even know for sure how much time has passed, do we? What if we've traveled through time? Our families may be dead."

"Why would you even think that?"

Suddenly the God of Mayhem was standing there between them, reaching out to touch them from his devastated Boston. Daniel couldn't even guess how far in the future they were. The God's seemingly compassionate eyes peered down from the separations in the multicolored layers of cloth. He might kill either of them simply because he had an impulse. Daniel turned his head, brought it back, and the image broke into scattered pieces. How was he going to tell Lenin about any of this?

"I don't know, Charles. I just have a feeling."

"It's okay, I get—I don't know—notions, myself. Because of the scenarios, and I think just because of being so far away from home and in this strange, unfathomable place. But evil will lie to you, you know that, don't you? And everything about this place is pure evil and of the devil."

"We can agree on that."

"So tell me, tell me about your family, and how you came here. Tell me what's troubling you."

Daniel told Lenin then about his wife, and Gordon, and Gordon's congenital heart disease and what it had meant, and how it had worn them all down.

"It was constant worry, constant self-examination. Were we

being too protective and ruining his quality of life, or were we not being protective enough and putting him at serious risk? Most of the time we were just exhausted, getting him ready for another surgery, trying to convince him that the clear liquids we were feeding him were for his own good and that he shouldn't cheat. He was just a kid, so of course he blamed us for not giving him the foods he wanted, and we'd tell him to be brave about it when he whined and then later we'd feel so terrible because why should a kid be asked to be that brave?

"They kept telling us to 'treat him normally,' but how can watching your child for signs of heart failure, developmental delays, and giving him all these medicines—how can that be normal? And if he throws up his medicine do you give him some more, or are you going to create an overdose? Or if he gets upset and spits half of it out? Sometimes I'd just want to shake him when he pulled a stunt like that.

"Neither one of us was getting enough sleep, and if his monitor went off we'd practically kill ourselves getting to his bedroom. And he hated going to the dentist, but some of the meds were pretty hard on his teeth, so he had to go more than most kids—he couldn't *afford* an infection. And he'd get mad, and yell at us, and even though we shouldn't have, sometimes we yelled back.

"His blue spells were the worst, when he couldn't get enough air, and he'd start grunting, and we were both convinced that would be it, he was going to die on us right there.

"And at our lowest, I'm ashamed to say, we'd blame each other—things in our families, our genetics, things she might have taken during the pregnancy, early signs we might have missed— and the marriage deteriorated. Once she said we should have divorced before he was born, and at that moment I thought she was right—we never should have had him."

"But a child, any child, is a gift. He wasn't—you can't look at your son as if he's a broken *toy*."

Daniel tried to keep the flash of anger to himself. "Of course not. Haven't you ever weakened? Especially in a moment of great pain? You have to understand, I grieved for my son for years—for his pain and for what I knew would be our eventual loss of him—while he was *still alive* and it felt like more than I could take. I couldn't imagine what it would be like when he was actually gone.

"But I became worse than that. My imagination, sometimes it could be such a hateful, evil thing. I'd see other people's children, and I'd hear them playing, their voices joyful and excited, and-I don't know, I'd imagine a car running them down, or I'd imagine them falling out of a tree, and it wasn't a fearful image for me, it was an image of justice being done, because why should we go through this and not they? I imagined that if my boy was taken, someone else's child needed to be taken as well, otherwise the world wasn't right."

"Daniel!"

"I know. I'm not proud of it. In fact I became so ashamed of myself I decided I shouldn't be near my son or my wife anymore. They deserved better. The day the roaches took me I was sitting in an airport with a plane ticket that would take me to the other side of the country. I hadn't boarded yet, but I think I probably was going to. I just needed to think about it some more. So I sat there while the others boarded, and they were calling my name, and I was thinking about whether I should stand up or not, when suddenly I was gone, and then in some giant insect's horrible embrace, and on my way here."

"Maybe you would have stayed. In fact, Daniel, I have great faith that you wouldn't have gotten on that plane."

"What difference does it make? My wife and son will never understand. As far as they know I just ran away like a coward. They will never know what happened to me."

The lights flickered. An electrified twitter travelled through the residents. A great rumbling sound filled the space and more pieces of the ceiling fell. Then the lights went out with a rapidly descending whine. Residents began to scream. It sounded unnatural. It sounded like a screeching of metal.

After the initial shock Daniel knew he could not be seeing them as they actually were. It was a scene from the end of the Second World War, and the concentration camps had been liberated. Several men were being helped out of a building, impossibly emaciated, skin stretched across the sharp edges of skeletons, the eyes looking huge in near-fleshless sockets, and on each broad bony pelvis where the narrow legs dangled, genitalia displayed as if stuck on as an afterthought. Many of the survivors would die within weeks from disease and malnutrition.

Then his vision cleared and the skin vanished from the skeletons, leaving metal armature arms, articulated rod hands, and cages of metal ribs, pivot joints and wheels, cables, tubing, metal pan skulls with artificial blinking eyes, snapping jaws with teeth attached. Lengths of gray human skin and pale muscle had been fastened to the frameworks in seemingly random arrangements.

The metal and flesh automations charged around the room in a panic, grabbing at each other, chattering and screaming in eerily human voices, their mechanical eyeballs jerking spastically as they acquired new glimpses of their changed realities.

"Daniel, Daniel, what is this?" The metal skull with the disturbingly alive eyeballs yapped in front of him, the mouth with all the wires and plastic and metal pieces used to articulate it.

It was Lenin's voice. Daniel reached out and touched the Leninbot, felt the metal bits, the tubes, and the squishy bits he assumed to be flesh, but he was too squeamish to look at what he touched. "Charles? Is that you?" He noticed an alpha-numeric label on the metal piece which emulated a clavicle, and other such labels—maybe the same label?—on the upper left arm, and on one of the flat metal ribs. "What's happened to you?"

"You, too, Daniel. Daniel, look at yourself."

Daniel lifted his arm. The rods that made up the various phalanges, the hinge joints, the larger metal lengths where the radius

227

and ulna should have been, responded minutely to commands he wasn't aware of issuing. The arm turned, the fingers wiggled at him. Packed inside the arm's framework were tubes, wires, heavier cable, junctions. And, etched onto the radius piece, the characters A-7713.

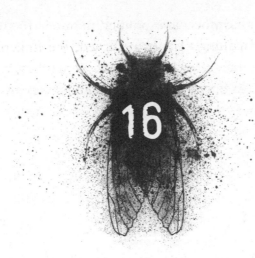

16

THEY WERE ALL men of metal and plastic now, all cyborgs now, automata, automations, androids, machines, robots, bots—none of the terms seemed all that right or acceptable or even possible. He considered whether it might be a trick—just another test, another experiment—but it didn't have the feel of a trick. Nor did it feel as if it had just happened, that they had suddenly transformed as if by magic.

It *might* be a hallucination, but he suspected not. It had the ring of truth. It felt like a confirmation of the peculiar incompleteness he'd felt ever since he'd come here. They'd ruined him. They'd devastated him. He wasn't even properly Daniel anymore. They'd taken his flesh, and now he was Danielbot, apparently only his brain left alive, but it probably wasn't even his brain, was it? Perhaps they'd only stolen his thoughts.

He didn't care that he was falling. He made a metallic sound as he hit the tile. A hollow thud and a rattle. He managed to sit up, metal arms holding onto metal legs, metal knees up. He leaned back against the wall and looked out.

The mechanical men he once knew but now could not recognize without their flesh continued to paw at each other in some sort of desperate attempt at recognition. They appeared to be both seeking familiar contact and trying to get away from these frightening, strange constructions. He recognized Lenin's voice in the crowd but couldn't determine which bot the voice was coming from. There were a few other vaguely familiar voices, but without a recognizable face to associate them to he wasn't sure what they'd actually looked like.

Suddenly several humans in skin-tight, dark blue uniforms rushed out of the observation room. They were slight in build, tired-eyed, with pale complexions, and carried longish, rifle-looking devices. They should have been mechanical men as well—it was only fair.

One of the bots approached these men, reaching out a gleaming, jittery arm and hand. Clearly he meant no harm—he radiated confusion, desperation.

One of the men spun around, shouted, and fumbled at a protruding tab on his rifle. A bluish white bolt flashed between the two and the bot fell. The air smelled like a lightning strike and burnt electrical components.

The remaining bots scattered, some of them gathering nearby. Daniel closed his eyes. Was he still Daniel? He felt like no one else, but he was afraid not. He repeatedly slapped his hand against the floor, then stopped, hating its clatter.

"Gather up!" He opened his eyes. The same human who had shot the bot approached them, sweeping his rifle. "Gather up! Make a line!"

Daniel struggled to his feet. *I'm not Daniel*, he thought. Not Daniel, Notdaniel. The more he repeated it in his head the more the two words together sounded like a single name.

The bots moved back and forth hesitantly. He could sense their confusion. Where to start? And why were they being ordered around by other… by these humans? The man came closer, raising his weapon.

"Better dial it down, Nathan," one of the other uniformed men said. "Looks like you killed this one."

"Stop!" Falstaff was running their way from the back of the room. He hadn't changed at all. "I can handle this!"

He watched as Falstaff pushed his way through the uniformed men. "I know them. I can handle this." The uniformed men slowly, somewhat reluctantly, backed off.

"John?" the bot next to him said. It was Lenin, judging by the voice. "What is this? What's happened to us?"

Falstaff was looking at the bot's number. EH-7384. "Charles," Falstaff said softly. "Just try to stay calm. There's a lot... a great number of things we'll all have to adjust to. Just give me a little time for explanations. We're working on the power issue—once there's sufficient power I think we can get you your old appearances back, then you'll all feel a lot better."

"Those fellows in the blue uniforms are the roaches, aren't they, John?" Daniel said. "This is what the roaches really look like, when they're not controlling how we see things. They're just people. Which, apparently, we are not. And which, apparently, you are."

"But we all *saw* them. They guarded us, took us down to the labs for our... our *scenarios*. They *brought* us here!" the Leninbot shouted.

"It was an illusion, Charlie. Probably using the same mechanism that made us look human to ourselves—am I correct, John?"

"Daniel—be careful."

"Don't call me that! I'm no more Daniel than you are!"

"What are you people talking about?" Charlie shouted. "John, what is he talking about?"

John grabbed Lenin and took him aside. "Daniel, just wait here." A couple of the guards moved closer. He supposed he still cared whether they shot him or not, because he didn't challenge them.

After several minutes of animated conversation with Lenin and some of the other bots, John returned.

"I'm sorry I lied to you, I really am. I know, I know, I lied to you all the time. I had to. Daniel—I—please, if you don't want me to use that name, what should I call you?"

Daniel held up his arm. "You could just use my number—that's what it's there for, isn't it?"

"Those numbers were meant for accurate records, matching... parts. We each have an implant," he said. "Which allows us to see you as you see yourselves, as your originals. We initially tried working without them, but the guards have always tended to treat you... more sensitively, when you appeared... more like them."

"I could have told you that—that was a lesson learned centuries ago."

"But I'm not going to call you by that serial number. I can't."

"Then if you must call me anything, refer to me as the Danielbot. I'm no more than an avatar, really, a voodoo doll. I would have said that you and your people have reduced me to that, but I was never really more, was I? Only your lies convinced me that I was more. I was never Daniel, was I? I was never even human. Was I a recording of some kind?"

"More or less—his memories, his feelings, a simulation of how he perceived things. I am truly sorry to have lied, but how could I have told you the complete truth? How would you have reacted?"

"No one ever figures it out?"

"They begin to, over time, and I try to confirm little bits, I drop hints. My job is to advocate, to somehow minimize the trauma. Otherwise their personalities begin to go off the rails. We cannot bring an entire person into the future, nor should we. I'm sure you would agree with that. So we bring a recording taken at a specific time, with all your beliefs and your past."

"And the real Daniel? The original?"

"He's completely unaware. His life goes on. But that recording is mapped here to an artificial brain, which we put into a body of sorts. It's invaluable, the knowledge it has, and the recording is so structured that it blends more easily with other recordings—the subjects, the characters it is asked to play. We've learned *so* much. So much raw data about who we are, how we behave."

"Why couldn't you have kept it all in a computer? Why put us in bodies at all?"

"The project has been going on for many years. We tried all that. But without a body the personalities simply would not be completely convinced they were real—they would not behave normally. By adding a bit of actual flesh to those bodies we were able to access a certain level of human vulnerability, a physical awareness of their mortality."

"Are you going to tell the others? Or is this supposed to be our little secret? Because I can't promise…"

"Let me try to bring them along as best I can. I've always tried to do my best to help, under the circumstances. I've always tried to tell my charges details I thought might comfort them, or satisfy enough of their curiosity that they wouldn't probe for more. I did that with Alan, with Walter, Charles, and certainly you. I've tried to make things better. Please let me continue to do that. This wasn't supposed to happen this way. I'm afraid it's going to be much too much for everyone."

The Danielbot examined his arms. The workings were quite intricate and responsive. Even though they looked like bits of machinery, they felt completely correct, completely real. Here and there were circles and oblongs of human flesh, like pads on a piece of furniture, like upholstery made of meat.

"So I'm never going home, John. That's pretty much the sum of it? No, don't answer. My beautiful wife, my lovely son… you do realize, don't you, that those memories were all I had to hold on to? And now to find out they don't even belong to me? My family is alive in the past with the original Daniel and none of them, in fact, have anything to do with me. So I have nothing? What am I going to do, John? Could you explain that?"

17

SOME OF THE bots had taken up pieces of blanket and were busy polishing themselves, wiping off dirt, rubbing out blemishes, bringing the metal and plastic to a high sheen. Some had concentrated particularly on their serial numbers, making them gleam like engraved trophy inscriptions. But for Danielbot the cleaner, the shinier they became, the more suggestive they were of death.

Danielbot spent his time examining his thought processes, his reactions. He certainly felt like more than a recording—he *felt* everything. He had an entire life to draw on, and a wide range of responses. And yet he also knew he was incomplete. By definition he had to be—those were all someone else's memories.

One of the other bots caught him staring and fixed his jaw into an exaggerated robotic smile. When he tilted his head he looked like a caricature of starvation.

Other bots sat collapsed together in the corners or folded up on themselves in resting positions that would have been impossible for a human being.

A great deal of physical self-examination was happening. The panic of the previous few hours had subsided—the bots appeared to be waiting for the promised return of power and their old, familiar, and comforting faces. But Danielbot had no desire to see his old skin again.

Various bots examined the mechanics of their new bodies with obvious fascination. Periodically the power flickered and he saw, ever so briefly, the old human faces of the other prisoners. The others were apparently having the same experience. They greeted these glimpses of the past with a kind of mechanical sigh, like the faint leak in an air compressor.

The human guards waited in their own little group, sitting against the wall beneath the observation window, their rifles vaguely pointed in the direction of the bots. They looked casual and relaxed, which was probably pretense. As roaches they'd been emotionless, their expressions alien and impenetrable. Now they seemed like nervous schoolboys.

Leninbot was nowhere to be seen. He had said nothing since Falstaff had spoken to them. Danielbot hoped he hadn't done anything foolish.

Ghostly imagery continued to overlay Danielbot's field of vision, intensifying and solidifying into three dimensional scenes during the power flickers, but always present to some degree, providing depth and subtext even to the most commonplace gestures and actions. At times he witnessed replays from his own scenarios, but a good number of the scenes and characters and terrible events were completely unfamiliar to him, as if the Ubo databanks had ruptured and were now flooding his brain, if brain was even the right word for whatever stored this information.

"You'll need to take that gear off." One of the ex-roaches was standing over him, his weapon aimed.

"What?"

"Those nodules on your head. They belong in one of the labs. You can't have them."

"They're—I don't know—*welded* to my head? I *can't* take them off."

The man sighed, reached over and began pulling on one.

Danielbot's head lifted with it. It didn't hurt, but it was a strange sensation. The cables that ran through Danielbot's neck stretched tightly. The fellow started shaking the nodule, making Danielbot's head wobble. He saw sparks, tiny explosions.

"Stop!" Falstaff was suddenly standing beside them, his hand on the man's arm. "They won't come off—you're going to damage the equipment!" Danielbot wondered if Falstaff meant the nodules, him, or both.

"Just doing my job." The man averted his eyes, looking angry.

"You're security. I'm technical. Let *me* worry about how the damn equipment is used. Just go… guard something." The guard strutted away. "I'm sorry, Daniel." Falstaff sat down on the floor beside him.

Danielbot gazed at the bots sprawled around the room. They looked like oversized toys whose batteries had run down, left scattered by a very bored and very large child. "I asked you not to call me by that name. I'm not Daniel anymore." He looked down at the number on his arm, and then showed it to Falstaff. "A7713. Or Danielbot."

"You're going to hear that number enough from the guards, but it's not going to come from me. I'm sorry—we didn't anticipate any of this. We were assured we would have independent power. These weren't things you were supposed to know about."

"So my… Daniel's life went on. He was about to make a terrible mistake, and I'll never know what he decided."

"We can't change the past. We don't even choose the moment at which we take the record. We send this bit of programming back inside a probe, and it recognizes a certain degree of anger, a particular sort of pathology—a matrix of hundreds of violence-related factors. Otherwise we'd be recording thousands of people. We record that person, and we retrieve the recording. There's one profile for the monsters of history, another for the ones we recruit to act like those monsters—the ones like you we can study and communicate with. I assure you they're not the same. You're not here because you're a bad person. It's based on probabilities, and hundreds of character traits."

"Why do you need us? Why make it so complicated? Why not use your own people, volunteers?"

"Well, we would, but they've made that illegal. It's considered human experimentation. I'm not sure the results would be as illuminating, in any case. With a recording we can suppress certain qualities and bring out others. We can make it a controlled experiment. But if we were to use—"

He paused. Danielbot filled in. "Real people?"

"I was going to say 'an original.' With people, you get what you get. You can't change them to fit the experiment better."

"I get it. I'm *clearly* not human, so you can feel free to fuck with my life."

"Daniel… Danielbot, please…"

"No *please* about it. *Please* would imply you made a polite request. You didn't." Being upset made him feel more human. "But you repeat the scenarios over and over again, using different ones of us?"

"It's part of the protocol. Each explorer experiences these scenarios slightly differently. We compile the results to get a more accurate glimpse into the violent personae."

"So, we're explorers now? Not prisoners?" Danielbot turned his head away from his ex-friend, this roach who hadn't had the decency to wear his roachness around them, and tried to close his eyes. It was then he realized that bot eyes had no lids, and that only a kind of unconsciousness would completely prevent him from seeing. "You're like little boys experimenting with pulling the wings off a fly. Once you discovered you could do it, you developed a need to do it."

"No, it's not like that. Daniel…"

"Stop calling me Daniel!" One of the guards rushed to respond but Falstaff waved him away. "I fail to see," Danielbot said, "what you have accomplished here. I've only had glimpses of the world out there, admittedly, but what I've seen, what I've heard, simply based on that I would say you've practically destroyed it."

The two sat in silence for a time. Finally Falstaff stirred. "We always thought we could fix what we'd broken. We were smart enough, we were clever enough. But sometimes the only practical solution is not to break things in the first place."

There was another rumbling and more of the ceiling came down. The bots jumped up and the guards rushed in to corral them into a semblance of order. Danielbot was separated from Falstaff but didn't object. He had no plan, and little desire to formulate one.

"We're moving to the roof to wait for rescue!" one of the guards shouted. The idea seemed ludicrous, but Danielbot had no choice but to go along with it.

Despite their obvious distress, the bots fell into line quickly. But something about the line bothered a few of the guards, who grabbed them, rearranged them, moved them aside like so much excess furniture, prodded them with the rifles. The bots acquiesced, terrified of a possible electrical charge. If one lagged, a charge against the base of the spine sent it sprawling forward, knocking the others out of line. The guards shouted angrily, as if the bots were being willfully disobedient. One of the bots fell and refused to move. Two guards blasted it until smoke issued from its targeted parts.

Eventually the guards herded them into the stairwell. The bots in back, rifles pointed at their heads, shoved those in front of them up the stairs. A bot near the top of the staircase fell, sliding back down with a static-filled howl.

One of the guards poked the fallen form with the end of his rifle. A quick blast at the base of the skull pan made the body jerk, climb to its knee joints, then fall back onto the floor. Another blast stilled it. When it wouldn't get up again despite determined prodding, two of the guards shoved it into a corner of the landing where it lay like a pile of stray parts.

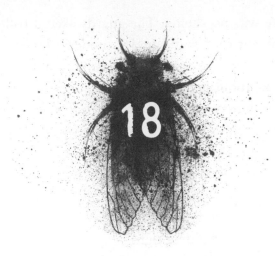

18

THE GUARDS WERE extremely nervous the first day or so as everyone camped out on the roof. They brandished their electric rifles at the slightest sign of resistance, screaming at the bots and threatening deadly force. It might have been the openness of the setting, without cover if there was a rebellion, although Danielbot could not imagine his fellow mechanical men organizing and attacking.

There must have been an adjustment in policy because no rifles were actually fired. What surprised Danielbot most was how quickly everyone fell into their roles: the guards standing up straight in their blue uniforms, attempting to walk and talk with authority and to devise humiliating games designed to keep the bots off-balance. After a few days they seldom brought their rifles down to a ready position. The bots, despite their larger size and heavy frames, developed a subservient posture, bowing their upper bodies to make themselves appear shorter, avoiding eye contact, and for the most part doing what they were told.

The skies were continuously gray with an occasional redness in the lower clouds, and black smoke hung just above the skyline. Far below, waves hit the building with a churning and shushing, but Danielbot had no intention of going close enough to the edge of the roof to steal a glimpse. Now and then the sky tore into rain and there was no shelter. The guards used a roll of plastic to create a makeshift roof they could sit under. Maybe the bots were waterproof. In any case they weren't offered a solution. Most of them just stood about in the downpour.

Some of the guards claimed that a helicopter would come to take them all off the roof. Danielbot would be surprised if anyone had that kind of fuel to spare. It wasn't stated openly, but he expected that only the guards were subject to rescue, leaving the "equipment" behind. He overheard one of them say they should just shoot the bots and escape before it was too late. Another said there was no such order, so he was holding tight.

The bots knew many of their fellows by voice, but the guards couldn't tell them apart without their fleshy mirages, and referred to the prisoners by their serial numbers or a truncated version thereof.

Danielbot—and to some degree Leninbot—kept to the edges of the groups, and thanks to Falstaff's occasional interventions, were left alone much of the time and protected from the pettier forms of harassment, although they weren't excluded from prisoner counts. The worse thing was bearing witness to the demeaning activities the guards devised to promote discipline and the bots quickly acquiesced to.

Count-offs happened an hour or so apart, or whenever there had been a minor altercation or disagreement, or whenever a guard decided to entertain a whim.

"Count off, alphabetical followed by numerical!"

"A7713!"

"A15510!"

"B10232!"

"B14368!"

"EH7384!"

If an error was made in the count, the bots had to repeat it twice. The guards would sometimes become creative with the counts, ordering the prisoners to deliver them backwards, or to skip every other numeral, or to call out a number thirteen more than their actual number. Sometimes physical movements were added to the count, push-ups or jumping jacks, activities not well suited to their mechanical frames.

Danielbot had begun to suspect that, besides personality and individual history, a certain amount of acquiescence had been programmed into their bot brains, a tendency to obey identified authority figures. Otherwise, he could not explain their willingness to follow orders, or his inability to even imagine a rebellion.

Some of the bots were made to stay in one spot for hours. Physically this was no challenge, but they had been provided with full memories of what pain and fatigue felt like, so after awhile they suffered accordingly.

When left alone, the bots returned to the same rooftop activities they'd participated in when they'd worn their human guises. They played their invented board games, danced and sang, or attempted to perform physical exercise. They subjected each other to petty abuse. The guards allowed the abuse to happen, but if too large a crowd gathered they would warn them off by punishing the first available offender. One of the guards discovered that a low level dose of electricity applied constantly to the back of the head pan might produce both delirium and persistent pain without death (or rather, "an irreversible shutdown"). There was no physical reason for the pain, but the bots felt it anyway. The guard looked excited to watch.

Around their fourth afternoon on the roof, there must have been a significant current surge in the systems below because some of the bots were suddenly refreshed with their old appearances, Leninbot included. He smiled as he rubbed at his pink, illusory skin. Danielbot returned the smile but neither made any attempt at more contact.

At this point the Danielbot didn't care much if he looked like Daniel ever again. It was all an ugly lie and to have his perfect disguise returned to him would have only made it worse. Somehow he needed to embrace who he was and not who he was not.

For Danielbot, along with the current surge had come a renewed onslaught of violent memories, highly fragmented and without his usual sense of participation. The memories played as a reel of vicious movie scenes spliced together with no sense of continuity or artistry. Urban gang wars blended into southern lynchings, then bits of Abu Grabe, suicide bombers in the Mideast, and Jim Jones exhorting parents to feed their children poisoned Kool-Aid. Danielbot wondered if whatever medium they'd used to store the threads of violent memories trawled from the past had become corrupted. It seemed he might be receiving the bottom-of-the-barrel bits, the test runs and the unsuccessful attempts, the events too old to retrieve cleanly—whatever was left over in the backwaters of the memory banks.

In the late afternoon dimness, the roof had become a broad field of prairie grass, low-lying hills on the horizon, a few distant twists of tree. Smoke and weeping, howls of pain.

The soldiers were aiming at a small brown-skinned running form, although the child was much too young to run properly, a toddler at most who staggered and fell and got himself up again. The Colorado Indian Wars. 1864 or thereabouts. The men were laughing, poking fun at each other's limited skills. "You shoot like my ol' granny, after she'd been drinkin' all day!"

The one with the scraggly red beard cursed, tried again, taking his time. The small form dropped. They cheered.

"In my neighborhood we called them the shadow people. They'd come in the middle of the night and the next day you'd find them camped out in the alley, or on a playground, sometimes even in your back yard. That was around the start of it." John had been sitting beside him, speaking, but Danielbot hadn't noticed him until now. "When they first reached the coast. Some of them had gone up into New York first, but the people from the southwestern states had gotten there first, so they came here."

"The people escaping South America," Danielbot said. "And Mexico."

"That's right. How did you—" John frowned. "Oh yes, your

last scenario was with the God of Mayhem. We used to share our contemporary criminal findings with law enforcement and the military, but that was back when those agencies were more functional.

"It's an odd thing, with all that we can do, the things we can make, the miracles we can accomplish—your very existence being one of them—that we can't seem to solve the food problem, or the overpopulation problem, or the environmental problem. We've had a helluva time just keeping our people sheltered, much less providing them with worthwhile things to do.

"How do you fault people for fleeing a burning house, whatever the immigration laws might be? And believe me, their house *was* burning. And you don't let your children get hurt, or die—you get them out of there, whatever the cost. The shadow people did what they had to do."

"So people are no better, no more generous, than they used to be in my day," Danielbot said.

"Human beings have greater powers of empathy than you might think. Their ability to mirror feelings, even quite dark feelings, to understand someone else's desperate situation, is really quite remarkable. That's why the scenarios work as well as they do."

Danielbot wondered. If he had a question, was it coming from him, or from the Daniel simulation inside him? He decided to ask it anyway. "Is this what you wanted to do with your life?"

Falstaff looked genuinely surprised. He stared at his hands, taking turns rubbing one with the other. Danielbot felt envious. He missed the human version of his hands. "It was never my goal. How could it be? Who could imagine such a thing? It's been okay. It's been interesting. It's kept body and soul together at a time when many are denied that benefit. But—human beings *settle*, you understand? That's much of what we spend our time on. Sometimes our imaginings are exquisitely detailed in that regard: what, specifically, we would accomplish, who we would be with, what they would look like, even down to the fine details of weather and the quality of the light that day. We also imagine what *we* would look like on such occasions, and it's usually somewhat different than the way we in fact look today.

"But we settle for less. Because we have no choice."

"Why? Why no choice?"

"Because no one can imagine reality, or would want to. That's the sad truth of it. Reality seems a poor substitute for what we dream. Most of us eventually accept that, even though it annoys and disappoints. But some of us become so angry, our frustration building over a period of years, that we erupt. We rage. And we destroy."

A bot was lying on the roof, one of the guards prodding him with the end of his rifle. "Can't you stop that?"

"I really have little influence over them," Falstaff said. "Security was never part of my responsibilities. In fact, there was always a certain amount of friction between the research team and the security team. The guards know what we do here, and they see how our subjects are after their scenarios."

"And to what end?" The Danielbot wanted to touch this man, to shake him, although he knew the guards would kill him before Falstaff could stop them. "What was the purpose of all this? What have you accomplished?"

Falstaff shrugged, looked at his hands. "I was just a little boy when the first waves of migrations hit the city. About ten years before I was born they discovered the process by which they could peek into the past and record a mind, partially or completely, depending on conditions. The average citizen didn't know about it—still doesn't— the government decided it might have security applications, and kept it secret. Some historians knew—they'd been hired by the government to play around with the technology, see what they could get it to do. And the scientists who developed it, my grandfather being one of those key figures. The government paid him well for that—he became a rich man, although he couldn't tell anyone how.

"I think there was shame attached to the enterprise from the beginning. Initially they targeted certain famous individuals, filling in the gaps of history with investigations into secrets, motivations, ambiguous events. The government didn't want any of that released, believing, quite accurately, I imagine, that if the citizens found out that their heroes had feet of clay it would reflect poorly on those in charge, whatever their politics. They might have shut the project down if not for the fact that a great deal of money, and certain cultural treasures, were located as a by-product of these investigations.

"The goal of the experiment was not necessarily to recreate an historical reality, although sometimes that might be useful, but to gain some understanding of the psychological dynamics involved.

"My grandfather had loftier goals. He thought these studies might lead to actual time travel, perhaps even a boost in human longevity. My father worked for him, but had concerns about the effects on the lives of the participants. He thought he might be able to ameliorate that, especially after he married my mother, my grandfather's only child.

"I was too young, really, to understand much about the food riots. I remember that my grandfather was sympathetic to the poor and all those people who had lost their homes, from whatever country. Then my grandmother and my mother and my sister were caught up in one of those riots. They were all killed. And my grandfather found a new purpose for the technology, and funded it himself. Violence—its causes and prevention. Not every culture has been violent, so he didn't believe it was innate. He felt if he could explore the causes he could root out the destroyer inside us."

"And? Any progress?"

"I...I certainly believe we're closer. Obviously if some needs aren't met, for the individual, for the group, violence occurs. But how do you meet those needs? *Can* you meet those needs? That's more difficult.

"My grandfather believed that at their core, human beings were a kind of possessed ape, haunted by intelligence and violent urges.

He believed that if we learned enough about these urges we might exorcise them, and create human beings capable of solving our problems.

"I think he should have focused instead on climate change, poverty, food shortages, and the creation of meaningful work. If these problems had been solved, or if enough progress had been made, well, I think there might not have been a need to probe the past for the answers to violence.

"We've created some remarkable things. We thought we were creating a kind of heaven, at least for those who could afford it, but the results have been a kind of hell.

"And everyone who has worked here realizes that it's far too late to apply what we might have learned to our current situation. We all understand it is too late for us. But what else can we do? We're committed."

Danielbot wanted to strike the man, but knew he would not. In fact he'd probably been rendered incapable. "You say human beings have empathy. Could you spare some of that empathy for me? I once was a person, or I thought I was. I once thought I had a family, but that has been taken away from me. I am nothing now, simply a recording device, and I am far more alone than I can fathom. And yet I ache for the wife I thought I had. I ache for that child. And I am devastated that the man whose memories I represent may have made a terrible mistake."

AFTER A FEW days some of the bots chose a resting place on the roof, any spot with a little bit of privacy or shade, where they became quiet, then motionless, and never woke up again. Danielbot came to understand that their bodies were powered by some kind of battery, and although he'd never been aware of being recharged, it was something that must have occurred on a regular basis and now was not happening anymore.

He wasn't the only one to figure this out. Leninbot showed him where a cord was hidden near the abdomen, and how it could be released and connected to one of several outlets in the roof. "But I don't know that any of them have any current. At least I don't feel anything. But I'd do it anyway, just in case." And he'd see other bots follow Leninbot's advice. Still, bots continued to become dormant. The fact that they all didn't freeze into immobility at the same time suggested that the batteries varied in terms of strength and quality, but eventually running out of power appeared inevitable.

Danielbot didn't complicate things by talking about how he was still seeing bits and ghosts of scenarios. The Ubo computers apparently had some power, perhaps from an independent source.

As reluctant as he was to lie down and remain still given what was happening to some of the others, it was clearly important to conserve power.

He had noticed that the roof had changed since the first time he'd come up here. It appeared slightly barren in comparison. A great deal of the old furniture was gone, perhaps tossed off the side by agitated bots after they were forced up here, or removed by the guards for security or safety purposes. He'd been aware of frantic activity around him that first day of their rooftop exile, but he'd been oblivious to much of it. He'd been too busy adjusting to this new sense of self, and missing the life he'd mistakenly thought he had.

There were still places to find shelter if the guards allowed it, even with a couple of hundred or so bots—more than he had ever before seen together at one time. Given how many had died, or had been gotten rid of, the population of Ubo must have been much larger than he ever knew.

This massive roof easily held them all. This field of gravel and discarded bits and old ruin went on forever.

He lay down for a while, his head propped up against some bricks, gazing across this roof which at times resembled an abandoned beach, at times a battlefield, depending on the temporary visions bleeding from his head into everything he saw. Flanders Fields,

Waterloo, Stalingrad, or Gettysburg, the thousands still buried beneath the battlefields of the Somme, the millions buried one upon the other all across Europe—it was hard to believe there could be enough dirt to contain them all, everyone who had once lived and breathed and sung and loved. And now out of reach. Yet he hadn't been one of them or even descended from one of them— all he'd ever been designed to do was observe. It was the worst injustice he could imagine.

The fields at Majdanek, at Auschwitz-Birkenau, at Płaszów, everywhere a concentration camp had been: now so peaceful. He could hear the birds sing, and some distant farmer's call for a wayward cow. He realized then he hadn't heard a bird since he'd been in Ubo, not even seen one. Was it possible they were all extinct? He hoped not, but maybe they were in some safer place where birds were better appreciated.

"Daydreaming again? Should a robot daydream?" He looked up—Leninbot was back, hovering. "I was afraid at first you might have died, run out of power. We've lost at least a dozen of our kind that way, by my count. It's murder, you know, to let us run out of power like that. These human beings, they're all murderers. We should have learned that from the scenarios. They're a plague upon the Earth which they are gradually destroying. I'm glad to discover I'm not one of them, are you?"

Could a robot feel weary? Danielbot found this line of conversation wearying. "I don't know—it's too soon for me. I liked the family I thought I had."

"So you miss your flesh?" Leninbot leaned over and stared at him intently with those lidless artificial eyes. Of course Danielbot knew he had the same eyes, but he did not imagine himself with those eyes—he imagined himself with Daniel's eyes. And perhaps that answered Leninbot's question.

"It was never my flesh. Or your flesh. It wasn't flesh at all—that was the delusion they planted in us."

"But you miss it, don't you?"

Danielbot sighed, but the sound was that unhuman-like, mechanical hiss which he hated. He cut it off. "Yes, I confess I do."

"Well, I've decided I don't anymore," Leninbot announced. "I think this—" He stood up and spread his metal arms. "Is an obvious improvement. It's so clear to me today. All those terrible things—we have observed them, but we didn't do those things, couldn't have, I don't believe, because we're not flesh. Nor do we possess all the weaknesses of skin flesh, organ flesh, and certainly not brain flesh. We're meant to replace all that."

Talking about this frightened him. "I understand what you're saying," he replied. He remembered the original Daniel using such a phrase when he didn't want to engage.

"But we are, all of us, running out of power! We're dying! And so many of us have died already." He lapsed into silence. This was true. As Danielbot looked out over the roof he could see so many of them lying about who hadn't moved in days. It didn't upset him as much as it should have. He was thinking too much like a human being. Stingy with his humanity, stunted in his empathy.

He turned to talk to Leninbot but the bot was already gone, wandering over the roof from bot to bot, seeing if they were still alive, attempting to wake them up, telling them the news of their superiority. The scene reminded him of other places. The fields rushed back into him, the peaceful fields where the camps had been, where birds had been.

These had not been safe places then, these fields where so many people died. Danielbot lay there for hours gazing across the roof, then across those fields, the sun rising over the distant rolling hills, the green, the pine trees, so different from this Boston, or anything else he had seen of this future world. But whose memory was this, and why here? And then he could see the transparent shapes of the thousands, their memories lost here beneath the grass, and feel the tears running down the face of the survivor who had come back to the old ruins of his concentration camp for answers. But the local townspeople seemed to have lost their own memories and denied knowledge of this place, except that once there had been Jews here, and they never came back. And there was no one who would talk to him about this annihilation.

As he'd turned away from the village he'd heard that one farmer muttering, "It was God's will, punishment for killing Christ."

There lay the long lines of the foundations where the prisoners were housed, the grass reaching up to cover the stones, to knock them back in time, to make them invisible, but someone kept it trimmed and the stones intact, so that people might remember. The very air began to rip, long gray splinters of wood pushing through the rents, and the crude barracks rose to fill the space. He remembered the beds, boards between bricks, sometimes holding three and sometimes five prisoners together. The constant trips to the latrine, unable to hold anything inside anymore, the stench so bad he eventually stopped smelling it. Lining up as you were told but still hoping the guards didn't see you. If you ended up on the outside of the group where they might notice you, your days were numbered. To stay invisible meant to stay alive. He remembered. He remembered.

He looked down at his arm and saw it clothed in flesh again. The number was covered up; he had a name again. Small ghostly flakes hit the skin and stayed without melting. He raised his arm to look at them—they were flakes of ash. In the distant city the flames stretched toward the sky, living, burning hands reaching up out of the crematoria, too late for any kind of help. That wouldn't be human beings out there burning, would it? He looked at the ash on his arm again. How could you tell a human's ash from that of a building's?

There the collapsed remains of the gas chambers, those dark rooms where they had imagined they would take a shower. The signs outside the showers: CLEAN IS GOOD! LICE CAN KILL! WASH YOURSELF! The German government was always generous with their helpful advice. The shower rooms had looked ordinary enough inside, except the ceilings were scarred by fingernails.

There the broken rubble of the crematoria, all that was left of the ovens where two thousand prisoners went up the chimney each day to Heaven, the flames turning the sky a blood color, the air full of screams, gunshots, and the barking of dogs. The devil was coming. The devil was coming to the camps. The devil had come to the Jews.

The sky grew darker, and Danielbot wondered if his power had run out and all his borrowed memories come to an end. But it was one of the guards, all jack boots and medals, leaning over him, blocking out the sun.

"You think you're a man of leisure, do you? Worthless piece of shit! Up, up! Time for exercise!"

What time was he in? Then he realized he was alive in both worlds. He joined a group of prisoners being forced to do push-ups, then jumping jacks, then running in place. Their flesh flashed to metal and then back to flesh again. Anyone refusing to cooperate was struck across the face, beaten to the ground. These abuses did not hurt his metal framework, but when the metal vanished and he was covered by a memory of skin, he was in agony. Deliberate misery was the rule of the day here, the strategy and the religion.

He could no longer tell anyone's age here. Most had been reduced to children of seventy, seventy-five pounds. They had become playthings, cures for the soldiers' boredom.

Still, some looked younger than the others. Not children anymore, but not yet adults. He thought he felt saddest for them, the ones who would never live long enough to have a story to tell.

But at some base level they all looked the same. They learned quickly. Hide yourself. Don't speak up. Eat when you can. Wash and dress yourself as cleanly as you can. And if you passed blood you were among the dying.

Some wanted to go into the hospital. They thought it would be easier for them there. Sometimes the patients would drop an extra crumb from a window for some poor soul waiting outside. But late at night from the hospital basement windows you could hear the screams. Because in there they ran tubes into you. They froze you, burned you, cut and cut and sewed. Outside you died by starvation and beatings. In the hospital you died by syringe.

"We need these shelters moved to the other side of the roof!"

These rickety configurations of boards and bricks and bits of canvas connected by odd metal strips looked more like art installations than any form of shelter, but the bots had no choice. When the shelters fell apart, as was inevitable, one bot was picked at random to receive shots of the electrical rifle charges until it smoked into immobility. Danielbot wasn't sure this was the same as termination, but no bot ever came back from it.

If a bot fell it was shot. If a bot refused it was shot. If a bot talked back it was shot. Some got back up after these punishments, some did not. Sometimes a bot was charged into a smoking ruin to let the others know that non-existence might come at any moment, without warning.

He woke up once in the dark, the sky moonless and starless, the only light the red reflection from distant fires. He sat up, gazed at all the recumbent forms—skulls in shadow, dark torsos, arms, legs. He could almost imagine himself human again, a real person again. A sudden yellow flare shimmered on the horizon in the direction of the city. Then the clouds moved and exposed a huge gibbous moon, one edge worn off.

Several bodies lay in the mud outside the prisoner's barracks. Two ragged, shambling figures dragged another one out to add to the pile.

The prisoners on grave detail were ordered to call them figures or dolls, never corpses. There were serious consequences if you failed to follow orders, if you used the wrong words or told the ones arriving what was about to happen to them. The guards might throw you into the ovens alive.

Once he saw some soldiers toss a crying baby into the air and use it as target practice. After this he believed that if he were ever to leave this place he would not leave as a human being.

He shook his head. The memory floated away. White robot eyes stared at him from a distant part of the roof—someone else was up. Then the woods closed in, and those eyes became stark white animal eyes, glowing in the light from the moon. Tall trees had grown up on either side, obscuring the distant ruins, the sky, the edges of the roof. A wide path lay between the two masses of trees, extending as far as he could see, past the roof's edge, and into nothing. It was what the Jews in the concentration camps had called the Road to Heaven.

He was still gazing into this hazy vision of the road when the dawn came. Phantasmal strands of barbed wire floated in the morning air, insubstantial as grass stalk and dandelion, until they solidified into metal. The low wooden barracks on the other side was bathed in snail-gray mist. This morning the air tasted of the dead. A naked body, and another, perhaps three, had crawled out during the night to join the bodies that already lay unmoving in the mud. Danielbot moved his arm forward and waved. The metal arm passed through the barbed wire, and the scene dissolved into one of a sprawl of mechanical men who did not need to sleep, but who slept anyway, out of choice or because their artificial brains no longer functioned. Some of the bots were leaking, dark stains spreading through the roof gravel.

More objects gradually manifested in his vision of the morning: the piles of suitcases and other possessions the Jews had been forced to abandon when they disembarked, the clothes piled thirty feet high. He saw the train empty, all the thousands forced down the road, and hours later he saw no one. None of those people came back.

Heat blasted his face. He was beyond weary. He looked down at his hands, covered in blood and grime. He threw another small form into the oven: a precious doll. Well-nourished corpses were burned with emaciated ones—for economy of time and saving fuel. It required a great deal of trial and error to find the most efficient combination. If he focused on the mechanics, the science of his job, he didn't have to think about what he was being made to do.

Several bots staggered their way up the ascension, the last road to the gas chamber, their shiny brain domes like shaved heads. They'd been here long enough to lose most of their fat, their flesh. They were like a cartoon of skeletons on their exhausted march, a silly jazz track playing in the background. Some of them disappeared then, having stepped off the edge of the roof.

Intruding into Danielbot's awareness like something he'd intended to remember: the devil was on his way to Ubo. The God of Mayhem was busying himself setting fires in a frenzy of excitement. Hardly able to contain himself, he'd begun to see the possibility of bringing the whole world down in flames. The sky turned a smoky red. He could hardly wait to find a boat and make his way to Ubo, like Charon crossing the river Styx.

Their shiny metal bodies, their translucent plastic parts, melting, burning with a white heat until not just their minds but their faces were gone.

Gone up the chimney and filling the late afternoon sky: all the memories, all the faces, the voices, all those who had disappeared from the planet.

Danielbot folded himself up on the rooftop. All this had happened less than twenty years before Daniel was born. How was it possible? Perhaps it was only history, but history was, in the end, a very small place. It was a foul history the entire planet owned.

He thought he saw Gordon running through the field, his small, broken heart forgotten. He stood up and tried to follow him with his eyes. Then he saw the boy on the rooftop, poking at the dead bird. Then the boy stood up, and took the knife from Happy Jack, and began slashing his way through his mother's womb.

A transparent train roared across the roof, its cattle cars loaded with masses of people standing, so close together they had to hold their arms over their heads, the sick and the babies underfoot, cooking in the heat and filth, unable to breathe. He glanced at the boy, whose gaze also was locked on the train. The boy looked at him and drew his finger across his neck.

"Lie down! All of you, hit the roof! Be still!" The guards were shouting, forcing the bots who were still on their feet to stretch out on the gravel. Danielbot hadn't seen exactly what happened, but apparently several bots were accused of grabbing the guards' electric rifles and they now lay in piles of smoking ruin. Again Danielbot wished he had the power to close his eyes, and settled for imagining himself lying in the darkness instead. Sometimes he cried but nothing came out, of course. The tears stayed there, invisible marks on his metal skin.

As he lay in the barracks, the dead and the dying all around him, stinking equally of filth and corrupted flesh, he knew that all normal fear had been driven completely out of him. He would attempt to stay alive, although death had lost its meaning. He was frequently in pain, but pain was what he expected. What he did fear were the *Muselmänner*, the soulless ones who ate very little, who reacted to nothing, doomed to selection, and yet still they walked, or shambled, most often at a snail's pace, always in the way, always underfoot. Not that he feared the *Muselmänner* themselves—they were pitiful, the best they could do was annoy and enrage. He abused them, as did many others. If one of them fell he had no embarrassment about stepping on his back. There had once been one in front of the barracks for days—they'd used him as a stepping stone, their feet pushing him further into the mud until he was like some piece of pavement.

But to become a *Muselmänner*, to transform into one of those silent, subhuman creatures, that was a terrifying possibility.

The soldiers gave the *Muselmänner* the hardest work to do, even though they were the weakest—a pack of five of them pushing a wagon, rolling a barrel. They did it slowly, and some would fall over dead in the process, but that didn't matter—they were supposed to die, this day or the next one. Often when they were beaten they appeared to feel no pain—they were a waste of brutality. Although sometimes they were good for a little cruel fun. You could make them do any shameful thing. A few managed to show them kindness—there were always a few saints around, giving up their own food, their own protection, for those who could not be saved. A waste of time, but they became like their pets.

Some said the *Muselmänner* were too empty to suffer—he didn't know about that. But he had his own miseries to worry about. He needed to forget about them.

In the beginning the Muselmänner ate anything—they'd eat shoe leather if there was nothing else. Toward the end, however, many of them couldn't eat anything, and yet they shuffled around without the strength to lift their feet. The weakest of the bunch had to bend down and use their hands to move their legs.

He sometimes spent a great deal of time trying to avoid them— they stank worse than anything he had ever encountered. Sometimes the other prisoners would push them out of the barracks so they had to sleep outside. He hated the way they got in the way all the time, the way they stared, the message they sent that all was lost.

It occurred to Danielbot that he himself hadn't eaten in days— of course he didn't need to. The so called protein paste had been largely for lubrication and conditioning purposes. What ill effects he might suffer without it, he had no idea. But the lack of power in the batteries—that was another—if he lost enough power a Muselmänn might be his fate.

He had never heard the term prisoner when everyone had been disguised and the guards had been roaches and unspeaking. They had called each other "residents." Now everyone used the word "prisoner."

Sometimes the punishments became an excuse to experiment with the bots' physical limits. Once a bot was down guards would surround the figure and apply electrical charges to various parts and observe which areas caused the most visible distress.

Witnessing this, Danielbot tried to go back and find the holocaust survivor inside himself, the one who had gone through so much and come out the other side. A meaning had to be found.

A vision of the future sometimes helped you survive.

With his family present inside him, he could feel genuine joy for a few moments at a time.

Despite a universe of pain it was possible for spiritual life to deepen.

A LARGE NUMBER of guards left during the next few days. He didn't see them go, but every morning when he woke up there were fewer of them. There also appeared to be fewer bots; Danielbot assumed they'd simply gone to the edge of the roof in the middle of the night and walked off. His own temptation to do so was outweighed by his need to see how the story ended.

The remaining guards no longer patrolled the roof perimeter. Perhaps they no longer had orders to prevent suicides. Perhaps it wasn't even considered suicide. Can an appliance kill itself?

He thought it odd that he still had sleep cycles. He doubted he needed them, unless sleep promoted sanity even in an artificial intelligence, and he still very much believed he was capable of losing his mind.

He could not explain his mental processing outside the context of Daniel. The best explanation his available mental tools could come up with was that he was a kind of dream of Daniel, a kind of nightmare. Was he the dreamer, or was it someone else? The troubling thing was that he was troubled at all.

Among the remaining guards the abusive treatment of the prisoners increased. There was no disciplinary reason for the abuse—the bots did not resist. Falstaff tried once or twice to stop the abuse and was beaten down for his trouble.

His battery life was rapidly coming to an end, but he saw nothing he could do about that. And perhaps he shouldn't bother, as he was a mere footnote in someone else's life.

"You," he said to Falstaff. "You came out of a womb. You had a family. You have a complete history. Your memories are your own and not someone else's. You should leave here while you still can."

"I'm going to hang on a bit longer. Who knows, maybe a helicopter will come and take us all out of here." Falstaff avoided eye contact.

"They won't take the bots, Falstaff. We're simply excess equipment."

"Falstaff?" He looked amused. "From Shakespeare?"

"When I first came here I didn't want to become too attached to anyone. I'd lost... Daniel had lost, enough people. I gave each of you new names, arbitrary names. Bogart, Lenin, Gandhi, Falstaff. Daniel enjoyed Shakespeare, particularly the histories."

"You're far more than a recording. You came up with those names on your own. These new memories are yours alone."

"The family was his. Gordon was his. If my only life is what I've experienced here, I'd rather not exist.

"Really, you should leave, John. Things will not end well here."

"Then come with me."

Danielbot could see the God of Mayhem wrapping his face in colorful rags, rising to his feet and spreading his arms. "No—look at us, think of what people would do to us. We would be less safe out among your kind."

"If you change your mind, just come. I'll find some way to help you. But before I leave—maybe there's enough power for me to find out if Daniel ever got on that plane."

"No. I don't think so—leave it be. It isn't always best to know."

That afternoon Danielbot became aware of crowd activity near one end of the roof, bots gathered into a wall, obscuring something on the other side, a flash of fast-moving metal and a mewling sound, like that of a failing engine or an animal in extremis. Danielbot maneuvered through the figures until he could get a better look: a bot struggling frantically, a chain attached from its frame to a large rusty ring embedded in the roof. Another bot was slapping him on the head, kicking him, then dodging out of his grasp at the last moment.

The chained bot snapped its teeth and shook its head. "Henry?"

The werewolfbot stopped, stared at him, then started shaking its head again. Danielbot studied the one who had been taunting him—that bot took one glance at him, turned his back and disappeared into the crowd. The werewolfbot made a high-pitched screeching sound. The chain was attached just below the neck joint. The bot kept running in circles, the chain stretched tightly to the ring. With each revolution he came perilously close to the edge of the roof. If he went off the edge he would hang himself.

When the manic figure wasn't running in circles it would stretch the chain as far as possible toward the crowd, supporting itself on its analogs of hands and knees, its segments and joints rigid with tension, its eye globes vibrating from the strain, and it would make a coughing, almost barking noise through its teeth, because it had clamped its jaw shut, as if it were trying to prevent the noise from coming out.

Danielbot approached within a few feet. "Henry? Do you recognize me?"

Again the bot twisted its head sideways in a dog-like movement. "Are you the king?" it asked. "Are you His Majesty?"

Danielbot thought a moment, then remembering, reached up and touched the cylinders attached to his skull. "These? It's not a crown. I was in an... accident."

"I've never had an accident," the werewolfbot said, "but I have made some." Its eyes wobbled sideways. "I know your face," the bot said. "It's like everyone's face."

"Are you trying to get free? I don't think they—"

"No! I have to be sure the chain is strong enough to hold me! I don't know who there is left to eat, but I would have to eat somebody! But can I eat them? I'm afraid they would break my teeth!"

The werewolfbot capered about then, snapping its jaws as if anxious for a ball. "Is there anything I can do for you?"

The werewolfbot stopped and grew very still, staring with its eyes frozen in place. "I can still feel my fur," he said. "But I can't see it! It still itches and grows beneath my skin, but I have no skin. I deserve to be in Hell, but I had no idea it would be this bad!"

"You're not in Hell. You're in the future we've made for ourselves."

"Are you a prophet? Jeanne d'Arc, that bitch, she was a prophet, among other things. Is it glorious being a prophet? Does it satisfy you? I crave such satisfaction, but it would seem I am far too itchy."

"No. I'm a ma—. I am just like you."

"A sorry end, isn't it, to be like me? I only wanted to be admired, or at least remembered. I only wanted to be greater than myself— doesn't every human being want to be greater than themselves? It's the only thing which would made life tolerable, the only possible compensation for the grinding boredom of it all! You start out so full of promise, and yet you end up a corpse!"

"There are other ways to look at it, I think," Danielbot said. The werewolfbot attempted to chew at its own parts with a rattling, metallic sound, and to howl, but the howl still came out muffled, which appeared to make the werewolfbot furious.

"I am the destroyer! I am the darkness at the end of time!" the werewolf screamed. "I am the slow corrupter, the rapid pestilence, the universal disassembler, the final stop on the journey! I am the madness without explanation! Love me and I will slaughter you! I will pick through your brains with my tongue!"

One of the guards pushed his way through the crowd of bots and aimed his electric rifle at the werewolfbot, who sniffed its barrel curiously, even though it lacked a nose. The guard pulled the trigger and held it as bolt after bolt wrapped the bot's frame. The other bots scattered. The Danielbot shouted "No!"

When the guard finally loosened his grip on the trigger, the werewolfbot collapsed into a motionless pile.

"Why did you do that? He was chained!" the Danielbot cried.

The guard turned and looked the bot over. "It malfunctioned," he said, and walked away.

Danielbot approached the werewolfbot's collapsed form. He prodded it with his foot. Bearings turned and pieces pivoted on their pins as the lifeless parts rearranged themselves with the shifting gravity, then stopped.

He was walking back through the crowd when he saw a bot staring at him, and then attempting to hide in the debris. It was the one who had been taunting Henry, and—he realized—the boy without a name he'd met on the roof what seemed a lifetime ago. He walked over slowly, trying not to scare him.

"It's okay," he said. "You can come out now. I know you don't recognize me, but we know each other. I met you on this roof a while back. You'd found a dead bird, remember?"

The bot came out. He looked no different than all the others, and they were all the same size. But he had the nameless boy's voice. "I know," the boy said. "I recognized you."

"How'd you manage that—we all look the same."

"I dunno." There was no shrug to see, but Danielbot could hear it in his voice. "Maybe just because of the way you are. We're all still different—at least I see differences."

"Why'd you run?"

"Because of what I did, to that crazy one on the chain."

"You tormented him. You were being cruel."

"I was just having fun. He was just so crazy. I was just letting off some steam! Killing time! I've just got way too much time! I didn't hurt him. That guard, he hurt him."

It seemed pointless to be having this conversation. What do you talk about when it's the end of the world? "So how are you doing?" he asked.

"How do you think? Look at what they done to me!" The boy's voice rose. He stood up and spread his mechanical arms. "Look at me!"

Danielbot turned and left. The bots who had been watching this drama scattered, as if embarrassed. That left only Falstaff standing there.

Danielbot walked quickly to Falstaff and grasped his hand, covering it with both of his metal ones, trying not to squeeze too hard, as if it were a wounded bird he was trying to save. "Henry is dead!" He was upset, and whatever else this man was—imprisoner or torturer or protector—he had been a companion through part of this journey. "One of your—one of the guards killed him. And the boy tormented him! The boy was almost gleeful!"

"It's adolescence. The boy holds onto our anger, and we hold onto the boy."

"He follows me everywhere!"

Falstaff shook his hand vigorously, as if they were two old friends saying goodbye forever. "Our murderous companion. Our provocateur, our sidekick! A huge part of our problem, I think, is that the human race has largely failed to reach its adulthood."

Danielbot could feel himself weeping, although he was aware that no actual tears were produced. "You're saying goodbye. I won't see you again. Be careful, my friend. God! Or the devil! I can see him in my head! The devil is on his way to Ubo!"

"I went down to the labs. I spent some time reconfiguring this bug in my head to your equipment." He gestured toward Danielbot's unwanted headgear. "Make yourself open to my signals. I'm going to rummage around below, see if I can take some of the electronic files with me. Maybe at some point someone can make better use of what we've done. Follow me if you can. At least maybe you'll know what it's like to escape this life." Falstaff's face began to break. "I'm so sorry." He was weeping. "You were never supposed to know. This was never supposed to happen."

"Haven't you been paying attention? Things that were never supposed to happen, they happen all the time."

19

THE CREATURE WHO called himself Danielbot sat on the edge of the roof struggling to organize all that flowed into his electronic brain into a kind of living and sensible collage. Recurrences of the characters he had played—from a frenzied Jack the Ripper to a stumbling and confused Stalin to a self-proclaimed god executing his killing spree from atop the accumulated trash of the world—interwove with other violent fragments to both obscure and illuminate the details of what he assumed to be his final resting place. Scattered bots both active and nonfunctional populated the dirt and gravel and asphalt rooftop of Ubo, a junkyard in the end.

At the moment very few were moving, but when they did each gesture made a ripple that stirred the images resting in what was left of his memory. His energy was at a very low ebb. He struggled to maintain coherence. He was receiving updates concerning Falstaff's descent through the disintegrating building, along with an intrusion of obsessive thoughts from the God of Mayhem across the water. His head ached, but he was unable to curtail the input.

None of this information was part of his memory or his life. It seemed to him now he lacked both a soul and a personal history. But these data was all he had as he came to the end of his time on the planet. For most human beings a soul was not much more practical than an imagined thing, given how little they appeared to speak to or use it, and for far too many a personal history was simply a record of how they had suffered. Better to be a machine with no expectations and no disappointments.

Danielbot's main problem was that he did not believe that. He grieved for his lost human life, imaginary or not.

He had watched as Falstaff descended from the roof door down a staircase that had been knocked dangerously askew during the last shuddering of the building, through the empty waiting room redolent of lives with endings unknown, then down another staircase which was dangerously broken, with missing treads and crumbling walls. Danielbot's view of Falstaff's activities was skewed at times, and tantalizingly incomplete.

At one point Falstaff entered a room Danielbot did not recognize or understand. What appeared to be a great pipe organ fashioned from crystal and silver wire hummed and glowed with colors which ebbed almost to nothing before exploding to such brilliance both Falstaff and Danielbot had to avert their eyes. Falstaff studiously unplugged various fragments from outlying parts of the crystalline structure. He grabbed a satchel off the floor and began filling it with what he had detached.

Several times Falstaff stopped and reconsidered, then he would take one of the fragments from his bag and replace it with another. Once the bag was full and almost too heavy to carry he secured the flap and slung it across his shoulder.

Dropping down to the next level over a ragged gap in the stairs, Falstaff paused. Danielbot could feel Falstaff's sudden wave of regret for all he had given up in order to work in this place. He'd never been married—all he had to go back to was an abandoned purpose and a city he hadn't lived in in years, and now on the verge of collapse.

But at least you have a life, Danielbot thought. He couldn't tell whether Falstaff had received the message or not—there was no reaction.

Still the apparatus attached to Danielbot's head fired intermittently with the last recorded memories of the most destructive human beings in history, both the brutes and the assassins who actually had a need to see blood on their hands, and the bureaucrats and administrators like King Leopold or Mao Zedong—murderers with quotas and a signature.

But clearest of all was the God across the water who now understood fully where Danielbot was, needing only to scratch an itch or two before coming to find him. Whether to kill or embrace him he hadn't yet decided.

THE GOD OF Mayhem had discovered a body in the trash. The rats had been at it. It wasn't one of his—for the most part he remembered where to find the bodies of those he was responsible for. And this was a child, a little girl clutching her doll, and he did not kill children. Children were largely innocent of the crimes of humanity, helpless against uncaring nature, and a consolation to the sting of death. And yet humanity was so careless with them, and they so precious they needed to be cared for until they too could become careless adults.

He examined her more closely. The doll had been tied to her wrist, and her pockets were stuffed with goodbye letters from mother and father, siblings and others, sad statements about how she had been loved and cared for, and expressions of grief over how death overtook her, at night and with no warning.

So she had been well loved, and still they had left her body here in the trash. Granted it was hard to know what to do with a body in these times, but the wrongness of this gnawed at him. Perhaps they had buried her and the seismic movement of trash and large debris had brought her to the surface again. This seemed unlikely but it was an explanation the God decided to believe.

The addicts and the alcoholics had had their higher power, the something greater than themselves they'd always wanted to be.

The God of Mayhem had no power higher than himself. If killing was an addiction (and certainly no drug could have eased his pain more efficiently) then he had no one else but himself to go to for a cure. This was unsatisfactory, but there was nothing to be done. The masses could never fully appreciate the lonely responsibilities of a god.

He was standing inside the church where he'd discovered the body. Perhaps the family had thought entombment unnecessary within these sanctified surroundings. The walls of the church still stood. Inside it was all trash and aggressive vegetation. He'd followed a young man here who'd disappeared into a pile of building debris where the congregation used to sit. Occasionally he would see a head peer out through some gap in the pile. The God thought the young man might actually live here.

The God left and continued on his way. He had other things to attend to. He'd recently become aware that he had a conscience. He was furious that his conscience refused to answer any of his questions, such as why a god even required a conscience. But he knew where his conscience was located: there, just offshore in the old mental hospital, or UBO as it was now signed. Apparently the God would have to take his questions there.

"I know who you are," the boy said behind him. "You can stay here with me."

The God of Mayhem ignored him. He talked too much, and he was a child. It was time for the God to put aside childish things.

As the God of Mayhem descended into the old north section, the Chinatown swamp and the partially-flooded government center and the abandoned inner harbor, the ground burned all around him. This did not particularly bother him, although he had to make some alterations in his route. If anything, the flames seemed appropriate to his mood. Perhaps his mood had even been the accelerant that had allowed these fires to spread.

Fire had expanded from some buildings in the distance behind him to the masses of trash, and now smoke was coming out of numerous fissures in the refuse ahead of him. Apparently it was burning beneath the surface. At scattered locations people were attempting to escape it, erupting like moles from holes in the ground. Blue smoke came out of the ground and wrapped around the trees. Boston had started its transformation into a Hell garden, and a final fitting sacrifice to him. Although footing was difficult, he picked up his pace.

As far as Danielbot could determine, the last of the guards was gone, leaving the bots to fend for themselves. "Good riddance, I'd say," Leninbot said beside him. "So do we leave, or do we stay?"

Danielbot looked at him. For a second he could see Lenin's flesh disguise, wrapping him completely, then unravelling to reveal the metal and plastic beneath. "We're free to do what we like, I suppose."

"Then I believe I want to live. I want something more than this. Human beings die, but what says we must?"

Danielbot could feel the God of Mayhem approaching the bay, searching for some kind of boat to take him across to Ubo. He tried to put that image out of his mind. He could feel Falstaff descending through yet another level of ruin and entering a level of doubt, worried about finding food, wondering whether he had time to search the lower levels for weapons or valuables, anything he could trade once he reached Boston, and still get out before the entire structure collapsed on him. Danielbot tried to put all that outside his mind as well.

"I never thought about any of that," he admitted. "I felt helpless. They made us all helpless, and not in control of our own fates. Like infants."

"But we aren't infants," Leninbot said. "Any more than the humans. Certainly, they have given themselves more things. More possessions, more culture. They have given themselves families who they can love and who will love them. They have their somethings to help them get over the fact that they will someday be nothing."

"I never considered whether a life on my own would be possible. I shared Daniel's life. I wanted Daniel's life. And although everything I see and touch tells me that I am not Daniel, that his things are not mine, I realize that I am not completely convinced. His memories are no longer intensely with me, but it's as if they are my memories of the past, my past."

"They're like any other scenario—eventually the memory will fade. You'll lose that connection. We all have a right to live," Leninbot said. "Doesn't it make you angry that you haven't? Doesn't it make you want to destroy something? This person you tried to be, he was about to walk away from everything. To hell with him and his life!"

"I understand, but I must ask you not to say that to me. I can still feel his wife in my arms, still smell his son's hair and feel his warmth against me. Those sensations—they are the most important things I have. They are all that I have."

DANIELBOT WATCHED AS Falstaff went one more level down, only to discover the staircase gone, dropped out of sight like a stone down a well. He couldn't see anything in the thick darkness below. He went through the rest of the level, desperate that his time might be running out. Opening a door, he found a room full of spare robot parts—arms, legs, rib cages, memory units, heads. A few had never been used, but most belonged to former residents, companions he had known and talked to. And most had never felt like anything less than real human beings. A few—James, Randall, Felix, Sarah—he had considered friends.

In an outer corridor he found a giant hole in the floor. Without hesitation, he dropped through it, rolling carefully when he hit the level below. As far as he could tell, the contents of his satchel remained secure.

*   *   *

"IF YOU WANT children, perhaps we can create some of our own," Leninbot was saying. His voice sounded weaker, so Danielbot suspected Leninbot's internal power supply was also fading. Certainly he himself felt somewhat lazy, with no desire to stand or move. And he had no other explanation for Leninbot's ridiculous idea.

"I'm not sure I understand you." It was not a subject he wished to discuss, but he had no one else to talk to.

"If we go into one of the labs, perhaps you can determine how our minds were built, how the memories were transferred. Then maybe you can turn one of these bots into a child."

"I'm afraid..." Danielbot searched for the words. "You're sounding like a human, willing to commit to the most ridiculous... fantasies. Simply because you wish it, doesn't make it possible."

But Leninbot continued, unfazed. "We could raise it to protect us. We could create many such children. Perhaps they left some of those electrical weapons behind. We could teach it that the human beings are our enemies..."

"Stop it! All this talk of violence! You talk just like a human! The future of any of us... depends on how our children are raised. And no, we cannot make children. We cannot make 'childbots.' And we should be thankful for it!"

He suddenly recalled something Daniel had worried over as a child. How the smallest mistakes he made only hid much larger, more terrible sins he hadn't yet recognized. Surely, certainly, he was going to Hell.

THE GOD OF Mayhem made it through the flooded neighborhoods jumping roof to roof, occasionally traversing rubbish piles that rose like mountain peaks above the water. In the twenty-first century, taking a note from the Dutch, they had started adding additional canals to allow the rising currents to enter the city without damage. But these projects had never been completed.

Suddenly he felt hands coming out of the water to grab him. He looked around: it was a sea of reaching arms, clutching hands, clawing fingers only inches from his boots. He tried to find Ubo with his eyes, and although he could sense its direction, the view of it was obscured. "Damn you." He gritted his teeth. "We will compare Hells when I arrive."

He kicked at some of the hands. His boot went right through them.

DANIELBOT WORRIED OVER Falstaff's labored progress as he maneuvered through collapsed corridors and lowered himself by strength alone over the gaps torn in the stairs of the lower levels. Water had begun to come in and more than once Falstaff had to swim across a room or dive beneath a partially-blocked passage. Danielbot could not contact him with any specificity, but he could send waves of warning concerning the God of Mayhem's steady approach.

Falstaff received the worry as a panic that flushed his face and fluttered his chest without knowing what it meant. But it sped him on anyway, thinking of the fires of Dresden, Hiroshima, and the Holocaust, all the lives and memories that could burn on the malice of a match.

WHEN THE GOD of Mayhem at last had a clear view of the harbor, it was close to sunset, the air chilly as it blew across the ocean from some places even worse than this, some places better. The abandoned inner harbor stretched across his vision, the three decaying tankers to one side, lower in the water than he remembered, the shadow of their oil stretching across the waters like the dark hand of the devil, prepared to grab and tear apart anything unlucky enough to stray into its path.

The God of Mayhem smiled, pleased with the little toy he had prepared for just such an opportunity.

He searched for Ubo then, and found it stranded there, the entire quarantine zone inundated in several feet of water connecting it to the harbor. He searched the shoreline. All the great wharves were long gone, in ruins or under the waves. But there were always scavenger boats, looking for anything to eat or trade, and he believed he knew a hidden spot where they docked.

"HAS HE REACHED the water yet? Is he on his way?"

He didn't know whether Leninbot meant Falstaff or the God of Mayhem, but he could see Falstaff as if he were right in front of him, retrieving a rubber raft from a storeroom almost underwater. It had been meant for the ocean behind them and had never been used.

Falstaff struggled with it, but at last had it free. As he pushed it through the gap in the wall into the water, he threw himself and the satchel safely inside.

"Tell him good luck, or Godspeed! What is it they used to say?"

"You forget, we're recorders, witnesses. We aren't meant to interact," Danielbot said, but still willed his hope Falstaff's way.

THE OLD MAN looked terrified, and when the God of Mayhem grabbed him by the throat the God could feel the geezer's will dissolving into the thin mud of his blood.

"You'll take me on your little boat, out there, you know the place? Where hope ends?" He gestured toward Ubo, and Danielbot, who realized now he hadn't heard his own heartbeat since he'd first awakened in Ubo and how that should have been a dead giveaway, could hear the God's heart beat like thunder.

"And if you do it well, I promise I will not burn you."

* * *

FALSTAFF WAS MORE than halfway across the water when he saw the little boat, the long white hair tortured by the wind as the old man hunched and dug in with the oars. Standing in the middle of the boat was a huge figure in an enormous black coat, face wrapped in multicolored rags. The figure turned its head as it passed and pointed at Falstaff with one long arm.

Falstaff could not be sure, what with the sound of the wind and his own loud heart, but he thought he heard laughter.

THE GOD OF Mayhem continued to laugh with his head thrown back. Eventually he stopped and gazed at the water, at the dark shadow of the devil's hand stretching behind and past them, the fingers curling, as if they might come back around and crush the boat.

He reached into his coat and pulled out his toy: an old flare strapped to a bottle full of jellied fuel. He lit the flare, stretched back and threw the bottle as hard as he could, hoping the devil would catch it in his overextended hand. If the oil here was too thin the cool ocean water would prevent ignition. But he had an instinct for such things, and sufficient faith the oil slick would be just thick enough.

"I figure we have about ten minutes, probably less. I seriously suggest you row, Grandad."

DANIELBOT SAW FALSTAFF land and pull his raft up on a jagged cluster of rocks resembling splintered tombstones. It was at that point that the sky all around them caught fire. The boom shook the building and Leninbot sprawled on top of him.

Fire filled his vision, so bright and hot he could not process anything he was seeing. He dragged himself to the edge of the roof, thinking all that water would wash the fire out of his eyes. Instead when he looked down what he saw was an ocean of fire, extending as far as he could see across the quarantine area to the near edges of the Boston ruin. A boat appeared in the midst of it, the God of Mayhem standing inside, and the flames did not appear to bother the God at all. If anything he reveled in it, his arms rising in triumph.

A ball of fire shot up from below and arced over and behind Danielbot, followed by another explosion. He twisted around. One of the bots had exploded. His torso looked like the ruptured shell of a giant metal insect.

Danielbot kept turning and was relieved to see Leninbot approaching, waving his arms. But when he arrived and began to speak Danielbot couldn't hear him, could barely make out his features. Instead he saw the God of Mayhem docked below, a rope in his hands and looped around the neck of the trembling old man. "My sincerest thank you for the rope, and see, you must have done a competent job. I'm not burning you."

And then he pulled on both sides of the rope until his hands were as far apart as he could make them. While behind him the brightly-colored souls of the dead raced from the flames.

A SMALL ARMY of people, their faces layered in strips of plastic and ragged cloth, greeted Falstaff as he made his way inland and up the first giant mound of trash. He thought at first they might be burn victims, because of their faces. They grabbed him on either side and helped him up the slope. He clutched the satchel strap on his shoulder and would not let go, willing to die rather than have it taken.

DANIELBOT LOOKED UP as the God of Mayhem strolled onto the roof, appearing even larger in person than what he'd imagined. Danielbot expected the God to come directly to him, pick him up and disassemble him in some crude and non-technical way, or perhaps just throw him into the flaming waters below. The air billowed with thick, particle-filled black smoke. He tasted the bitterness and foulness of it with each reluctant breath. Even though he had no lungs and so no need to breathe, he had been breathing, smelling, and tasting ever since he had awakened here.

But the God of Mayhem simply looked confused. He unwrapped his head and threw his rags away. He looked older in person, his beard matted and streaked heavily with gray, his soft eyes watering like those of a sick child.

The God seemed not to see the bots at all at first. They stood still enough—the Danielbot thought they might resemble some artistic assemblage. The God kept turning his head, searching the roof with his eyes, seeking, Danielbot supposed, for real human beings.

Finally the God of Mayhem paused and stared at them. Leninbot and some of the other bots around Danielbot began to move restlessly, as if swaying to some internal electrical rhythm.

The God came to them and looked down, taller by a head. Suddenly he fell to his knees and folded his hands together. He looked from one bot to the other, finally focusing on Danielbot as if he expected him to be the spokesman.

"Are you gods, or devils? What are you?" the God of Mayhem asked.

The other bots moved their eye fixtures around, confused. Danielbot eased closer to the God, far enough away that he couldn't be grabbed. It was raining in his head, fragments of the wife and son who were not his, whom he once had thought he loved and perhaps still did.

"We're the ones who remember."

20

Each morning during Falstaff's stay in the trash pickers' home, the father prepared his smaller children for the day's work by first liberally kissing their dark faces—a thorough covering of forehead, cheeks, nose, and chin.

It reminded Falstaff that for a parent every inch of your child was a precious thing to be cherished. And although he loved watching, Falstaff was vaguely embarrassed by this unadulterated outpouring of love. He didn't deserve to witness such affection after the things he had done. Daniel... Danielbot should have been here instead. Or would this family have seen the bot as a monster and a threat?

It wasn't just, and Falstaff hated his part in it. This father understood what was needed in desperate times, and those in charge of Ubo had not. In Ubo they had witnessed a great deal, and yet they had not witnessed enough.

Then, the children still giggling, the father pasted the strips of cloth and plastic to their skin in random layers. It vividly recalled Halloweens when Falstaff was very young, and his mother had dressed him for the night. He wasn't sure if the pickers' get-up was a costume, exactly, but obscuring the wearer's identity was part of the design. It also suggested damage and disease to predators—

wild dogs and rogue humans—so that they tended to leave the ones dressed this way alone. The colors and methods of disguise distinguished among the various tribes and clarified who belonged to whom. There were occasional disagreements among these groups, but little actual violence.

Falstaff usually went with the family when they picked; customarily no family member was ever left alone. He also wore the layered strips, and it was an odd sensation, especially the way they came down partially over the eyes, like hanging skin as the result of some disastrous burn.

But he wanted to earn his keep, even though he had no idea what he was doing. There were fellows who went around to the various tribes with lists of what was in demand, what could be traded, and that's what set the priorities. Falstaff assumed they were brokers of some sort, but he didn't know the economics involved or how these lists were compiled.

The family he stayed with spoke a little Spanish, a little English, but also used a lot of other words he wasn't familiar with, or words which had acquired additional meanings. A "dolly," for example, was any impractical thing that made you feel better. A toy could be a dolly, but so could a photograph, or a good luck charm.

For the most part these people remained silent, relying on looks, gestures, touches. And they listened—to each other, and to the sounds outside.

He owed this family everything. They'd given him a soft, warm and dry place to sleep, and although it did smell a bit, he had become used to it. They fed him. They provided companionship, and they gave no indication that they were anxious for him to leave. He hesitated to call it love, although it was a reasonable facsimile thereof. It was an answer, a way to approach the world that worked for them. But he was a stranger, and he didn't deserve such kindness.

When the family wasn't working, they were reading—one room was almost filled with battered and stained but readable paperbacks. At certain hours of the day, when the parents had determined it was relatively safe, the children played music. There was a kind of violin made out of a stick, a can, and some wire, a square wooden guitar, a wind instrument constructed out of pipe and oval bits of metal. He assumed the children had practiced a great deal—the music was slightly jangly and nervous, but he found it oddly soothing.

Their "house" might have been an actual house at one time. They lived on the edge of a huge debris and trash field—their primary workspace. A stream of the trash had eddied down among some older structures, exploding the walls out, knocking them off foundations. The parents had hollowed out a hidden, womb-like space among all that. The structure was seemingly stable. There was an escape tunnel in the back, big enough for the family to crawl through in case of emergencies, although certainly not large enough for Falstaff.

He thought he might keep the name Falstaff. He didn't know if Danielbot had understood what he was doing when he'd assigned him the name, but it might be his judgment and his punishment for what he'd done these past few years. Ironically he had little sense of humor anymore—it had been scoured out of him during his time in Ubo. Like Falstaff, he had been a liar and a coward. He'd lied to all of them. It had been his job, but now that seemed a pathetic excuse.

Sometimes, however, when these little children rode his back—four or more at the same time seemingly unable to get enough of him—he'd felt the high humor of Falstaff inside him, eager to come out.

Today the oldest daughter kept gesturing that she wanted to show him something. They'd been through this many times before—she was proud of this world of hers. He kept reminding himself that she'd never known anything better. She wanted to show it off to the newcomer. And the things she had revealed to him so far had been quite impressive. She'd taken him down into the old subway system where a jungle of vegetation and even a vegetable garden or two filled the abandoned cars. Another afternoon she took him into a friend's abode where the fellow had filled several canvases with rotting organic matter. They stank badly, of course, but the colorful visual effect had been quite beautiful.

Today they walked a couple of miles through a series of ghostly abandoned neighborhoods—she was unable or unwilling to tell him why no one wanted to live there—to a towering apartment complex rising out of acres of rubbish. The pickers were out on the trash field in force, dressed in a variety of bright colors as well as the usual white, dull gray, and brown.

The front doors were heavily graffitied and so deeply scarred Falstaff wondered if at one point someone might have tried to drive a vehicle through them. Two guards were stationed on either side, armed with old-fashioned assault rifles. They eyed him suspiciously but smiled warmly when they saw his young companion, who greeted all four by name. Inside, the lobby was packed with pickers in their signature tribal outfits, food vendors, and a variety of other people he assumed to be guests of the pickers or hangers on like himself. All were animated and obviously excited.

That happy excitement was perhaps the most surprising thing he'd encountered since he'd left Ubo. Most of the faces he had seen before he got here had been guarded, suspicious, or simply afraid.

The elevators, not surprisingly, didn't work, so they took the stairs, which were jammed with people in both directions. And although Falstaff felt some anxiety about the close proximity of so many strangers, everyone appeared to be in a celebratory mood. The landings were crowded as each had an out-facing window with people lined up to see whatever it was they were there to see.

Occasionally his young companion would clutch his hand. At first he thought maybe this was a childhood thing, a reach for adult support and comfort. But then he realized she was the comfortable one here. He was the outsider, and when she saw that he was a little uneasy or nervous in this vast crowd she was offering him support. He'd been aware of her watching him ever since they left her home—she knew what he was feeling better than he did.

This trip to the apartment tower was about more than bragging—it was her gift to him. He would really need to leave soon—he couldn't bear such kindness, such love. He wasn't worthy of it.

They exited onto the eighteenth floor near the top of the building. They stopped at an old woman's apartment where they traded for some cold but tasty spiced burritos, three batteries for two burritos. A few more batteries and some quiet but firm bargaining (this lovely almond-skinned young girl was a force to be reckoned with) got them into the apartment down the hall, and two rickety chairs out on the balcony.

Falstaff peered out over the field of rubbish and the surrounding backdrop of buildings. In one sense it was Boston as he was afraid it had become, a dismaying ruin of trash and disintegrating structures and the fires beyond and the black boil of acrid smoke hanging above. He was high up enough to see what was left of Ubo out in the bay: like a ruined castle in the middle of a shallow polluted lake, its walls collapsed and blackened by the fire that had only recently expired. But there might still have been survivors, and maybe someday he would find them, if they didn't find him first.

The field of trash spread out below him was not dismaying, but an amazing display of frantic activity as figures swarmed over the ground in a maelstrom of color, accompanied by a roar of cheered anticipation so loud and thunderous it frightened him with how the building shook. He kept looking at the girl for some kind of explanation—he had no real context for what he was seeing—but she simply pointed at his eyes and indicated that he needed to watch what was happening below.

There appeared to be one person in charge, a young man in a bright red T-shirt, long hair and a beard, who ran around at the base of the tower shouting orders to the pickers out in the field and various subordinates along the sidelines. But then Falstaff heard the yelling from above, and he leaned out from the balcony craning his neck up to see, and there was an arm coming out from the edge of the roof waving and gesturing with accompanying shouted orders. So whoever was directing this spectacle, whatever it was, did so from the roof, and his commands were relayed to the folks on the ground.

It occurred to him then that the field of trash the pickers were walking on wasn't random—anything but, because the color showing to those in the apartment tower was an overall gradient of white or pale gray. It was a deliberate thing. Obviously you couldn't get a random distribution of gray trash, and now and then when a gust of wind or the action of the picker's feet caused some disturbance in the color palette, there were children dressed in white and gray who ran across the field with long sticks in their hands to make the correction.

Suddenly a great shout echoed across the field as a burst of bright red exploded in the middle of all that gray. Falstaff leaned forward to try to determine what was happening. The red appeared to be a great pulsing of flame and leaves like a rose made out of fire. But if he concentrated he could see that it was a mass of pickers with varying shades and shapes of red, pink, and orange on their costumes gyrating in a circle and showing different portions of their bodies to the audience above.

He hadn't noticed them gather, but he now realized most of the field was covered with standing pickers, milling, moving about in both geometric and spiraling patterns, showing the gray predominantly, but there were glimpses of other colors in their costumes as well, further down their bodies and mostly hidden.

The entire field burst into a fireball, then blinked out. The crowd roared.

The people around him on the balcony began to chatter excitedly, pointing at the field, laughing, gesturing. The girl put her hand over his and smiled. "It's animation, am I right?" he asked. "Like a cartoon?" The girl looked slightly confused, then nodded.

He'd seen somewhat the same principle at sporting events, decades ago. A group of people in the stands would turn over cards to say something a letter at a time, or to make a picture. But what he'd just seen involved dance and precise physical manipulation, a tight choreography. A thousand times more elaborate than what he'd seen at those old sporting events. It struck him then how all his years in Ubo had been as much a prison for him as it had been for the subjects. Life had gone on, people had loved and imaginations had evolved, and he'd had no idea. It was like putting on a new pair of glasses and discovering that your entire field of vision transformed. The sudden change in perspective was dizzying.

An old man nearby looked at him, put his hands to his head and made an exploding gesture. He laughed and Falstaff laughed with him. He didn't deserve this, but he remembered that Danielbot had sent him here. He had permission to enjoy himself, to live. It was the only sane thing to do under the circumstances.

A resonating hum rose through the air, becoming rounder and more prayer-like as the mouths below gradually opened. Then the ground beneath the pickers appeared to be breaking apart to reveal the glowing coals underneath and the remaining ground turning black around them.

It was the pickers scuffling their feet, turning over the carefully-placed gray layers of trash to uncover the reddish layers and the black layers buried underneath.

A sharp-edged fissure appeared near the upper left corner of the field. It travelled down, widening, becoming a sword that crashed against another sword. Then there were fists and knives and a struggle of giant warring forms. The animation grew more violent as explosions of color were used to heighten the effect. A large bird escaped the center of the conflict but just as it almost achieved the impossible and left the boundaries of ground to soar up into the audience, a final slash severed its head.

The style of the animation was jittery and shaky, but the resulting energy was palpable. Every figure appeared electrified.

The field went to a mottled blue and black darkness except for one relatively small explosion of blood. But then that blood began to drip in linear horizontals and verticals as a geometric representation of a city rendered in red on a black canvas appeared, the details filling in until it might have been Boston or some other city on the old eastern seaboard. Falstaff could hear the girl's small gasps and cries of excitement beside him.

The aural chorus had continued quite without his being aware of it, and then flames appeared scattered inside the lines of buildings and windows and within seconds another brightly animated fire had consumed it all with a resulting gasp from both audience and performers.

The dawn of pale yellows that next appeared was only an animation, a simulation laid over a skin above a nearly unlimited supply of waste, destruction, and loss, and yet no less thrilling for all that.

A small bird appeared above that yellow, flying jerkily from one side of the field to the other, as if battered by the wind. It disappeared off the far edge as the field turned so white it hurt the eyes. Years later surrounded by his friends Falstaff would still wonder if that bird had been real.

Afterwards they descended the stairs into the lobby. People seemed reluctant to leave. Falstaff understood this—they'd all seen something unique and magical, involving almost unimaginable cooperation. He wanted to stay close for a while, maybe meet the creator of the piece, see if any of the magic rubbed off on him.

There were tables of goods to trade—it appeared these vendors never missed an opportunity. Falstaff stopped abruptly. There on a table was one of the bot power packs.

"So you got out too. I'm glad. There are only two or three of us, far as I know."

Falstaff stared into the stranger's face, thinking he was familiar, but he couldn't place him. His young companion gazed up at them, wide-eyed, but saying nothing. Then he saw the collar of the dark blue uniform under the gray parka he wore. "You were one of the guards, um ..."

"Clemmons."

"That's right, Clemmons. We never talked, for some reason."

"I kept to myself, pretty much. I never felt... comfortable there, doing what we did. No excuse of course, but still."

"Well. Well." Falstaff had no idea what to say.

"It's better here. I wasn't expecting that. This is my table. These people, they're so generous."

"Yes, yes they are," Falstaff said. "They've found their answer, and generosity's definitely part of it. Well, I hope to see you again." He turned, feeling embarrassed, feeling caught, and hoping he never saw this man again.

"Wait! I have something for you." The ex-guard held a battered pack out to him. Falstaff took it—it was heavy. He rested it gently on the table, loosened the top flap. It was the head of one of the bots. He felt himself recoil, but he didn't let it go. He imagined how awful it would be if it slipped out and landed on the floor.

"I don't know which one it was. I know I should, but I just don't. It got pretty well blasted—the ID is heavily scarred over. I was going to trade it, figured I could get a great deal for it, but I just couldn't. I hope you'll take it, maybe you can wake it up somehow."

Falstaff shook his head. "I don't—"

"Please. We shouldn't forget what happened there. Maybe some of that information, well, you should have this, you should keep it safe."

Falstaff looked down. The girl was gazing into the bag. She reached into her pocket and pulled out half a burrito and put it into the man's hand.

"Why, thank you," the ex-guard said to the girl, then to Falstaff, "What is she doing? What does she want?"

"I think she wants the head, actually. She wants to trade you for it."

"Surely you can't—"

"If you'll throw in the battery pack we'll take both of them off your hands. For the burrito. Or rather, the half of the burrito."

"But what would she do with it?"

"She'll love it—that's one of the things she does. And she's curious, and very bright. I'll help her—we'll see what we can do, what we can salvage. I want to do that. I'd love to do that."

Falstaff helped her carry it home.

"Love is the only sane and satisfactory answer to the problem of human existence."
— Erich Fromm, *The Art of Loving*

Author's Note: A-7713, the serial number of the "Danielbot," was the number tattooed at Auschwitz-Birkenau on the arm of Elie Wiesel in his *Night*, one of the most important documents written about the Holocaust.